Rukmini

Saiswaroopa Iyer holds an MBA from the Indian Institute of Technology, Kharagpur, and has worked as an investment professional before turning to her passion of storytelling. Her love for the epics, Puranas and philosophy made her become a full-time author. She has written five novels, *Abhaya, Avishi, Mauri, Draupadi* and *Rukmini,* all based on strong female characters from the ancient past of India. She also holds a certificate in the Puranas from The Oxford Centre for Hindu Studies, University of Oxford, England. She runs a mentorship programme for aspiring novelists and is also a Carnatic Classical singer.

She lives in Bengaluru

Praise for the book

India is the last surviving, ancient Goddess-worshipping culture. Saiswaroopa, and all her books till now, give us the quintessential archetype of the Indian approach to the feminine: strong and wise, fierce when necessary, gentle when possible. For those who want to understand the Indian way, her books are a must-read.

—**Amish Tripathi**, Director, Nehru Centre London and bestselling, award-winning author

All Saiswaroopa Iyer's books are wonderful and this one, on Rukmini, is no different. Among Krishna's eight major wives, Rukmini is the most important. Rukmini is a powerful and impressive lady and the author makes her come alive. A deeply engrossing book.

—**Dr Bibek Debroy**, author, translator of *Itihasa* and *Puranas*

Engrossing...seamless blending of the original text and the layered portrayal of an indomitable, extraordinary woman...

—**Kavita Kané**, bestselling author

Indian civilization stays alive through its epics. Here Saiswaroopa has retold the story of Krishna and Rukmini for our times. Just like Krishna promised that he would reappear to protect Dharma in each era, our civilizational memory is kept alive in each generation by storytellers like Saiswaroopa.

—**Sanjeev Sanyal**, writer and economist

In this striking story of Rukmini, Saiswaroopa, once again draws us into a fascinating bygone world, part history, part legend, part sacred lore. Rukmini, Krishna's primary consort, emerges as a strong, contemporary woman in this retelling, as much human as divine.

—**Professor Makarand R. Paranjape**, A.M., Ph.D. (Illinois) Director, Indian Institute of Advanced Study

A saga of two journeys, one in ancient India and the other within, Sai's *Rukmini* is a well-crafted blend of physical and psychological adventures—and her finest work so far.

—**Gautam Chikermane**, author and economist

Saiswaroopa Iyer has swiftly emerged as the subtle chronicler of a feminist perspective to Indian mythology and proto-history.

—**Hindol Sengupta**, award-winning author and journalist

The novel brings out the dimensions of Rukmini hitherto unspoken about in popular imagination. What we have in *Rukmini* is the continuation in the process of building through literary discourse an attempt to bring the Dharmic Feminine in all her traditional independence, intelligence, indominance, love and patience to the modern generation of girls.

—**Aravindan Neelakanthan,** author and historian

Saiswarooopa handles the complex storyline with consummate ease, weaving the multitude of strands deftly into a beguiling tapestry.

—**Sumedha Verma Ojha**, author, historian, former IRS

Rukmini

Krishna's Wife

SAISWAROOPA IYER

RUPA

Published by
Rupa Publications India Pvt. Ltd 2021
161-B/4, Gulmohar House,
Yusuf Sarai Community Centre,
New Delhi 110049

Sales centres:
Bengaluru Chennai
Hyderabad Kolkata Mumbai

This is a work of fiction. Names, characters, places and incidents are either the product of the author's imagination or are used fictitiously and any resemblance to any actual person, living or dead, events or locales is entirely coincidental.

P-ISBN: 978-93-9035-608-9
E-ISBN: 978-93-9035-616-4

Seventeenth impression 2026

20 19 18 17

Printed in India

To Shakti, the Supreme Feminine, the very vitality that runs in my veins and yours

To Krishna, the joy that fills every heart and the reason that guides us

To every woman who has made a choice and had the courage to stand by the same

Author's Note

The Rukmini Kalyanam episode of Bhagavatam is a part and parcel of every household in my part of the country. The story of how the princess of Vidarbha braved all odds in making her choice and in making sure that her choice prevailed is considered as an auspicious read and traditionally, unmarried girls are encouraged to read the episode to be blessed with a suitable spouse. In Bhagavatam and Hari Vamsham, the story of Rukmini is established as that of a great devotee, apart from being a beloved bride of Lord Krishna. But often her story, post her wedding, is eclipsed by the macro plot of the Mahabharata and the exploits of Lord Krishna. I considered it a matter of fortune to retell the story of the woman believed to be the incarnation of Goddess Lakshmi. The result is this book in your hands, a labour of all my love for Krishna, the Mahabharata and Bhagavatam.

Writing the story of Lord Krishna's household proved to be a tricky and yet fulfilling challenge. While Bhagavatam and Harivamsham extol his householder life to be full of delightful leelas, the Mahabharata shows a grim macro picture of the whole of Bharatavarsha walking towards sure doom—the battle of Kurukshetra. Was Rukmini's life after she wed this delightful champion of dharma only filled with household intrigues and co-wife rivalries, where she emerged as the epitome of forbearance and bhakti? Or was she an active part of Krishna's endeavours to establish dharma in the whole of Bharata? This novel is also my humble attempt to reconcile the contrasting narratives of the Bhagavatam and the Mahabharata. As I mentioned, a challenging endeavour that required me to take many liberties as well as a fulfilling one that blessed me with a vision of Lord Krishna's household, of what went behind his serene smile that keeps the faith of his bhaktas going.

To my poetical mind, Rukmini manifested as the irresistible feminine energy, the Shakti in human form, growing every minute to match her divine husband. The wedding of Rukmini is a game changer even in the plot of the Mahabharata, though we don't find explicit mentions. With Jarasandha, the Emperor of Magadha, flexing his muscles, the future of the smaller kingdoms was under his mercy. Extending his hegemony through marital relationships, be it giving away his own daughters to Kamsa so that he could raise a powerful neighbour in the vicinity of the Kurus or binding his own followers like Shishupala of Chedi and Rukma of Vidarbha by betrothing Rukmini to Shishupala. The stance of Princess Rukmini to choose Krishna, a rising Yadava leader, instead of bowing down to Jarasandha's designs is the first act of rebellion the Magadha king encountered among his own followers. The patriarchal bounds could not stop the avatara of Goddess Lakshmi from reuniting with that of Lord Vishnu and in the form of this wedding, adharma, which was entrenched in the polity of Bharatavarsha, found a challenge.

There are also aspects of the Yadava and Vrishni sociopolitical structures, which escape many readers of the epics, and have been explored in the book. The republican structure of Sudharma, the gathering of Yadava lords, the active participation of women in the state affairs, and the voice and strength they wielded would leave even those in the twenty-first century wonderstruck.

In Adi Parva of the Mahabharata, Shakuntala lectures Dushyanta about the status of a wife,

Ardha bharya manushyasya bharya srestatamah sakhaa
Bhaaryaa moolam trivargasya bharya mitramarishyatam

(A wife is half the man. A wife is the best of friends. A wife is the source of three objectives—dharma, artha, kama. A wife is a friend till the very end)

—*The Mahabharata Volume 1* by Dr Bibek Debroy

In this book, Goddess Rukmini willed me to explore her life after her wedding, which was in no way less adventurous than her husband's. I attempted to plot her trajectory from a rebellious princess, to a committed lover and wife, and finally to a towering lady in the Lord's household, who held his fortress when he was absent. It is also about her journey of gradual realization of the divinity that surrounded her and sprouted within her, which made her a fitting goddess by Krishna's side.

My story is but a humble script of how the divine couple chose to manifest in my words. I humbly pray to Goddess Rukmini and Lord Krishna to bless every reader with a joyful and fulfilled life led in the path of dharma.

Namostu nandatmaja vallabhaayaih
(I bow down to the beloved of the son of Nanda)

Prologue

Saurashtra

'Arise, brother Arjuna,' Rukmini said softly. Those around her could only wonder how she could compose herself in the face of what she had lost.

'Of all the people, I expected you to face this better. He isn't dead. He can never be. Death doesn't have a chance against him,' Rukmini repeated what she had kept on saying the past week. Others called it her sullen defiance of the inevitable. But try as they did, none could convince her otherwise.

Arjuna recovered from the faint that had overtaken him and realized that he was lying on the very bed of the man who once meant everything to him. 'He is indeed capable of outwitting Death himself, sister Rukmini. Death was, but a change of garments for the Atman, he used to say.' The words were philosophical but bereavement shook his voice. The darkening crimson rays of the fast setting sun mirrored the gloom of everyone at Dwaraka. Like a nightmare that refused to end.

Rukmini looked at him. The warrior who had single-handedly overcome every opponent he faced in battle, the invincible Maharathi who did not break at the worst of miseries now seemed on the edge.

'Brother Arjuna...'

Arjuna rose to his feet with an effort. It was a visible struggle on his face to gather resolve in the face of bereavement that he had never even dreamt of. Holding Rukmini by her arm, he implored, 'Come with me to Indraprastha, Rukmini. We need each other in this hour.'

Rukmini shook her head and pulled her arm back. 'Brother, I can't leave Dwaraka.' She stepped away. Softening, she added, 'He promised to come for me. And he will...'

Arjuna walked up to the threshold and stopped, clutching at the ornate projections of the enormous doors of her palace. Even the inanimate objects of this household seemed to grieve. But the woman before him stuck to her obstinate belief. *Enviable obstinacy*. If that was madness, he wished he shared it with her. But no, he could not escape reality. Not when all he had of his dearest charioteer, his best friend, advisor, guru and god was that last message to save the Yadavas. At least whoever remained of them. And Arjuna knew his own sanity was fast fading. He had to take them all to safety while he still could.

'And he made me promise him to keep you all safe, Rukmini. Pray, come with me sister.'

'Yes, take everyone else with you back to Indraprastha, my brother. That will fulfil my responsibility too. But I cannot come.' Rukmini's closed her eyes. The sound of a large wave thrashing against the high walls of the palace startled them both. The next moment, she saw Arjuna stagger, losing his balance. She herself felt shaken at the unexpected impact. Steadying themselves, they looked at each other; realization dawned upon both. *It had come much before they had expected it to!*

Arjuna saw a transformation in her face. Grit and authority making their way into her otherwise tranquil eyes.

'Follow me!' she urged and he had to comply.

'Malathi! Mrinalini! Towards the backyard! The backyard!' Instructions kept pouring out of her mouth and Arjuna found himself mechanically following what he could. More palace folk joined them.

Rukmini called out to the guards like one possessed. 'The worse has come! Open that! Quick!' She pointed at the inconspicuous doors of a seldom-used corridor towards the southern direction. 'Get in there and move southward everyone.'

Arjuna saw an old guard take the cue and ring an enormous bell to warn those in the furthest corners of the palace. More family members and attendants joined. They had been preparing for this journey, and still, the sea managed to surprise them. Rumbling sounds followed. The world seemed like it was in a hurry to merge into a deluge. Rukmini and Arjuna fought on with every bit of energy, trying to save every life they could. They stopped at a cracking sound at the western wall of the city visible from her garden. The sea had begun to attack Dwaraka! The earth quaked again.

A few minutes were all it needed for the earth to show her arrogant denizens their place. Helpless cries rented the air. Suppressing every other emotion, Rukmini raised her hand to gather themselves and led the way through the corridor.

'The pillar triads will hold the palace walls in place for a while. We shall reach the southern creek from where we can wade into mainland Saurashtra.'

Others, too numb to give in to any emotion, followed her. She had led them all to safety once, this way. They could trust her to save them once again now. They had to.

❦

It was past midnight when the carts and chariots were ready for the journey. The horrific riot at Prabhasa and Nature's sudden onslaught had left them too little to bother carrying along with themselves. But the valuables and wealth had already reached the mainland under a heavy guard, thanks to Rukmini's early preparations.

'Brother…' Rukmini halted. But Arjuna, too, was determined and she could not offer much resistance lest he crumbled under his own anguish. He helped Rukmini board the chariot. Unfurling the eagle banner that violently fluttered in the gale, Arjuna cracked the whip.

Memories of the times when the sight of this very eagle banner brought unspeakable joy to his heart were still fresh in his mind. Neither of them spoke. Rukmini surveyed the line of bullock carts that followed them.

'Go slow. They should be able to keep up.'

Arjuna nodded. With one last look at the glorious city that changed the face of western Bharatavarsha, the retinue proceeded eastwards. Before long, Rukmini heard Arjuna cry.

'My Gandiva! It was in your palace!'

He could speak no more. Rukmini pressed his arm. It was a painful sight to see the warrior in him disintegrate.

'Brother, look at me,' she implored. 'Gandiva served you well. You wielded it and honoured it. Let Lord Varuna claim the legendary weapon now. The battle ahead of us has little use of conventional weapons.'

Arjuna sighed, a wry chuckle racking him. 'Fool that I am. Mourning a bow when my friend, my cousin, my... everything that kept me together has left me!'

That was when Rukmini gave him an angry shove. 'He has not left! You don't believe me, son of Kunti!'

It was Arjuna's turn to steady himself and gather her in an embrace. 'I burnt his remains with these hands, Rukmini.'

Rukmini shook her head, extricating herself. 'Is this all you know of him, Arjuna?'

Arjuna suppressed another cry and set the horses to a gallop. He could not afford to cry till he reached the ramparts of Indraprastha. Ignoring Rukmini was the best he could do. But it was a tough task as she kept on repeating those words all through the way.

'He can appear right here. If he wished. Any moment.'

Arjuna shook his head and cracked the whip again. That

moment, they heard a cry. An ominous one. Arjuna's arms froze. The horses came to a standstill. The sound of a horn followed. Bullocks bellowed from behind.

Hell broke loose.

'Abhiras! The merciless barbarians!' someone shouted from behind. 'Women! Protect the women!'

Arjuna scrambled for the handy sword. He almost caught the hilt when something whizzed past him and pain seared through his left arm.

'Rukmini!'

'Brother Arjuna!' Rukmini felt his arm and gasped. The arrow had cut deep. She doubted if he could lift the weapon.

'By Mahadeva, why aren't the horses moving?'

They had stopped, sensing hostile figures surrounding the chariot.

'Stay away!' Arjuna warned, cracking the whip in the air.

But fate was not on the side of the once invincible warrior. Rukmini was overcome with pity at the helplessness in his tone.

'Arjuna,' she said tenderly. 'You've suffered enough.'

'Rukmini!'

'Don't blame yourself, my brother.'

Arjuna could hardly reply when two rough hands yanked him off the chariot.

'Spare him. Take me.'

'Dare you low lives even approach her... Rukmini!'

She stood, stoically holding on to the flagstaff as the chariot came under the mercy of the attackers, speeding into darkness.

She heard Arjuna bellow, but in vain.

'Krishna!' His name escaped both their lips, but laden with different emotions.

Rukmini felt a strange sense of familiarity, the memory of being 'abducted' on this very chariot. It was decades ago, but she remembered it like yesterday. She also remembered the delirious abandon she had felt. Laughter shook her. A hysterical laughter that echoed across the wilderness and reached the high skies.

Part One

At Avanti, Many Decades Earlier

'Stop that laughter! Pray, that's the least you can do.'

But Rukmini was not in a mood to heed that request, or anything else that told her to slow the horses she drove.

'Rukmini, please! Unless you have something so against me that you want me to get thrown off the chariot and die.'

'By Mahadeva!' Rukmini sighed at the continuous outpour of nagging. 'I expected the Princess of Avanti to be a sport.' She finally pulled on the reins, bringing the chariot to a halt.

For a long moment, Mitravinda did not move, still hugging the flag post, and shielding her eyes from the swirls of dust that arose from Rukmini's feverish pace of driving the steeds. When she finally moved, she coughed, inhaling the remnants of dust enveloping them. 'Mahakala save us indeed! We have lost the guard!' Annoyance replaced fear in her tone. The fourteen-year-old Princess of Avanti had heard a lot about her guest, the Princess of Vidarbha. But when Rukmini insisted upon accompanying her to the forest ashram of Sandipani and that she would drive the chariot herself, Mitravinda had not bargained for this mad ride that drained her off her energy.

'Did we?' Rukmini's eyes grew wider as she surveyed the path they had travelled along. Her parted lips met again after a moment when she turned back and saw Mitravinda frowning. 'At last!' Rukmini laughed again, oblivious to the dangers that might threaten them in the wild.

'I am walking back,' Mitravinda declared, alighting from the chariot. The feel of her feet on the firm ground was comforting.

'Don't you worry, Mitra. They are bound to follow us till here. Perhaps a muhurta or two later,' Rukmini called after her. 'Do you hear that?' She stopped.

Mitravinda halted and turned back. 'That's the waters!' She sighed; relief visible at the gurgling sound. 'We must be close to the ashram. These tiny rivulets spring to life post monsoon.'

Rukmini's eyes lit up at the mention of 'rivulet'. 'Let's go to the water. Pray, I am dying of thirst. We can also have a quick bath and get rid of the dust on us before meeting Guru Sandipani.'

Mitravinda's mood lifted at the idea. The guard that accompanied them from Ujjayini would soon find the empty chariot and look for them. 'We have just the time for a relieving bath.'

Mitravinda agreed and they hurried towards the water. Soon, they were splashing water against each other, unmindful of the wilderness around them. Rukmini though, kept a close watch on her weapons—a dagger and a sword.

'To think that I was so unwilling to come to this ashram itself, much less, bringing you with me. By the whole pantheon, Rukmini, I never thought you were this wild!'

Rukmini laughed again. 'I don't let go of the smallest opportunity to break free of the suffocating royal guard. Be it of Avanti or of Vidarbha. And why were you unwilling to visit the ashram? Aren't you looking forward to meeting your brothers, Vinda and Anuvinda?'

Mitra rolled her eyes, shrugging, and Rukmini needed no more insight into the relationship she shared with her brothers. Something that Rukmini could very well connect to. Her own brother Rukma had reservations about her 'unladylike' habits and she never let his remarks against her go without stiff contentions. Every exchange only soured the relationship between them. So much so that other family members openly wished for her to get married and go away so that they were spared of these squabbles.

'Brothers are supposed to make their sister feel cared for,'

Mitravinda remarked, almost continuing Rukmini's unexpressed thoughts. She then pursed her lips and shook her head, not wanting to say more in front of a maiden she had met only a couple of days before.

'We need to take charge of our lives, little one,' Rukmini smiled, drying her hair with her upper garment. 'That is exactly the reason I came with you to the ashram.' She winked.

Mitravinda's curiosity was piqued.

'Have you considered the kingdoms you may get married into? The princes who would make prospective grooms?' Rukmini continued.

The thought of getting married was not new to Mitravinda. But narrowing down the options was something she had not done yet. She looked at Rukmini and shook her head, the mixed feelings of her heart showing up.

Rukmini patted her cheek. 'Trying to deny the reality, Mitra?'

The response was a sigh. Rukmini shrugged and continued, 'Kuru, Panchala, Kashi, Kalinga, Kekaya, Madra, Gandhara, Kambhoja, Magadha, Chedi, Pundra, Pragjyotisha. The princes of these kingdoms are all what we are left to choose from.'

Mitravinda nodded, thoughtful. 'So, you made a choice. Did you not?'

'I did. And none of the above, including your brothers, seem to fit.' Rukmini fanned her upper garment and leaned against a boulder.

'Waiting for a god now. Aren't you?' Mitravinda teased.

'We don't have much time, Mitra.' Rukmini refused to be humoured. 'If we don't make the first move, someone else will do it, seal our fates for their narrow ends.'

'How can anyone do that!' Mitravinda looked up. 'We get to make our choice in a swayamvara. That has been the way of our ancestors. That is what the codes and Shastras prescribe.'

Rukmini stared into the vacuum. 'Ancestors. Codes. Shastras. If they were truly valued and cherished, we would not face what we do today, Princess of Avanti. Decades ago, the princesses of Kashi were carried away from their swayamvara. One of them protested and perished searching for justice. Two others were made to marry the brother of their abductor. When their husband died childless, they were made to go through niyoga. Can you imagine yourself in their place?'

Mitravinda shook her head. 'That abductor is now a revered patriarch whose ways are looked up to.'

'At the other end, there are people like Jarasandha of Magadha. That abomination of a man can go to any extent to spread his dominion. Political to marital, he forges any alliance at his will.'

Mitravinda nodded, aware of the recent developments at Vidarbha and Rukmini's distaste for the King of Magadha. 'Panchala and Kuru. Possibly the only kingdoms yet to fall under his sway.'

'That means Avanti too…' Rukmini frowned. Mitravinda only sighed in response.

Another kingdom. That can't be good!

A splash of water behind the bushes drew their attention. Rukmini almost reached for her dagger when sounds of laughter fell upon her ears. Merry laughter of a man and a woman. Filled with an abandon that made her smile and follow the voices. Mitravinda too followed her.

'Balarama, how I wish I were not bound by my promise to my father.'

'No, beloved Princess. Trust me, I shall never make you choose between the two.'

Rukmini halted, sensing that the lovers were close by.

'It is dangerous, Balarama. I am on a hopeless mission that will take me to my death. Don't follow me there.'

'Ah Death! He is an old friend, Revathi. A frequent visitor, almost like family. My brother and I shall convince him to visit us later. Like we've been doing all our lives.'

The sheer mixture of mirth and confidence made Rukmini and Mitravinda exchange smiles.

'And besides, I can't break my brahmacharya or yours, Princess. We shall wait till I win your hand, fair and square.'

Brahmacharis? They must be the students of Sandipani. Rukmini cautiously walked around the thickets to seek directions from the couple the very moment Revathi chose to throw herself into Balarama's arms. Rukmini and Mitravinda gasped aloud, startling them.

'For—forgive us, we did not mean to interrupt,' said Rukmini.

'We are just seeking our way to Guru Sandipani's ashram. I am Mitravinda from Avanti and she is Rukmini, the Princess of Vidarbha,' Mitravinda added.

They saw the male brahmachari grin. 'Mitra! Cousin, what a pleasant surprise! How are aunt Rajadhi and uncle Jayatsena?'

Rukmini saw Mitra wonder for a moment and then grin back at him. 'Cousin Balarama.'

Rukmini started walking away to not intrude into what looked like a family reunion, but Mitravinda pulled her back.

'Come with us to the ashram. We shall send out some of the students to inform your guard in case they are looking for you,' Revathi beamed. There was something warm about her and her lover that instantly drew Rukmini.

'Where is Krishna?' Mitravinda asked Balarama as the little party made its way towards the ashram.

'Somewhere around,' Rukmini heard Balarama reply. It seemed a bit strange that the Princess of Avanti, who was overjoyed to meet her cousins, did not enquire as much about her own brothers Vinda and Anuvinda. The conversation around her had the typical joy of a long-due family reunion. Mitravinda's every second sentence seemed to be around this Krishna. Rukmini halted in her steps due to a memory of what she had overheard her brother Rukma saying to an envoy from Magadha, a few weeks before. They had spoken of brothers Balarama and Krishna. And that the Emperor of Magadha wanted to kill the brothers in order to avenge his son-in-law Kamsa of Mathura.

Eavesdropping on conversations around state affairs started as a childhood pastime for Rukmini. Her father did not mind at first. When her brother started objecting, Rukmini was only incensed enough to rebel and do it more and as a result, she got to know of most of Rukma's plans. She secretly enjoyed it when they failed. And now, she was face to face with someone whose killing was being plotted by Jarasandha, the man who she hated and her brother worshipped. Rukmini was brought back from her thoughts when Mitravinda waved at her and she realized that they had reached the ashram.

Krishna

The stay at the ashram was more comfortable than Rukmini had imagined. The spacious cottages were tastefully painted and decorated with inexpensive pottery. The simplicity was endearing. And Gurupatni Sughosha took care about their basic comforts. It was only in the middle of the night that Rukmini awoke with a start. She had dreamt of a certain assassin attempting to kill the good-natured Balarama and his brother whose face she could not see before she woke up. Sighing with relief, Rukmini reached out for the water jug beside the lamp. It was empty.

Rukmini groaned. It wasn't even midnight, but her thirst showed no signs of being quenched. The lightning, thunder and rain outside did not help. Unable to bear the dehydration anymore, she walked out of the hut into the incessant drizzle, hoping to find a student of the ashram who she could request for water. But the weather had made sure that there were none around. Everyone had retired.

Her eyes fell upon the residence of Guru Sandipani. Rukmini did not want to disturb the Gurupatni at this hour. But she also felt it would not hurt to check out just in case there was someone awake. Cautiously, she made her way to Sandipani's hut. She could hear voices. *Good! I could ask them for water without having to disturb their sleep.* But what fell upon her ears made her next step hesitant and unsure.

'I am really worried, Sughosha. The boys should have returned by now.' It was the Kulapati, Guru Sandipani.

Rukmini heard Gurupatni sigh. 'The weather can be so treacherous. Even a slight clue about the rain, and I would have forbidden the boys from leaving the ashram.'

'First thing in the morning, I want to transfer the duty of fetching firewood to someone else. We cannot risk Krishna's safety this way. Much depends on him.'

'In fact, Kulapati, Krishna himself came asking if there was enough firewood to cook for the large group of guests. The detail had slipped my mind too. He can be so thoughtful while being engaged in study and practice too!'

'He is made for bigger things, Sughosha. His insights into Shastric tenets, his focus, his attention to detail—everything leaves me wonderstruck. He gives me the hope of a change that this land of Bharata badly needs.'

'Blessed are his parents to have a son like him.'

'He is the saviour of his clan. He killed Kamsa, that son-in-law of Jarasandha. That King of Magadha is bent upon revenge. There might be forces that may want to harm Krishna.' Sandipani lowered his tone. 'That Princess of Vidarbha who is visiting us, her brother is close to Jarasandha. Her guard may have spies or even assassins. Who knows why she tagged along with Princess Mitravinda here?'

'Princess Rukmini? She doesn't look like she means any harm, Kulapati,' Sughosha almost chided Sandipani. 'Besides, I am more worried about the boys missing their meal in the evening. Hope they don't feel weak or faint!'

Rukmini bit her lip. Her brother's reputation as a mindless minion of that Jarasandha had preceded her and now, she herself was being doubted of malice when she meant none.

'Maybe I am rash in my suspicions. But we better be paranoid than be sorry, Sughosha. We know the pain of losing our child. We cannot let it happen again to the parents of those under our care. Certainly not to the parents of Krishna and Balarama. I shall go in search of them at the break of dawn.'

There was no way Rukmini could talk to them. Not at least till her anger had subsided. Anger against that unfair suspicion.

Anger against her brother and that monster at Magadha who her brother worshipped. Struggling to get a grip over herself, she turned around to walk back to her cottage. A part of her wanted to wake up Mitravinda and leave the ashram immediately. But there was no need to for that. The horses of the chariot they drove in would know their way back to Avanti and from there, she could leave for Vidarbha and confront her brother.

Or…

Rukmini halted at the whiff of familiar fragrance of the meal she had eaten in the evening. To her right, was the hut that served as the store for the food left over after the meal.

Or she could…

In a saner frame of mind, Rukmini would not have considered that as a foolhardy thought. But her indignation got the better of her. So did the resolve to prove to Sandipani that she came with no malice. And to make everyone around her realize that she was no puppet in the hands of the men of her family.

The rain was not going to stop her.

By the time sense kicked in, Rukmini had gone too far with her plan. Too far to even consider regretting. She frantically glanced around the treacherous wilder paths off the ashram. *How could she find the two boys lost in the wilderness who she had never seen in her life? And why did she spend the rainy night in search of them?* Thankfully, she had ridden the chariot and had stuck to the beaten path in the jungle. The rain had sent the predators too deeper towards shelter. Rukmini considered the recklessness she had resorted to. Her hosts, both Mitravinda and Sandipani, would be worried about her absence and Sandipani was already worried about Krishna not returning.

The fatigue of the long night began to catch up with her. Rukmini thought of drinking water from the nearest source and exploring ways to return to the ashram, hopefully before the break of dawn. She would have to invent an excuse for her wet garments. The rain had finally stopped and locating the stream of water was simpler with the gurgling sound reaching her ears clearly. Rukmini alighted from the chariot and walked across the muddy pathway. The sky had begun to brighten and the forest looked much more benign. That was when she saw the enormous boulder that had caved in towards the bottom, almost providing a hood-like shelter to someone reclining below. Rukmini let out a gasp of surprise. He did look like a brahmachari from the ashram.

No sooner did the shape of the boulder remind her of a cobra's hood, Rukmini actually spotted a real one, dangerously close to him, and hardly a few feet away from his head. The reptile drew itself to its full height and spread its hood. Holding her breath, Rukmini hurried closer, hoping not to be spotted by the cobra. But to her horror, she saw the hood turn towards her. Rukmini froze and collapsed to the ground. The cobra stood still, showing no signs of retreating; as still as the youth sleeping blissfully, oblivious to the venomous creature at his head. Gathering her wits, Rukmini inched closer, till she could try and shake him awake. The cobra hissed and she froze again. Only after a long pause did Rukmini exhale and reached out to shake him awake, by his leg.

'Wake up,' she managed to whisper. 'There is a cobra a yard away from your head... Stay still.'

Before he even stirred, a shrill cry startled Rukmini from behind, making her clutch at his knee. A furious flutter followed and she became aware of a presence behind her. Possibly of some bird, an enormous one.

Goddess Gauri!

'You stay with me as well,' Rukmini heard his calm words—unrealistically calm in the face of almost certain death. She saw him turn her way. The first ray of dawn had penetrated through the wild cover. Her gaze, which had stuck to the treacherous reptile all this while, turned to his face and paused at his eyes. He opened them. Her lips parted. It felt like she had known the spark in his eyes for long. A smile appeared on his lips, reaching his eyes and she let out the breath she had arrested till then.

'What's behind me?'

His smile was more pronounced. Reaching out to hold her hand that was still clutching his leg, he replied, 'An unrealistically large eagle.'

Rukmini resisted the urge to turn around, and nodded. It felt better to look into his eyes that spoke of something beyond her comprehension. In a trice, he sat up and rolled away from the boulder, pulling Rukmini away too.

The legendary enemies, the serpent and the eagle, were now locked in a battle of gazes. Rukmini watched them with bated breath. The eagle was truly enormous. The serpent moved, slithering along the boulder and the eagle fluttered its wings, gliding forward. They almost crossed each other's paths. But then, the snake crawled away, disappearing into the wilderness. The eagle also flew away, out of her sight. The day became brighter. As if what she had seen till now had also been a dream. If anything was real, it was this young man before her. *Was he...?*

'Krishna!' A third voice interrupted their wordless conversation.

'Sudama! Glad you found me.'

'Who is this?'

Rukmini shook herself of her reverie and introduced herself to the two brahmacharis, conscious of her gaze refusing to tear away from Krishna. 'Guru Sandipani and Gurupatni were worried all night about you both not returning.'

'And you came searching for us, Princess?' Sudama stared at her, eyes wide. 'Alone?' he added, looking around.

Rukmini found herself almost cornered. Which princess or

even young woman would go in the middle of the night in search of a stranger who she had never met in a strange land?

'My...horses ... they gain speed early,' she lied pointing towards the path where her chariot stood, and hoping that there was some group searching for Krishna and Sudama behind her.

'Glad they did, Princess Rukmini,' Krishna beamed. 'I was almost faint with hunger.'

Rukmini felt her heart miss a beat, out of concern.

'I happened to bring a potful of the parched rice that Gurupatni prepared yesterday evening! Let me bring that...' But as she sprinted towards the chariot, they followed her.

As she watched them have the parched rice, Rukmini could not help but remember her dream. It felt all the more disturbing now. If what she overheard her brother saying about Jarasandha's vengeful motive was true ... Rukmini shuddered inwardly. That very moment, Krishna looked up at her and smiled. Did he know of the danger that loomed over his head? Rukmini had heard bits and pieces of his past from Mitravinda as a tough survivor against multiple attempts on his life. But now, the threat came from a monster against whom nobody in Bharatavarsha could stand. The least that this brave youth deserved was some knowledge of what awaited him. Rukmini realized that Krishna was looking at her askance as she stared at him and sighed inwardly. Pursing her lips for a moment, she gathered herself enough to say, 'Stay in the ashram for another year. At least. The King of Magadha plans to attack your Mathura soon. I overheard my brother Prince Rukma talking about this.'

She saw his brows come together in a furrow and his eyes widen with what looked like surprise, but his lips too curved in what looked like amusement. *Which of them was true?*

'And you dared to commit what some would call espionage, because?'

Rukmini felt indignation rise within. In a span of a few hours, she had gone from an insane maiden riding out in the rain searching for strangers to someone betraying her own family. *Well, she had not leaked out military secrets of Vidarbha,* she angrily thought to herself.

'Is that how a person gets rewarded for sharing some life-saving information?' she retorted, making no attempt to hide her annoyance.

Krishna shook his head. 'I meant, a favour of this order warrants... what can I pay you back for this?' His smile was disarming enough to make all her anger melt away. But the thought of Jarasandha made Rukmini feel more defiant than ever.

'Just frustrate every attempt of Jarasandha who meddles in affairs that don't concern him. He has had an unchallenged run for far too long.'

As the words rolled out of her mouth, Rukmini realized how unrealistic they sounded. She dearly hoped that he would choose to leave the conversation and to her relief, he and Sudama finished their food and rose to return to the ashram.

❦

'Jarasandha plans to attack Mathura?' Balarama sounded surprised as well as angry. 'That old...' evidently, he restrained himself from mouthing an abuse. 'And that Princess of Vidarbha told you this? Why?'

'What should be done during his attack is the question that needs an immediate answer, brother. I say, we bid farewell to brahmacharya now, return to Mathura and lead a retaliation. I know Mathura will prevail this time.'

'As much as I would love to put an end to Jarasandha, how are you this sure, Krishna?'

Unknown to Balarama, Rukmini too waited for an answer. Just that she was hiding below the window of the cottage that housed them in the ashram. She almost regretted sharing the information now. What was the use if Krishna was going to throw himself in the way of danger this way?

'The Kingdom of Panchala lies in Jarasandha's way. And King Drupada is hostile to Magadha. And Jarasandha's motive is personal now. He would not plan a military attack with full strength. He would bear in mind a submissive Mathura, with fearful Yadavas against who he had a dominating run all these years. If we return and motivate the Yadavas to unite and retaliate, he would be in for a surprise and that would enable us to best him,' said Krishna, putting forth his analysis.

Rukmini found herself smiling at the very thought of someone besting Jarasandha.

'Sounds like a plan,' she heard Balarama agree. 'And if I may ask, what is with that smile of yours since this morning, Krishna? I am reminded of our days in Vrindavan.' There was no reply from Krishna.

Rukmini heard Balarama approach Krishna. 'Is there a reason other than Jarasandha for you to bid farewell to brahmacharya?'

Rukmini's lips parted as she waited for Krishna to answer. There was a teasing silence that followed. Almost frustrating.

'Rukmini!' Mitravinda's sudden call almost made her jump out of her skin. 'What are you doing here?'

Years of eavesdropping on Rukma's conversations had prepared Rukmini to generate believable excuses right on her feet. Letting the earring she held fall to the ground, she pretended to search for the jewel.

'Rukmini, what are you searching for...By Mahadeva, you are standing on it!' Mitravinda came and retrieved the earring as Rukmini backed away, acting her best to look sheepish. 'Let us leave.'

Rukmini wordlessly followed Mitravinda, now fully aware that the brothers knew of her presence around their hut. Mitravinda had accepted her excuse as she was unaware of the whole thing, but Krishna and Balarama were not fools to believe in her earring story. All she could hope was to beat a hasty retreat before the last bits of her reputation were shredded. But to her embarrassment, Krishna and Balarama walked out of the hut. She avoided looking at them and let Mitravinda bid her farewell. It was almost like they knew her predicament when they did not try and look her in the eye—a gesture that made her breathe easy till she boarded the chariot. She turned around to find Krishna's gaze fixed upon her. He beamed and she felt compelled to smile back before the chariot departed.

Shishupala

Vidarbha

'Mid-day meal in the garden? Just because there is a guest? Why can't he be hosted in the dining chamber?' Rukmini frowned. The chief of female attendants of the palace did not reply. Her duty had been to just convey Crown Prince Rukma's order and not justify them. Even if she tried, the older woman knew that justifying any of Rukma's actions to Rukmini was a task unachievable even by the Gods. So notorious was their rivalry. Though Rukmini always had the upper hand in the palace matters, it was not so today.

Rukmini stared at the maid and shook her head. 'Well, send for Malathi then.'

'She is already there, helping out with the arrangements, my Princess. Let me help with braiding your hair,' she smiled. 'Experience has taught me a thing or two about braiding that your friend Malathi may not know.'

Rukmini's mind remained troubled. Royal guests were not new to Vidarbha. She herself had hosted rishis and travelling bards many times. It was the guests from royal and noble backgrounds that she kept away from. Mostly because they all belonged under the political umbrella of Jarasandha, the man who controlled the bulk of Bharatavarsha, not through rightful emperorship, but through other shady means that included managing and taking advantage of mutual dependencies through forging marital alliances. Today's guest, according to what she heard, was no different from a minion of Jarasandha.

Prince Shishupala of Chedi.

The name and kingdom did not matter to Rukmini. She just loathe to be a part of one of her brother's extravagant lunches that reeked of political appeasement.

'A smile on that blooming face would top it all, my Princess.' The senior maid concluded as she secured a freshly woven string of jasmines along the length of Rukmini's braid with a golden pin.

Rukmini controlled her frown out of respect for the maid's age. But unsolicited advice regarding her etiquette was not something Rukmini tolerated.

'Alright, let us get this over with,' Rukmini nodded, making a mental note to give a piece of her mind to Rukma later. He had no right to commit her presence without consulting her. Rukmini strode towards the garden in front of King Bhishmaka's mansion, ignoring the maid's suggestions about her pace and gait.

Nearing the garden, she considered having a word with her father first and was about to enter his chamber when a cry fell upon her ears. It came from one of the resthouses at the southwestern corner of the garden. Rukmini hurried in the direction. The sight of the couple of guards who stood at a distance tested her temper. 'Why aren't you rushing to whoever that is...' Rukmini said, as her eyes narrowed at the sight that met her.

'Malathi!'

Her companion since childhood and keeper of her secrets, Malathi seemed to be struggling against a man. He had pinned her against a pillar.

Rukmini raced to the spot, not bothering to order the guards to follow her. 'Let her GO! How dare you!'

The youth turned around. The contempt at the intervening voice changed into something else—a smile; no, a smirk. And an unapologetic one that only multiplied Rukmini's rage.

'Princess!' Malathi said, struggling to break free of his grip.

Perhaps it was something in Rukmini's glare that made the

youth let go of Malathi, who hurried to take shield behind Rukmini.

'Princess Rukmini, is it? Heard about you…' He smiled, eyes still narrowing at the way Rukmini comforted Malathi.

His silks and jewels suggested a royal birth. Rukmini guessed that this was that Prince of Chedi who was visiting them. She exhaled, bringing her voice down to normal with an effort. 'I may be unaware of the way women are treated in your place, but here at Vidarbha, holding a woman against her will is a crime. But as a guest who may be unaware of what we may consider a given, you can get away by apologizing to my companion.'

The senior maid of the palace had now caught up with Rukmini. Panting, she exclaimed, 'Princess Rukmini, that is Prince Shishupala of Chedi.'

'Prince Shishupala,' Rukmini acknowledged without blinking. 'Apologize.'

Shishupala smirked in response, his intense gaze starting to make Rukmini uncomfortable. *And Rukma was hosting this man!* There was no way she was going to play host to such a brute.

'You are brave.' Shishupala came forward, stepping too close for comfort. 'But don't maids and servants here follow the orders of their masters? My Princess, you ought to visit Chedi to have a taste of their obedience.'

Rukmini stood her ground. After a long pause, she turned to the guards. 'Escort him to the outskirts of Kundina,' she said to them. The lone pair of guards as well as the maids who had collected there looked shocked. 'You heard me. And you, Shishupala, back off.'

The menace in Shishupala's smirk only increased as he remained unmoved, challenging her authority. The inaction from the guards added to her frustration and then, Rukmini's patience snapped. The next moment, Shishupala staggered back by a pace, clutching his cheek where she had delivered a resounding slap.

'What's going on?' a voice interrupted. The guards visibly

straightened at the entrance of the Crown Prince Rukma. 'Rukmini!'

'What's going on? Eldest, your guards have turned blind and deaf! Or they are forced to, when you bring undesirable and undeserving guests to our kingdom.' Rukmini's anger was now directed at her brother.

The senior maid conveyed what happened in broken phrases. Rukma glared at Rukmini and then turned to Shishupala. 'The midday meal shall be served in the royal dining hall itself, Yuvaraja Shishupala... My father, King Bhishmaka, shall join us too,' he added in a hurry.

'Count me out of it,' Rukmini declared and walked away, not caring for the reaction of either. Only Malathi scuttled away behind her.

'Seek out the King and request his audience,' Rukmini instructed another guard on the way as they passed the western entrance of King Bhishmaka's mansion. 'And you, Malathi, shall tell my father what exactly happened.'

Malathi nodded, now looking like she would break into tears any moment. Rukmini took her to her chambers. But there was no message from her father all day. Instead, there was a message from Rukma summoning Malathi, which Rukmini angrily told Malathi to ignore. When she could not stand it any longer, Rukmini stormed towards Bhishmaka's chambers.

There, she caught up with a tired Bhishmaka, seeking to retire early. 'Can we sleep when our "honoured guest" lusts after innocent palace maids?' She shook Bhishmaka's arm.

Though used to his daughter's ways, the force of her tug was more than what Bhishmaka was prepared for. 'Rukmini!' He frowned, realizing that she was angrier than ever before. The matter was obviously more important than her usual quarrels with Rukma.

'Shishupala nearly molested poor Malathi. And this imbecile son of yours, Rukma... Don't even make me say what his reaction was! In your place, Father, I would have disowned him.'

Bhishmaka sighed. Prince Shishupala of Chedi was not just a royal guest, but also a chosen protégé of Emperor Jarasandha. Angering him would not just mean hostility from Chedi, but it would also earn the ire of Jarasandha. 'Rukmini.' He gently patted her shoulder, motioning her to sit by his side. 'I have always indulged you in your quarrels against your brother. It always made me proud to have a headstrong daughter. But the matter now is more serious.'

'Exactly, Father. The matter is now of the honour of women working for us, trusting our capability to protect them.'

'Wait,' Bhishmaka shook his head. 'Shishupala is not just a guest, Rukmini.'

'He is a predator, evil and malicious! Send him away at once and try knocking some sense into Rukma's hard skull.'

Bhishmaka cringed. Things were definitely not going the way they all had hoped. It was hardly a week since Jarasandha's messenger had come, carrying the Emperor's message suggesting Shishupala as a prospective groom for Rukmini. Bhishmaka sadly had to admit that the Emperor of Magadha did not just mean to suggest, he meant to order. And Rukmini now was in no position to receive the news without throwing a tantrum. He would have to appeal to her sense of duty, hiding the news from her and hoping that a day would come when she would understand. He could negotiate a year or two before the wedding could be held.

'Shishupala is a young prince. We shall keep his father, Damaghosha, the King of Chedi, appraised of his behaviour. Boys do change as they grow.'

Rukmini had almost calmed down but the last statement ended up angering her even more. There was something more to Bhishmaka's reaction—or the lack of it; a sense of foreboding that she herself could not comprehend.

'Why is he a guest here anyway?' she asked, in a bid to gather any information that she was not aware of. 'There is no celebration or a festival for him to participate in. Nor has he achieved anything great for us to host him and show any appreciation. Nor does Vidarbha owe Chedi any favours. Father,' her voice fell to a whisper, though her eyes were fierce. 'Tell me why is the Prince of Chedi here at all? Why is this fool Rukma falling head over heels to impress him?'

'First of all, you need to stop talking about your eldest that way, Rukmini,' Bhishmaka cautioned. 'As my youngest child, your childhood, where you could just have things go your way, just extended beyond sixteen springs. Isn't it time you paid attention to your role, my child?'

It was the first time that Rukmini found Bhishmaka complaining about her faults. She loved her father dearly and would have listened to him any other day. But this deliberate change of topic was untimely. Still, Rukmini pursed her lips, arresting her next reaction and inhaled. 'Father, which duty did I fail to fulfil?'

'There is no shortcoming that I see in you, my child. But you are a princess, educated in the Shastras, in the statecraft, Rukmini. It is time you are also exposed to the intricacies and intrigues that surround the lives of royals.'

He saw her frown. Bhishmaka weighed his next few sentences. He was wading into tricky waters and had to hold back as much information from Rukmini as he could.

'You know that we are friends with an emperor like Jarasandha.' He nervously smiled. 'And friendships with great kings like him bring with it a large base of supporters to deal with. Do you comprehend, Rukmini?'

'King Damaghosha of Chedi is a friend of Jarasandha, which makes him our friend. I get that.' Rukmini gritted her teeth. 'That does not say we bear Shishupala's overtures without showing that we can stand up for our daughters. Does it?'

'As I said, we shall let the fact be known to Damaghosha, Rukmini. But you have to remember that you can't jeopardize our friendship—the friendship between three kingdoms—for one companion of yours.'

Rukmini sprang to her feet and backed away like she had seen a ghost. The disbelief that screamed through her eyes needed no words.

'Like I am aware of Shishupala's inappropriate behaviour, I am also aware of your thoughtless reaction, Rukmini.'

'I gave him what he deserved!'

'Slapping a guest prince for the sake of a maid... Well, well, let us even say we don't treat the women working for us as slaves, but here is where you need to apply nuance.'

'Nuance—meaning, I don't react, smiling at this "guest" like he did nothing.'

'You love your companions and maids like your own sisters, and I am proud of you for that, Rukmini,' Bhishmaka persisted. 'But sometimes, smaller things need to be sacrificed for larger causes. Haven't you studied the story of Lord Ramachandra? He sacrificed his own wife—' Bhishmaka was silenced when Rukmini protested, again with a force he had not seen coming.

'I studied about a Ramachandra who waged a battle for his wife, who ensured a rule where women could wander even in the middle of the night with no fear. Father,' Rukmini stopped to catch her breath, her voice turning hoarse, 'and those undeserving ones who cannot speak up for those under their protection need to stop taking his name!'

'Rukmini!' Bhishmaka thundered.

'Rama's sacrifices were made from a position of strength. Not as a spineless man who fears a more powerful king. Stop subverting history to suit your weaknesses.' Rukmini was like someone possessed, undeterred.

'Rukmini, I am your father.' Bhishmaka gasped and shook her arm as hard as his anger let him.

Rukmini shook, but because of her own anger that threatened to get the better of her. But the anger was overpowered by shame, of being caught in a situation this helpless. The pressure in her chest broke into a sob and Rukmini backed away, forbidding Bhishmaka from following her. She raced towards her room but the tears sprang much before, her sobs getting stronger and louder. Running into her room she closed her door, seeking the comfort of solitude, her only companion when everyone around her seemed hell-bent on doing the wrong thing—some even finding excuses from history. She had never felt this weak and alone. A part of her could not even comprehend this strong wave of grief engulfing her.

At that moment two hands held her shoulders from behind and Rukmini threw herself into them and sobbed for a brief moment before she realized she was in the embrace of a stranger, a man. Well, not so much a stranger.

A Surprise Visitor

Krishna! Here at Vidarbha!

The next moment, fear and shock replaced the rest of her emotions. Rukmini was almost sure it was a dream. It had to be, for none could enter her heavily guarded chambers. But when Krishna's hand reached out to wipe her tears, she gasped, shaking herself alert.

'What are you doing here?' she managed to blurt out.

'Searching for a safe place,' Krishna smiled. 'And I was sure to find it under your protection, Princess.'

'Under my protection, by Mahadeva! My brother Rukma hates you, Krishna!'

'That's exactly the reason why I came to your chambers instead of going to his.'

Rukmini stared at him, still not believing what was happening. Which man would be this foolhardy to come to the house of his sworn enemy, searching for a safe place? Certainly not someone who faced and overcame intrigues by the minute, like Krishna Vaasudeva. And still, here he was, trusting her. Rukmini found it hard to come to terms with that. *Or was he?*

'Tell me everything, Krishna. What brings you to Vidarbha. I am no fool to believe that you would throw yourself in harm's way without a good reason.'

'Trust me, he does that way too often, defying all logic,' a third voice interjected.

'Just when I thought it would not get more surprising!' Rukmini blurted out seeing Balarama emerging from a dark corner of the portico. Gathering herself, she showed him a seat and turned to Krishna.

'We are on our way southward, Princess Rukmini. This is the only way we could stave Jarasandha's second attack on Mathura, this time with a greater military strength than the last one. He would spare Mathura if he did not find us there,' Krishna continued as Rukmini's gaze locked with his. 'And we need a shelter for the night. I could not think of a better place than yours.'

Rukmini stared and abruptly averted her gaze. She still remembered the flutter in her heart at her first meeting with Krishna in the ashram. She had uprooted strands of hope in her heart, considering the irreconcilable hatred that her brother had for Krishna. And now, he trusted her despite her brother. Rukmini had to make a conscious effort to conceal that spring of joy at the realization. But the next moment, reality hit her. 'Any public guesthouse could have kept you safer, noble Yadava. What made you trust this chamber, which is, a stone's throw away from Rukma's. By Mahadeva, he will get you killed if he even senses that you are here!'

'*If* he senses…' Krishna waved and chuckled. 'Besides, the guesthouses are full of Jarasandha's spies. Just for your information.' Krishna shrugged. 'To gauge how faithful Vidarbha is to Magadha, they can even smell traces of any rebellion against the "emperor". And some of them also know of the welcome you gave to the Prince of Chedi this afternoon.'

Balarama suddenly rose to his feet. 'This isn't working, Krishna. I was a fool to listen to you. Let us not trouble her.'

Rukmini wanted to deny that it was a trouble. But it all seemed so much beyond all borders of sanity. How can the guards not sense the presence of two young men? Someone was bound to suspect if she ordered the maids to bring in two extra meals. 'Wait, did you even eat today?' she asked Balarama.

'Not a concern, Princess. We have seen worse.' Turning to Krishna, his voice became stern. 'We must leave.'

Krishna shrugged and went to the door, unbolting it.

'That is the front corridor! Wait!' Rukmini called after him, horrified. But Krishna had opened the door and there was someone standing there. Rukmini's heart was in her mouth for a moment before she realized it was only Malathi, who ran in like she was fleeing from someone. Obviously Shishupala.

'Princess, that Prince of Chedi again—' Malathi stopped speaking on seeing the two strangers, her jaws wide open.

Rukmini flew to the door, securing it. 'Dare not breathe a word about their presence!' She raised a forbidding finger at Malathi.

Malathi stood rooted, still unable to believe that two strangers had made their way right into the chamber. Her face was still pale with remnants of fear and now, this new shock of finding two handsome young men who her princess was fiercely protective of.

'But do breathe,' Krishna added, looking kindly at Malathi. 'Just breathe.'

Malathi nodded at him and exhaled. Krishna grinned.

'Humour?' Rukmini and Balarama exclaimed in unison.

'At this moment?' Rukmini added softly.

Before any of them could react, there was a knock at the giant wooden door of the chamber. Rukmini held on to the bolt and looked at Malathi, who swallowed and went to the door.

'The Princess is resting!' Malathi said, trying to muster as much authority as she could.

There was a sigh of uncertainty from the other side. Malathi then found the courage to rotate the wooden shutter that revealed the face of the person on the other side through the small opening. Her courage came back when she saw that it was just the senior maid who looked after the other wing of the palace.

'Prince Rukma wanted to talk to the Princess,' she said curtly.

Rukmini saw Malathi look up at her and slowly moved to shield Krishna from view. Behind the closed doors, it was unnecessary but she could not take chances. She shook her head at Malathi, thinking of excuses to reject audience with Rukma. But knowing Rukma, she feared that her brother would force his way in. *Unless she could think of something that could keep him away too.*

'I think even you were summoned, Malathi,' the woman at the door added after a long pause. It was Malathi who hit upon the perfect excuse.

'It is that time of the month!' Malathi uttered. 'For the Princess. I need to be with her in case...'

'Alright…' came the not-so-pleased response. 'Isn't it sooner this time? And why haven't you taken her to the Ritu Griha?'

'Th—there are rats there!' Malathi replied uncertainly, looking at Rukmini's miming. There was another loud sigh from the other side of the door. Probably about the disappointment of having to cleanse the chamber of the Princess after the 'cycle' passed.

Rukmini came to the door this time. 'Send us the evening meal here itself. And some fruit in case I don't relish the preparations.' The maid acknowledged and left.

Rukmini's heart slowed down at the sound of the receding footsteps and then she turned to the two men. Balarama stared at a blank wall trying his best to look like he had not heard anything and Krishna looked at Malathi appreciatively.

'What was that?' Rukmini looked at Malathi. 'Was there no better excuse?'

Malathi shrugged and shook her head. 'We could have faked illness but who knows? No man will dare to enter the room of a menstruating woman for sure!' She looked at her mistress and then at Krishna who suddenly seemed lost, almost like something disturbed him but only for a moment before he was normal.

'Alright. This has crossed the borders of insanity,' Balarama interjected, nudging Krishna. 'We can't stay here, Krishna. This is beyond troubling.'

'Rather, after all that has happened, better stay back and have a good night's sleep,' Rukmini protested. 'Much needed before your long travel ahead... brother Balarama,' she added remembering that was how Mitravinda had addressed him during their visit to the ashram.

Malathi brought in the meal and fruits, which the four of them shared. 'May I ask where in the southern part of the land are you both headed to?' Rukmini asked, unable to bear the uncomfortable silence. 'Wait, don't answer. Strategic reasons and all, I can understand.'

Krishna looked up and beamed. 'Wish we knew the answer. But yes, it has to be somewhere safe enough even after Jarasandha comes to know that we have passed this way.'

'How would he come to know?' Rukmini raised her brows.

'Because we will let him know that we passed through Vidarbha down south,' Krishna grinned. Before anyone could say anything, he produced a copper seal and handed it to Malathi. 'The seal of Mathura. If I can ask of another favour of you, sister Malathi. Drop it outside any of the public guesthouses after we've had a three-to-four-day lead. The spies of Jarasandha would know we have passed through Vidarbha. That should keep Jarasandha away from Mathura for sure.'

'And right on your pursuit for sure!' Rukmini exclaimed. 'And a whole army will come to fight just you both!'

Krishna and Balarama exchanged a glance and smiled at each other. 'That's the plan,' Balarama nodded.

Rukmini continued to stare at Krishna, searching for other topics of conversation, but none seemed appropriate. She had to be content with just their presence, trying to rein in the various springs of hope and desire arising in her heart. She signalled to Malathi and the latter started making beds for the guests. The night wasn't going to be kind to Rukmini.

An hour passed and she could hear Balarama snoring. Malathi too had fallen asleep. When the second quarter of the night arrived, Rukmini was done tossing on her bed and sat up, glancing at her balcony. She saw Krishna seated on the steps leading to it, staring at the stars.

Wasn't the bed comfortable?' she whispered, approaching him.

Krishna waved the concern away, moving to a side. Rukmini sat by his side, trying to gauge his expression in the moonlight. It did not betray any trace of worry at the uncertainty that faced him. *How can one seem so unaffected? Has he given up? Has he resigned to the possibility of being caught by Jarasandha?* 'I have heard a lot about you,' Rukmini remarked. The flutter in her heart had calmed down, making it seem like they had known each other since forever. 'About the sacrifices and ordeals your parents faced to keep you and brother Balarama safe.'

'And the deaths that happened in my pursuit?' The words betrayed no expression. *Except that he acknowledged all the costs that had been paid in blood in his favour. Or perhaps he did not show what he truly felt.*

Rukmini inched closer. 'Would it all not go in vain if, Mahadeva forbid, Jarasandha gets to you?'

'It would all definitely go in vain if he gets to Mathura and destroys the city for sheltering me,' Krishna replied.

Rukmini had nothing to say to counter that. Except that she strongly wanted him to survive whatever that was threatening him. 'Jarasandha needs a nemesis,' she said, hoping to make him change his mind. 'Rather, this land needs a nemesis to stand up to him, maybe destroy him.' Involuntarily, her hand patted his knee and his held hers. *Almost like he knew what her heart felt for him. Just that he showed no response other than a grateful acknowledgment.*

They stayed that way for most of the night, except for an occasional quip or a remark. When the bell rang announcing the fourth quarter of the night Krishna rose to wake Balarama. Rukmini woke up Malathi to lead them safely outside the palace. 'If the guards at the city gates bother you, tell them you were visiting the royal scholar Agnidyotana,' she advised. 'I trust him to keep my secrets.'

It was an inexplicable pang of grief that struck her at their departure. Balarama gratefully patted her head and the sheer affection in his eyes compelled her to touch his feet, though he stopped her midway.

'Come back safe—no, victorious. That would be the price of my hospitality,' she managed to steel herself enough to say, in a tone of mock authority. Krishna turned around and grinned at her.

She knew it then. She loved him. And she could not stop him from leaving!

❦

'When is he expected?' Rukmini asked impatiently, glancing at the humble doorway for the umpteenth time.

'By Mahadeva, even I have never waited with this much anxiety for my father to return!' a chirpy Lilavati remarked with a chuckle. The chubby daughter of the royal purohita Agnidyotana could not help but be amused at the importance her father commanded.

'You will!' Rukmini snapped. 'When he is about to bring you news about a man you love.' She rose and paced across the doorway. 'Did you not say that he would be back much before sunset?'

'Sshhhh!' Lilavati cautioned. 'Princess, can I remind you that the matter is to be kept confidential. And that my neighbours aren't supposed to know that their Princess is in love with the man her family hates?'

Rukmini stood on her toes and surveyed the neighbourhood. But thanks to the loud chirping of the birds returning to their nests at sunset, her words did not seem to fall upon any unwelcome pair of ears.

'There! Father has returned!' Lilavati pointed at the familiar figure coming home. The wide smile that appeared on the lips of the brahmin past sixty springs was a sufficient indicator to Rukmini about the news he had brought.

Agnidyotana cleared his throat with an indulgent wink. 'Isn't there a royal decree by His Highness the Crown Prince Rukma that the women of the palace should reach back home by sunset?' The mock authority in his tone almost made Lilavati giggle and drop the pitcher of water she was about to hand him to wash his feet.

'Acharya!' Rukmini protested, wringing her hands. 'Tease me later, but pray, what did you find out?'

'That two youth, strange to the lands lying to the south of Vindhyas, gave a whole army the run of their lives and shamed them while eluding everyone. Let us say that the King of Magadha has encountered his nemesis.'

That made it two consecutive victories for Krishna against Jarasandha.

Rukmini leaned against the threshold, glancing at the sky, and grateful to those who had heeded her prayers in the past months. Her lips then curved with a hint of glee. She could not wait for Rukma to return, sour faced at his failure.

The Engagement

Kashi

The sunrise at the sacred city of Kashi was a delightful sight. But what added to Rukmini's delight was the sight of encampments behind her that occupied the empty fields till the end of the horizon. To the eyes of a layman, it was just a celebration thrown by the King of Magadha for all his supporters, vassals and allies in the honour of Lord Vishvanatha. But Rukmini was privy to the reason behind this gathering. It was a rattled emperor who sought to brainstorm solutions to his problem. It was her Krishna whose sheer wit and capability sent this powerful emperor and his minions into such a tizzy that they were forced to seek the grace of the God of gods.

There was still time before the morning gathering that happened before the midday harathi and continued through a sumptuous lunch followed by some serious discussion, which happened only among the kings and select nobles and princes. Rukmini remembered how exulted Rukma was to be included in the elite group. *Spineless coward.*

A familiar scent greeted her nostrils. Just a whiff before it was gone. Rukmini's eyes grew wide for a moment before she shook her head. *Not Possible.* But to her pleasant surprise, the fragrance came back and lingered. Still unable to believe, Rukmini stood rooted to the spot. She knew she was definitely not alone. But the long-drawn quiet brought a wave of uncertainty. Losing her patience, she whirled around, her long plait following the force of the movement and hitting a hand that held her arm. She had waited for this for too long.

'I knew I could find you here.' Krishna beamed.

'Because it was I who sent you the message!' Rukmini retorted with a teasing grin.

'But you spoke about certain rats collecting here to pray for their war against a lion, and…' Krishna exclaimed, glancing at the ground.

'My lion is here. I would not worry about rats. I am a princess of royal birth, you see?' Rukmini winked, inching closer.

A bout of silence followed, for words felt unnecessary when her eyes met his. Rukmini tore her gaze only at the sudden sound of a chirping bird. Krishna looked into the waters of the Ganga. 'There is also a guest here who you would not want to dismiss as a rat.' When Rukmini looked at him askance, Krishna continued. 'King Drupada of Panchala. His sons and daughter Draupadi, accompany him.'

'What about him, Krishna?'

'Jarasandha planned his first attack on Mathura when Drupada faced a crisis because of the Kuru preceptor, Dronacharya. But his second attack has been blocked because Drupada refused him and his armies a free pass.'

'That sounds courageous and hostile!' Rukmini remarked. 'But why would he grace a gathering like this?'

Krishna shrugged, though the arch of his right brow suggested a clue. 'Hostilities and amicabilities in power games are like day and night.'

Rukmini frowned. 'Trust Jarasandha to coerce even the strongest-minded into submission, Krishna. What if he succeeds in negotiating with Drupada?'

Krishna nodded, quietly acknowledging the possibility. 'We need to get closer to the royal family of Drupada.'

Rukmini looked at him and smiled, saying nothing for a while. 'Thank you, Krishna.'

'For?'

'For the answer I was searching for all these months. It came when you said "we".' Her lips pouted into what looked like a bud the night before it blossomed. She turned her gaze away, beaming. 'Well, what would you know about the troubles of a maiden whose family shows no intentions of marrying her to a worthy groom? When I lost all hopes from them, I conducted my own swayamvara in my mind.' She turned back to meet Krishna's gaze with a grin. 'What happened at the battle near Gomantaka when two young men defied a whole army and left the so-called emperor "red faced" made me decide. And when you said *we*...' Rukmini averted her gaze again and walked ahead, expecting him to follow her. *I got my answer.*

It was a sudden shuffling of footsteps that startled Rukmini. Concerned, she whirled around and did not find Krishna. The ghat was empty. It was almost like she had imagined his arrival. *Had she?* Rukmini frantically glanced around and found no signs of Krishna. The next moment, she thanked all the Gods for that. It was a flustered Rukma who hurried towards her. 'What on earth are you doing here?' He grasped her hand. 'Come, Rukmini, the Emperor wants to see you.'

'Will you stop calling him that?' Rukmini retorted, hurriedly walking behind him.

She reached the giant tent that had served as a place for all the kings to gather under Jarasandha's banner. Ostentatiously decorated with expensive furniture on raised platforms erected to seat them, it almost looked like a palatial courtroom from the inside. Rukmini saw her father Bhishmaka seated and hurried up to him. On a platform further raised to their left, she saw Jarasandha address the gathering, casting a wide smile at her and acknowledging her arrival.

'Bow down to him!' Rukma whispered fiercely. Rukmini pretended to not listen and inched closer to Bhishmaka. Jarasandha then turned to another royal family seated to his left. 'I want to begin by thanking the esteemed King of Panchala who graced this humble celebration of ours with his family. And what can one say about his children? A father has to have done some tapasya and a score of yajnas to beget these.' He pointed to the two princes and a young princess who stood by Drupada's side.

Rukmini smiled to herself, realizing that she had not imagined Krishna's arrival there. Drupada was indeed in the gathering. The Princess of Panchala was majestic, elegant and graceful in every way, and enough to arrest Rukmini's attention for the rest of Jarasandha's talk, in which she was anyway not interested. Till he uttered her name, that is. Rukmini looked at him like she had been rudely awoken from her sleep.

'Go.' Rukma nudged her from behind. 'He is calling you.'

Rukmini could not decide whether she hated Jarasandha more or his ability to fake that sophistication, which made him look almost saintly, like someone born to save the whole world, while in fact, he was a monster who only sought control. She found all eyes on her. 'Go, child.' Bhishmaka patted her shoulder. Rukmini was overcome with a sense of foreboding. The attention of Jarasandha on her could not mean well. Cautiously, she made her way towards him. Jarasandha patted her head.

'Wish I had a granddaughter like you, Rukmini,' he remarked with a chuckle and then flicked his hand. Rukmini saw who he pointed to and her heart missed a beat. 'I am delighted to announce the engagement of this gem of a princess to none other than our very promising Prince of Chedi. Come, Shishupala.'

Rukmini stared at him and then at her father and brother who stood deferentially at the foot of the platform where Jarasandha stood. Bhishmaka avoided meeting her eye. Telling Rukma anything seemed to be of no use from the way he was grinning. In a moment, her eyes were filled with tears. *Wrong! Wrong! How do I stop it?*

But there was clearly no way out and she saw Shishupala making his way towards them, closer to her. Rukmini turned away, her furious gaze again seeking Bhishmaka's, but in vain. When Shishupala ascended the platform, coming dangerously close to her, Rukmini broke from Jarasandha's grip and hurried down the platform. She looked at Rukma for a moment and then ran out of the gathering. She heard Jarasandha remarking about how coyness overcame even the most upright of girls when it came to their wedding.

'I don't consent. I don't!' she shouted, but the cheer that followed Jarasandha's announcement drowned her voice. Rukmini ran out towards the ghats. She wanted to seek out Krishna that very moment and elope with him. But her frantic search yielded no result. It was post sunset that she saw Malathi who led her back to their camp. She had all the mind to lash out at her father and brother, but a sense of fatigue overcame her as the world went dark.

❦

It stung. Rukmini's eyes blurred, not at the stinging pain in her cheek when Rukma slapped her, but at the way her own family acted like hers was a life that could be bartered to suit interests that were neither hers nor of the citizens of Vidarbha.

'Imbeciles of the highest order. I am ashamed that the blood that runs in your veins, also runs in mine!' she had lashed out at Rukma, whose response was a tight slap across her cheek. He had caught her hair, still angry at her outburst when someone came to the entrance of their camp.

'Stop that!'

It was the Princess of Panchala visibly distressed at what she was seeing.

'What is going on?'

Rukma immediately released his grip, the change in him visible. Rukmini's attention too was on their guest. The daughter of Drupada looked even more beautiful today. Her well-groomed hair, lustrous and long, braided perhaps by the best of sairandhris, made Rukmini try and set right hers, dishevelled at Rukma's manhandling. She brushed aside her tears, but made no attempt to smile or hide her anger against her brother. Then Rukmini heard Rukma offering to drive the Princess of Panchala back to their camp on his chariot.

'Brother Rukma,' Rukmini intervened, glaring at him when he turned towards her. 'Sister-in-law awaits you at the banks of the Ganga. I shall, instead, keep your word and take the Princess of Panchala back in my chariot.' This, she hoped, would send him away and give her some minutes with the princess. Krishna seemed to think highly of this family and she had to befriend this elegant guest of hers.

To Rukmini's delight, the Princess of Panchala also insisted that Rukma leave to join his wife while Rukmini could drive her back on her chariot. Rukma left in a huff.

'I shall be back soon,' Rukmini spoke softly and slipped behind a latticed partition where she could see her image in a wide-mouthed pot of water. Her hair needed some attention. She was angry with Rukma for messing it up that way. But Malathi had left to bring refreshments for the Princess of Panchala and Rukmini had to do her hair by herself. At that moment, she saw the daughter of Drupada come near her and take the comb from her, kindly offering to braid her hair. There was a sense of warmth that almost made her want to cry again. But Rukmini held back.

Giving a single-lined answer to the questions asked, Rukmini asked the Princess of Panchala her name. 'You can call me Krishnaa, though everyone calls me Draupadi.' For the first time, Rukmini smiled. Like she felt the presence of her Krishna. She had to befriend Draupadi. And the best way to do so was to warn Draupadi of the consequences of her father, Drupada, befriending Jarasandha.

She finally expressed her thoughts to the princess, while she drove the chariot towards the Panchala camp. Draupadi smiled her worries away when Rukmini cautioned her about Jarasandha's capability to also take Draupadi's future into his hands and set up an alliance with his selfish interests at the helm. For a moment, Rukmini almost envied Draupadi for the protective father and siblings she had. After arriving at the Panchala camp Draupadi patted Rukmini's arm, admiring her lone fight for what was right. 'Remember Rukmini, you have a sister at Panchala, in case I can be of any help in your fight. Small or big, any help.'

Rukmini nodded with gratitude and turned the chariot around. Her part of befriending the family of Drupada was done. But how was she going to find her way out of this engagement with Shishupala? Where was Krishna when she needed him? Another futile round of search for him went by. Not that Rukmini expected to find him in the open when his enemies swarmed the city of Kashi. But nothing about Krishna was predictable and she did not want to leave any stone unturned. Her level of frustration only increased at what Malathi told her upon returning to the camp.

'The King invited Shishupala over to Kundinapura in the month of Magha.' Malathi was almost terrified, reliving what happened during Shishupala's last visit. 'And he readily agreed!'

'Of course, he will!' Rukmini retorted.

'Your father wanted you both to reconcile.'

'Mahadeva!' Rukmini tried to gather her thoughts. 'Did you say the month of Magha?' None of her family members could be trusted to give her a solution for this. And Krishna was nowhere to be found. She needed a counsel from someone who sympathized with her. Rukmini stopped at a thought. *Probably it was too soon to trust?* But think as much as she could, she found no other way. Finally, she made up her mind. The risk was worth taking. 'Malathi, go to the Panchala camp and request Princess Draupadi to meet me at the temple before the midday harathi tomorrow.'

At Panchala

The visit to Panchala had almost come to an end. While Rukmini was happy and grateful to have escaped hosting Shishupala and be a guest of Princess Draupadi, there were more serious things cropping up. Draupadi was always a part of strategic discussions in her family and Rukmini got to know bits and pieces about what happened around Panchala. More importantly, some detail about their neighbour Jarasandha's plans. There was some news about a messenger from Magadha visiting Kampilya, the capital of Panchala. Rukmini was alarmed to hear of a possibility of Jarasandha passing through Panchala. It meant only one thing—another attack on Mathura. After two crushing defeats, Jarasandha would be like a serpent whose hood had been kicked. She was sure he would now attack Mathura with all his might.

'It starts like this, with trading favours that seem "harmless". But Jarasandha cannot be trusted, Draupadi. Trust me, I have seen a lot of his other side!' she frantically tried to caution Draupadi.

'Princess Rukmini, I have heard about it from my very gurus. My father is no stranger to Jarasandha's ways. But trust me, it is much more complicated than this. The recent developments have distressed me. But after his defeat at the hands of the Kuru princes, my father has not been himself.'

Rukmini would have loved to lend a patient ear to Draupadi's past, but at the moment, she had to do anything that could stop Drupada from granting a free pass to Jarasandha's armies. Hearing nothing from Krishna in the interim had only added to her impatience. 'Can anything be done to stop Jarasandha from freely passing through your kingdom and attacking Mathura, Draupadi? Anything?'

Draupadi pursed her lips, like something troubled her.

Grasping Rukmini's hand, she nodded. 'I shall try reasoning with Father once more tomorrow.' Seeing Rukmini's almost crestfallen face, she could not help but express her curiosity, 'What's your interest in the well-being of Mathura, Rukmini?'

Rukmini knew that she could not keep many secrets from Draupadi now. Especially not after the latter had helped her during her hour of need, like a sister. 'If you concur with me about the threat that Jarasandha represents to this land of Bharata, his nemesis is at Mathura. Someone we should all stand by.' She averted her gaze, still debating with herself about revealing more.

'Does that someone mean even more to you than just a nemesis to the "monster" you hate?' Draupadi beamed with a twinkle in her eyes.

Rukmini was compelled to smile back. 'Right now, he is eluding me and I can't keep my peace.'

'And you still press his issue to whatever end you can.' Draupadi's eyes hinted admiration. 'I pray you succeed, Rukmini. I pray you succeed in teaching a fitting lesson to these adharmic patriarchs. Mahadeva forbid, but if you are forced to wed that Shishupala or whoever against your wish, I shall arrange for your escape.'

Rukmini nodded in gratitude. But before she could say anything, her attention was drawn to something making its way inside through a latticed window. Rukmini thought it was a reptile at first. But it turned out to be something that surprised her. *A Peacock feather?* There was someone on the other side of the latticed wall trying to insert the feather. *It was a message!* Her heart leapt and she hoped that Draupadi would leave on some pretext.

Like the Gods had heard her prayers, Draupadi's brother sent for her some time later. As soon as she was alone, Rukmini rushed to the wall and picked up the feather. It was dipped in that unique mixture of musk and sandalwood. Something totally unique to him—her Krishna! *Was he in that very palace? Had he tracked her all the way from Vidarbha to Panchala?*

Before Rukmini could peep through the holes, she heard a strange voice from the other side.

'Tomorrow, in the second quarter of the night, by the rear entrance of this garden.'

Rukmini rushed out of the chamber towards the corridor to see who it was. But she spotted no one. *So tomorrow it was.* Rukmini had to exert all her efforts to contain her excitement for the rest of the day.

Only Rukmini knew how she managed to keep herself together for the whole of the next day. She counted the moments of the first quarter of the night. Draupadi returned late from her unsuccessful attempt to convince her father Drupada to not cooperate with Jarasandha. She waited for Draupadi to fall asleep and no sooner had the bell rang to announce the second quarter of the night, did she hurry to see Krishna.

And he was waiting for her!

True to her expectation, the moment she ran into his arms, the world around her seemed to freeze. Before she could lose herself in savouring the warmth of the embrace, she remembered the grim news she had to share with him. But even as her face fell before updating Krishna about the developments, she saw him smile. A smile of accomplishment!

'We are almost successful in securing a safe home for the Yadavas, Rukmini. A home where you can step in with no fear of an unforeseen attack. Brother Balarama and Princess Revathi have succeeded in freeing the coastal lands of Saurashtra from her enemies. It will be the new home of the Yadavas.'

'When are you going to take me there?'

'Perhaps in a year. If things fructify and there is no attack from

Jarasandha before we evacuate Mathura.'

'I am afraid, he is not going to let you do that, Krishna.' Rukmini looked crestfallen. 'King Drupada has consented for his free pass through Panchala, Krishna. I tried to influence Princess Draupadi to persuade her father against it, and she did her best too, but in vain.'

Krishna considered the news and nodded reassuringly.

'Forget it, Krishna. Take me to Mathura, now. Hold me ransom for Jarasandha to halt his attack. We can evacuate Mathura in peace.'

Krishna laughed with an abandon that made Rukmini glance around for any guards who could be alerted at the sound. 'What is so funny about that!'

Krishna shook his head. 'Not this way, Rukmini. Not from Panchala. It would create more problems for King Drupada and his family. He has suffered enough.'

'He does not seem to have an iota of concern for you, Krishna. And you on the other hand ...'

'Our mind cares for our limbs, though *they* don't care for it. Doesn't it, Rukmini?

Rukmini looked at Krishna, realizing what had made her fall in love with him in the first place. *It was like everyone belonged to him. The Yadavas, the Panchalas.*

'Krishna, Shishupala is at Kundinapura now. In all probability, he is pressing my father to declare a date for the wedding! This is the month of Magha. They would not wait beyond Shraavana. We don't have a year, as you want.'

Krishna shook his head. 'If we can stop Jarasandha's quick pass through Panchala, he would have to circumvent the borders of this kingdom and would avoid doing that during the summer as that would dehydrate his armies, which are already disgruntled. This means his attack would coincide with the monsoons and that would be too close to the month of Shraavana. They would not fix your wedding—if I can guess—not before the next Magha or even Vaisakha after that.'

Rukmini nodded, relieved. But there was a big 'if' on which this assurance depended on. 'We have already tried convincing Drupada.'

'Let me try.' Krishna smiled. 'You have made more progress than you think you have, Rukmini. Drupada now knows he is not on a strong moral ground. All he needs is an assurance and time to heal his wounds.'

Rukmini knew that Krishna had a plan. When he reached out to caress her cheek, she also knew it was time to part. And only Mahadeva knew when they would meet again. Standing on her toes, she held his face close and kissed him on the forehead. She knew she would not live separated from him. She also knew he knew that. There was his dharma, and there was hers. The very same dharma would unite them even if it meant they had to part at the moment. She would hang on to this till the next moment came.

Kalayavana

Vidarbha

It was not a peaceful year for Rukmini after her brief visit to Panchala. She could never forgive Rukma and her father for meekly giving into Jarasandha's dominion even in their personal lives. Rukma's attitude worsened the differences and it often spilled into the other parts of their life too. At times, she could not help thinking about how Draupadi's family at Panchala stood together through all their differences, tried keeping political affairs away during their dining hours, succeeded in spending time together as a family. Something that was grossly missing in hers. The only person who truly felt like family was the royal purohita and her guru, Agnidyotana.

While there was also some heartening news about Jarasandha's plans getting delayed, something she was sure was the result of Krishna's intervention at Panchala, references to her impending wedding to Shishupala were testing her patience. Rukmini tried to keep her calm doing the one activity that she always liked—driving her chariot around the city of Kundina like a whirlwind. Something that also helped her stay closer to the common people of the city. While they did not have much to complain about, Rukmini sensed the increased presence of officials and various nobles from Magadha and Chedi and the inconvenience her people went through in providing for these guests. After the summer passed, Rukma left for Magadha to again take part in the attack on Mathura, which they all had been waiting to do. It did not help when she cautioned Rukma that they would not meet with success.

A restless couple of months passed with her waiting for news about what had happened at Mathura. Through Malathi and her own interactions with the travellers who came to Vidarbha, she gathered bits and pieces of information that only created more confusion. Some said Jarasandha had burnt the city. Some said the Yadavas actually averted the tragedy and escaped to a safe haven. There was no clear news about Krishna. When Rukma returned from his 'campaign', Rukmini could make out that they were not sure about their success either. All that Jarasandha's army could be sure of was that they had razed a whole city to the ground. But there was a lack of clear jubilance in her brother, which gave her clues about the successful Yadava exodus. Of course, she knew which way they had gone and she was never going to reveal that.

One evening as she returned from her usual rounds in the chariot, Rukmini found Bhishmaka, Rukma, her other brothers and councillors meeting. General meetings like that never stretched beyond sunset and this looked unusual. *Was it an emergency?* Rukmini debated whether to enter the Sabha room. But knowing how Rukma had begun to get more and more secretive in the recent months, she decided to eavesdrop. The discussion seemed cheerful. The next words came from the astrologer that made her heart stop. It was indeed an emergency!

'The brighter Ekadashi of Jyeshta then,' the astrologer declared. 'Ideal for our Princess' planetary position as well as for the Prince of Chedi.'

Rukmini backed away in the dimly lit corridor and almost bumped into Malathi who caught her arm, her face gone pale.

'It is bad news, Malathi.'

'I am afraid there is worse news, Princess,' Malathi whispered pulling Rukmini towards the rear of the royal mansion where, in one of the inconspicuous resthouses, a young brahmin waited for them.

'Vasantaka from Avanti,' Malathi introduced. 'He studied in

the ashrama of Sandipani, my Princess.'

Rukmini did not remember him, but before she could say more, Vasantaka spoke, 'It is about the Yadava exodus towards Saurashtra, My Princess. The worst has happened.'

'Tell me everything, Vasantaka!' Rukmini clutched Malathi's arm. Something did not bode well.

There was an ambush upon the Yadava division by a certain mercenary called Kalayavana. And Krishna took him on, leading him away from the rest… all by himself.'

'And?'

Vasantaka hung his head. 'Krishna did not reach the new shore city that houses the Yadavas now. It has been a month since they saw him last.' He could not continue.

Rukmini saw him struggle for words and give up, imploring her to understand what was unspoken. She slowly shook her head. 'No, that does not prove anything.'

Vasantaka could not speak any more. Malathi squeezed Rukmini's hands.

'Stop that!' Rukmini hissed. 'And yes, the news *is* of no relevance, Vasantaka! It proves nothing of the sort you are all fearing!'

'My Princess!'

Rukmini raised a forbidding hand and with an effort, lowered her tone to a fierce whisper. 'There is no proof of Krishna's death.'

She hurried away, locking herself in her room for the rest of the day. *Who was this Kalayavana and how could people think Krishna would fall to him? The Krishna who could vanquish Jarasandha's army in an open field.* Determined to get to the bottom of this, Rukmini barged into her brother's chamber the first thing in the morning. Rukma had just woken up and was not prepared to handle an angry Rukmini then. 'Who is Kalayavana?'

'Rukmini!'

'Who is he? Do you fools think he can even harm Krishna?'

Rukma frowned, realizing that Rukmini was not a stranger to whatever was going on. But it was her uncontrollable rage that made him uncomfortable. 'How does that concern you, Rukmini?'

'It doesn't. And it will never. Because that fly cannot harm my Krishna! Get that into your hard skull!'

'What did you say, foolish girl?'

'I said I am in love with your enemy. The man who you, your emperor and his worthless minions can't even dream to vanquish. I love Krishna Vaasudeva.' Even as Rukma tried to come to terms with what she had just said, Rukmini quickly added, 'As for that Prince of Chedi, if you love him so much, you marry him on that date you all fixed without as much as caring for my consent. Because I am not even going to look at his cursed face!'

Rukma's eyes narrowed. Grasping Rukmini's arms roughly, he warned, 'This is the last time you are going to take the name of that pseudo-noble son of a slave, Rukmini!'

'I love Krishna! I love Krishna and Krishna is the only man I am going to wed! What are you going to do? Kill me?'

'May not be a bad idea if you go on this way!' Rukma held her neck in a bid to strangulate her.

'Rukma!' Bhishmaka had rushed in along with Rukma's wife who had sneaked away to bring him to intervene. 'Is that what being the eldest means to you? Kill your own sister?'

'Marrying me off to that Shishupala is not very different from that!' Rukmini angrily retorted. 'And you, Father, aren't different from him.'

'Tell me, how would you handle this spitfire!' Rukma shoved Rukmini towards Bhishmaka. 'I am afraid we will need to drug her to get her married.'

'Stop wanting to "handle"me and go back to gurukula to revise your Shastras. Drugging a bride to force a wedding upon her is Paisachika Vivaha. Gods will curse you both!'

'Enough, Rukmini!' Bhishmaka raised a finger. 'Don't add to the complications here. I know you are a worthy daughter. Don't become a bad example, my child. Think of what the populace of Vidarbha would say.'

Rukmini clenched her fists. With Rukma, she could still fight, telling him things on his face; but her father disappointed her more. Reining in her anger with some effort, she turned to go, but halted to add, 'I had to make myself clear. The choice is yours, whether to follow dharma, the word of the ancient seers or the decree of your "emperor".'

She raced back to her room. Something told her that Krishna was alive. He would contact her. He definitely would. But she had to buy time for him.

❦

The news of another late evening council made Rukmini hope against hope. She had convinced Agnidyotana to oppose this wedding and impress the Shastraic merit of securing the bride's consent for any marital ritual to be blessed by Gods. Agnidyotana's wisdom was respected by many in the court. They would think before defying his words. Or so Rukmini hoped, as she waited for Malathi to bring her the news of the final outcome. When her companion finally came back with a crestfallen face, Rukmini's heart sank.

'Acharya Agnidyotana tried his best, my Princess. But he was a lone voice,' Malathi reported. 'When he threatened to not officiate this wedding as the priest, your brother said he could easily be replaced.'

'What?'

'The Acharya gave up his position.'

Rukmini collapsed onto her couch. There went her last resort, now powerless, and thanks to her, removed from his position too.

Worst of all, there was no news of Krishna.

Draupadi! Rukmini knew she could appeal to Draupadi. But the idea of being a refugee at Panchala was not acceptable to her. And it was not like Krishna to be absent for this long. He had contacted her in times that had been much more dangerous. Rukmini fought back the part of her that believed the worst. Her characteristic determination won. After a sleepless night, she hit upon a plan that seemed more like a fantasy, given the number of assumptions. But this was all she could do. Rukmini was not prepared to give it up till the last moment.

'If Agnidyotana has indeed given up his position, he really loves me like a daughter,' she thought aloud to Malathi. 'He can go to Saurashtra and ascertain facts. And if he can meet Krishna, and if Krishna agrees to my plan, he'll just have enough time to come to Vidarbha and take me away before the wedding!'

If Agnidyotana agreed to go for her sake.

If he could successfully complete the arduous journey alone, despite his age.

If he finds Krishna at all.

If he could convey this to Krishna, what would happen at Vidarbha?

If Krishna did not have more pressing issues like the security of his newly found home.

Rukmini felt dizzy at the sheer number of uncertainties that lay in her plan. Gathering herself with an effort, she decided to focus on the task in hand, and go one step at a time.

'Let us visit Acharya Agnidyotana, Malathi.'

Agnidyotana, the Messenger

It was well past sunset by the time Rukmini finished briefing Acharya Agnidyotana. To her delight he agreed to take on the journey. After taking her side had cost him his position, she had expected him to at least resist the idea. But Agnidyotana lived by the Shastras, and swore by the ancient code of conduct as seen by the immortal rishis. There was no way he would officiate a wedding that did not have the bride's consent. If that adharmic wedding was anyway taking place, he would do all he could to help Rukmini out of it.

But he, Agnidyotana, did not want to rush. The callousness of the royal family had bothered him alright, but Rukmini had been a delightful disciple and he loved her as much as he loved his own daughter, Lilavati. With Bhishmaka and Rukma being mere puppets to the whims of Jarasandha, he, Agnidyotana, too had his duty.

'Princess Rukmini, my child. You have indeed honoured me by considering me as a pitru tulya, one equivalent to a father. But Rukmini, I would fail in my duty if I don't ask you about your choice in the face of this oppression. Are you really sure about the man you love, Rukmini?'

'Acharya, after everything we have seen…'

'No, I trust your wisdom to assess Vaasudeva's character, my child. But have you envisioned what life would be, wedded to such a man?'

Rukmini nodded with a confident smile. 'Trust me, Acharya, I have. Despite the mayhem I fought against in my own family, I also fought against the fear of uncertainties that would envelope my life, if all Gods willing, I wed Krishna. I am no stranger to the fact that life would become only more challenging at Dwaraka.'

Agnidyotana considered her words. He, too, was no stranger to the unfolding political vortex in the northern part of Bharata, which would engulf the neighbouring and lesser provinces too.

'There is no escape from the political intrigue that is gathering, Acharya. Our country, this Bharatavarsha, is going to pay the price of letting an adharmi like Jarasandha run his course for more than a generation. The choice to "stay out of it" simply does not exist.'

'This is my fear, Rukmini,' Agnidyotana remarked. 'Your vision of your own future is so focussed on stopping Jarasandha, that you are not pausing to visualize your life, what it would transform into when you become one among the Yadava noble ladies than a queen, as you should be if you wed any prince of Bharatavarsha.'

'You talk of the Yadavas as if they are a different clan altogether, Acharya,' Rukmini beamed. 'I learnt my history from you. My own family is an offshoot of the grand old genealogical tree of Yadu. Am I not a Yadava myself?

'Acharya, I know that the Vrishni clan of the Yadavas has stuck to its age-old republican system of governance while many of the offshoot clans have turned monarchical. Rukma and his likes will, of course, disagree. But can we actually state with authority that a monarchy that does not consider a maiden's consent to be important is superior to a republic where nobody stands on a pedestal?'

Agnidyotana smiled at the discourse. He had seen Rukmini take a lot of interest in statecraft even as a child while being vociferously opinionated at times. But try as he might, it was hard to find a flaw in her judgment. When she came to a conclusion, there was nothing that could make her change her mind.

'Living the ideal is not always as simple as stating them, my child,' he gently cautioned. 'But I am sure your strong will and grit are going to help you face whatever destiny throws at you.'

A bout of silence was filled with the chirping of birds from outside. Agnidyotana keenly observed Rukmini's face for the slightest sign of doubt. But there was none.

'Have you considered this, Rukmini, there would be situations when many married women do have to turn to their natal homes for support. All Gods forbid you face such a situation, who will you turn to? Given that the women of our land have grown up listening to the tales of powerful women like Savitri who faced even the God of Death without needing the slightest support from her natal family. But in this age, Rukmini, do you, in your pragmatic sense, see a woman surviving an intrigue-filled complex household without her brothers supporting her?'

Rukmini pursed her lips, letting a lone tear flow before she brushed it away. 'Acharya, do you see me having a natal home at all today, which I have to worry about after my marriage?'

It was the surge of pain that surfaced in her eyes, which stirred something within Agnidyotana, and he felt small for even broaching the question. Having known Rukmini since her days as a toddler, this was the one time she let her vulnerability show. He reached out to pat her head. When she looked at him again, Rukmini was her older self. 'I am not a fool to think I can survive without support, Acharya. Today, I turned to you, because you are the lone person in Vidarbha who understands the adharma being committed by my family. There was a time when I sought the support of a near stranger, Princess Draupadi, because she understood what the maiden in me was going through. There will always be men and women of dharma who will stand by their kind. That, not just the Vrishni clan, is the true family of my Krishna. That is my family too.'

That was the softest tone that Agnidyotana had seen Rukmini speak in. But the sheer strength in her words were, he had to admit, energizing. So much that an unexplainable enthusiasm filled within himself, to undertake this journey to Saurashtra, carrying her message to Krishna.

'Lilavati,' he called out to his daughter. 'Help me prepare for the journey ahead. I shall start for Saurashtra at dawn after two days.'

Rukmini smiled with gratitude and left Agnidyotana's abode.

The Wedding Date Approaches

More than a month passed by. Rukmini's restlessness increased with each day. She would only pretend to go about her day, but glance at the entrance of the mansion for any sign of Agnidyotana's return. His daughter Lilavati too had no clue about the whereabouts of her father. Meanwhile, the courtesy visits from the royal family of Chedi increased in frequency, much to Rukmini's distress.

'Why did I not leave with Acharya Agnidyotana? Gods willing, I would have found Krishna and stayed back with him. Else I would have lived the rest of my life in seclusion at Prabhasa or some remote place, performing tapasya so that I am reunited with Krishna at least in the next life. What was I even thinking of, staying back here!'

'Princess!' Malathi exclaimed hurrying to her. 'You have now started talking aloud to yourself. People may think you have gone mad!'

'Well, I am going mad.' Rukmini wrung her hands. 'Or wait! If I do this more, will the King of Chedi think I won't be a bride befitting his son and cancel the wedding?'

'Rukmini, my Princess.' Malathi held her arms. 'They don't care about your state of mind. All they want is a token of alliance, that is, you alive, in any state of mind. Living with you, I have begun to understand how these royal minds think. And you are beginning to lose your mind. I can't see you like this.'

Rukmini sighed. 'Looks like the Gods have willed it that I face my doom, Malathi. Else why would Krishna, who used to appear in the most unexpected moments, desert me this way? Why would Acharya Agnidyotana not even send a message about his journey or at least his well-being? Every time I see Lilavati, I am overcome with guilt and fear that I might have sent her father away on his last journey!'

'Perhaps, the Acharya ascertained the bitter truth and did not have the heart to return?' Malathi added.

'Why am I even alive, Malathi? To see adharma inch its way to victory each day? To see everyone I love, everyone I revere, leave me? To hear every day, that I am an unworthy daughter and sister, when in fact…'

'What about Princess Draupadi?' Malathi suggested.

'What do I tell her? "Draupadi, the man I loved is dead now and I have nowhere to go"? And how long before this monster Jarasandha reaches out for her too?' Rukmini paused for breath, her chest feeling heavier. She then looked up with determination. 'I will not let Jarasandha get away with this. He will not play with a maiden's future. This wedding has to be stopped, at all costs.' Rising to her feet, she asked Malathi to follow her. 'I shall talk to the King of Chedi this very moment. I shall tell him I hate his son and have no desire to enter his household. And don't dare stop me!'

Not bothering to heed any of Malathi's pleas to pause and think twice, Rukmini stormed into the royal guesthouse where King Damaghosha of Chedi was housed.

'Lord of Chedi, this wedding has to be stopped. I don't want to marry your son,' Rukmini blurted out, ignoring any protocol that was due. Damaghosha, who looked older by a decade for his age, stared at her outburst, but kept his calm. He then turned to Malathi who just caught up with Rukmini. 'Secure the entrance. Let the Princess of Vidarbha vent this out.'

'King Damaghosha. There is nothing left for me to say except for what I made clear just now. I am in love with another man. How can I wed your son? How can I step into the household of Chedi with my heart given to someone else? Forget me, would you feel secure with a daughter-in-law who is not prepared to swear by your family?'

'Have a seat, child Rukmini.'

Rukmini had not expected King Damaghosha to stay this unaffected. She sat on the seat offered, trying to steady her breath.

'The news is not new to me, Rukmini. I knew it at Kashi itself when you ran out of the gathering the moment your engagement was announced. That was not an act of coyness. It was a brave rebellion. Wish some kings of my generation had half your courage in our times.' But this acknowledgment of her courage was all the support that Damaghosha had to offer. 'But I am afraid, it is too late, my child. Your consent, or for that matter, mine, Bhishmaka's or anyone else's does not matter before the will of Jarasandha.'

The lack of any reverent prefix to Jarasandha told Rukmini of how Damaghosha truly regarded him. She considered his stoic eyes and looked into them directly. 'Doesn't your heart rebel at the thought, Lord of Chedi?'

Damaghosha's jaw tightened for a moment before he let out a sigh. 'Let me tell you a story, Rukmini. The Vrishnis of Mathura were a flourishing republic. Their diplomatic stances, their valour, their enterprising abilities, it gave them a sort of immunity from the neighbouring monarchies. All was well till a certain Jarasandha of Magadha set his eyes on expanding his kingdom. In a bid to neutralize his rivals, the Kurus, he aimed at having an ally close to them. Mathura was his target. Mathura, where the dominant clan was the Shoora household, known for its valour; the household to which my wife, Queen Shrutashrava, belonged.'

Rukmini listened intently, choosing to not interrupt. She knew of the marital relationships of the Yadavas, which was reputed to have spread wider than the span of the sun.

Damaghosha continued, 'My father-in-law, the old patriarch Shoora, was true to his name. He had five daughters and a son, Vasudeva. Jarasandha started his interference, initially with some trade grants, which soon extended to familial visits. Before long, a mysterious illness killed the old Shoora. And Jarasandha's daughters wed Kamsa, the son of another clan lord, Ugrasena. He then played godfather to the orphaned daughters of Shoora, getting them married to the kings of his choice. I was one of them. The vast wealth of the household got divided into the dowries given away to their daughters, Shruta, Shrutakirti, Shrutashrava and Rajadhi. And Jarasandha's son-in-law Kamsa went from strength to strength. Mathura became a captive of Magadhan power, their proxy garrison. Vasudeva, the young son of Shoora was rendered helpless as Kamsa heaped his atrocities upon him, killing his newborn children. We, the brothers-in-law of Vasudeva, could not even dare to raise our voice for fear of angering Jarasandha. He even created minor strife in our own families to keep us from uniting. Princess Rukmini, you may be wondering what makes me narrate this to you. I want to caution you about the force you are rebelling against. Do you think you stand a chance where the kings of four powerful dynasties failed?'

'Kings of four powerful dynasties indeed!' Rukmini shook her head. 'Shoora's daughters and wealth were accepted by you all. But you shied away from your dharma, King Damaghosha. I now blame not Jarasandha, but you. All of you who failed the household of Shoora. All of you who let this monster go from strength to strength under your watch. For had you shown the commitment to your dharma then, I would have been studying about your heroic deeds instead of hearing the story of your failure from your own lips.' Contempt filling her gaze, she rose. 'And your son would have regarded you with greater respect than become a minion of another king.'

Rukmini made her way towards the exit, but turned back. 'King Damaghosha, accept my gratitude for telling me this. And stay assured, I shall stop Jarasandha's marital conquests. I shall fight the battle you should have done long back. This Princess of Vidarbha shall not enter the household of Chedi. Your preparations shall be in vain.'

'I wish I had the hope left in me to bless you, child. But…'

Rukmini left before he could complete his sentence. She could not have made it clearer. If Damaghosha had an iota of self-respect, he would try and dissuade his son from this wedding. Rukmini now had her own family to convince. But it would not happen till late in the evening, given how busy Bhishmaka and Rukma were, in arranging for the wedding. *The wedding that would never take place.* Shaking her head, Rukmini retired to her chamber, waiting for them to return. It was when Malathi spotted an extra battalion of guards around their wing of the palace that Rukmini got uncomfortable. It was unusual. The battalion looked like they belonged to the army and not the regular guard. Rukmini stepped out to investigate, only to be advised to go back inside by the new guard outside.

'Prince Rukma wishes that you don't leave the palace till the date of the wedding, my Princess,' The burly man said. 'I have the order to stop you even by force if required. Pray, don't make me do that, my Princess.'

Rukmini glared at him. *Rukma resorted to this?* Rukmini guessed that the news of her confronting Damaghosha could have reached Rukma and her cowardly brother would have taken this step in response. But before she could lash out, a voice interrupted her.

'My Princess!' Malathi hurried to the entrance, leading a familiar figure. *Vasantaka!* 'The Princess needs to perform a ritual worship of a Brahmachari,' she told the soldier guard with a straight face and managed to get Vasantaka inside. Her discrete grip over Rukmini's arm told her that Vasantaka had brought some news and she followed a visibly excited Malathi towards her chamber.

'The Yadava warriors are camped two yojanas away from the borders of Kundinapura!' Malathi could hardly hold herself back till she secured the door. 'Vasantaka brought the news.'

Vasantaka nodded. 'The news of your impending wedding reached Dwaraka, Princess Rukmini.'

Rukmini's face lit up. 'Krishna has come! So, Acharya Agnidyotana reached Dwaraka?'

Vasantaka's face fell. 'We still don't know anything about Krishna, my Princess. Balarama leads the Yadava contingent.'

Rukmini's heart sank for a moment. Staring into a vacuum as a deluge of sorrow engulfed her, she suddenly saw a ray of light. 'Vasantaka! Were you told to tell me and others that you haven't heard about Krishna? Tell me the truth! If what you all say about Krishna is right, why would the Yadava contingent bother about rescuing me when they are drowned in grief and bereavement?' Before Vasantaka could react, Rukmini abruptly turned to Malathi. 'I know! Krishna wants everyone to think that he is dead. Rukma, Jarasandha and all his minions would have decreased their guard. They will come with lesser army strength. Brother Balarama will launch a surprise attack on them and Krishna would come from a different direction to take me away! Malathi, my Krishna—this is all his strategy!'

She stared at the two exchanging unsure glances.

'All I know is that Balarama is stationed at the southernmost borders of Avanti, ready to enter Vidarbha even by force if required. The reason behind this is not hard to guess, my Princess. I cannot give you any more hopes than that,' Vasantaka reiterated.

'What do you want to do, my Princess? It is three days to the wedding now.' Malathi gently squeezed Rukmini's arm. 'Perhaps, we can find a way to slip out and get you to the northern borders? That seems like a safe thing to do. These new soldiers who replaced our usual guards, they are battle hardened, but they don't know the palace walls as much as we do. There are those recesses where we can slip out and escape unnoticed. Just lay low till—'

'I am going to follow my plan,' Rukmini declared. 'I know it.

I can sense it. He has entered Vidarbha, Malathi.'

Malathi wrung her hands, feeling helpless at Rukmini's delusion. She sensed Vasantaka's sideward glance and shook her head. But the brahmin youth seemed persistent. 'Not now, Vasantaka. Not at this juncture.'

Rukmini turned around and looked at both of them.

'Princess Rukmini, I... I love Malathi,' Vasantaka explained. 'I thought I could get you both out of Vidarbha to safety tonight.'

Rukmini's lips curved into a smile the next moment and she held Malathi's arms. Malathi turned away. 'Look at me, Malathi. Do you love Vasantaka?'

'Later, my Princess.' Malathi tried to move away but Rukmini held her firmly. 'I shall not leave Vidarbha till you are safely out of that Shishupala's grip. I shall not leave your side.'

'Don't be a fool.' Rukmini patted Malathi's cheek. 'Very few women are this fortunate, Malathi. Your lover has carried out dangerous missions of spying for us, just because he loves you. Honour that. Leave with him. I can fend for myself.'

'I am your friend since we were toddlers, Rukmini!' Malathi protested, dropping the protocol. 'I can't leave your side during such a crisis just because there is a man to take me away. I love Vasantaka too, but he needs to understand my dharma too.' Malathi extricated herself from Rukmini's grip and turned to Vasantaka. 'Pray, wait for me till this dies down, Vasantaka. Our lives will not know joy if we desert the one who looked after me like a sister since childhood. You have studied the Shastras, I am sure there is no heaven waiting for those who desert their friends in the hour of need.'

For the first time in her life, Rukmini found herself tongue-tied in front of her companion's resolve. Malathi left for her chamber and Rukmini was left staring at a tense Vasantaka. 'I guess I know how that feels…' she remarked in a soft tone.

Vasantaka nodded with a sad smile. 'Pray, tell her that I shall wait for her, Princess. I'll beg in the streets of Vidarbha for my sustenance but I shall not leave without Malathi.'

It was another long day for Rukmini, and all the while, hope and despair were battling with all their intensity for their place in her heart. She mentally mapped the routes between Saurashtra and Vidarbha that she knew of. She speculated where Krishna could camp on the way. She thought about the obstacles that would have come in his way. She thought about the possible tactics he would have applied to overcome them, the possible disguises he would have resorted to, so that he could hoodwink the armies of Vidarbha, Magadha and Chedi, and the possible places he would stay so that he could surface at the right time, near the temple of Goddess Gauri. She would conclude her ritual worship of the universal Mother who married the lord of this universe and succeeded in her love. And Rukmini's lover would come, with the blessing of the Mother.

But what if her assumptions were in vain? Rukmini could not help fearing that there was truth in what Vasantaka and the others believed. *Probably that was the reason why Agnidyotana did not return.* The old Acharya loved her like his own daughter. *He may not have had the heart to see her crumble under the weight of the harsh truth. She would conclude her worship of Goddess Gauri, but probably the Goddess would not consider her worthy of any blessings. And she would be in the clutches of those guards who would escort her to that wedding arena where...* Rukmini's breathing got heavier and heavier as terrifying images of the grim future played in her mind, with Jarasandha laughing his way to be the lord of Bharatavarsha.

Malathi was a silent spectator of Rukmini's oscillating states of mind. At times, she had to even force the princess to eat at least enough to have the energy to run. The night before the wedding, she led Rukmini to the royal dining hall where Bhishmaka wanted all his sons to dine with their sister before she left Vidarbha with her groom the next day. Rukmini mutely followed her, showing the least interest in the food or in interacting with her brothers and father. Bhishmaka tried to banter, invoking emotional moments since Rukmini's childhood. But neither Rukma nor Rukmini softened. The old man gave up, disheartened.

A tense bout of silence continued till Rukma finally got up to leave, citing the remaining preparations. Rukmini looked up. Their cold stares met, more like those of enemies rather than a brother and sister.

'Rukma!' Rukmini's voice had become coldly husky. 'Brother Balarama has camped outside the northern border of Vidarbha, with the Yadava forces. They shall swoop down upon your armies tonight and rescue me.'

'Rukmini!' Bhishmaka exclaimed.

'And I shall leave with them.'

Malathi rushed to her side. 'She has been saying this since morning, my King. I think she has just dreamt it! A night's sleep will do good to her.'

Rukmini glared at Malathi. Before she could say anything, Rukma grabbed her arm, forcing her to face him.

'Rukma, I forbid you!' Bhishmaka warned, trying to restrain his son.

'You aren't going to have this one your way, Rukma,' Rukmini declared in barely a whisper.

'Malathi, take the Princess back to her chamber!' Bhishmaka ordered, putting himself between Rukmini and his son.

Smiling at her father, Rukmini patted his arm. 'This is the night, Father. I shall stop being a trouble from tomorrow onwards. I shall be a bride of Krishna either at Dwaraka or in the land of Gods where he truly belongs. You will not lose sleep over me.'

At that moment, when Bhishmaka was almost close to breaking down, Rukmini let herself be led away by Malathi, sparing him the indignity.

'What—did—you—just—do?' Malathi almost screamed at her, securing the doors. 'Ruined your only chance of escaping this marriage? Rukmini, pray, don't take leave of your senses this way.'

'Sshhhh!' Rukmini frowned. 'I know exactly what I did. And it perfectly falls into the plan.'

'What plan? Rukmini, there is no plan. When are you going to realize that?' Malathi held her in a tight embrace. 'There was this one opportunity to escape and join Lord Balarama. You could have lived in Dwaraka as a daughter. You could have found another eligible young man. Anything could have happened in your favour, but you had to ruin that one opportunity by blowing their cover?'

Rukmini chuckled at Malathi's anxiety. 'Blowing their cover? They came well prepared for a battle, Malathi. And that is the army that even defeated Jarasandha once. That is the army that reclaimed Saurashtra from dreadful robbers and pirates. That is my Krishna's army, *my* army.'

Malathi collapsed onto a smaller couch, giving up any hopes about her mistress' sanity returning.

'My dearest Malathi.' Rukmini squeezed her shoulders. 'You should have left with Vasantaka. That would have spared you of all this worry. That poor boy is begging on the streets of Vidarbha, waiting for you.'

Malathi shook her head and refused to react, praying to every god whose name she knew of to save Princess Rukmini.

'Alright, let us get some sleep. The Gauri Pooja has to take place in the Brahma Muhurta tomorrow. I don't want my Krishna to see dark circles under my eyes when we meet.'

Gauri Pooja

For the first time in the past one year, Rukmini felt a sense of abandon as she decked herself up. Bell after bell she had counted, waiting for the night to pass, and she wasted no time in bathing and adorning herself. Fussing over the jewellery that lay before her, she almost annoyed Malathi out of her wits till the maid wept aloud.

Feeling compelled to pause, Rukmini smiled at her. 'I have thought of every possibility, my sweet friend. If things don't go according to my plan, I shall escape through the southern side of Vidarbha. The jewels may come of use in negotiating my way through. There are ashramas, temple towns and a hundred other places where I can spend the rest of my life in dignified seclusion, Malathi. But you have to find Vasantaka as soon as possible and start your life together. Take the rest of my jewellery with you. Have a joyful life.'

Malathi smiled through a tear that succeeded in flowing out of her eye and shook her head. 'He is gone. I went to where Vasantaka stayed last evening, Princess. He was not there.' She turned away. 'Men after all.' She shrugged and selected a string of freshly bloomed jasmines to weave around Rukmini's long braid. 'My Princess, you still cannot braid your hair by yourself. I shall come with you, wherever you go. We'll survive without the boys.'

They smiled at each other, silently promising to maintain camaraderie that had kept them together through all these times. Before long, a knock was heard and the palace maids on the other side of the door informed them it was time for Gauri Pooja.

The thirty-strong guard, not to mention the womenfolk of the noble households, none of who she could trust, made Rukmini hesitate for a moment. Malathi quietly concluded Rukmini's braiding, securing it with a golden fastener and helped her with the plates of worship materials required for the ritual worship of Gauri.

It was a widespread belief that the worship of Goddess Gauri would grant a bride the husband of her choice, and the Goddess who succeeded in reuniting with her love, Lord Mahadeva, would bless the couple with a long life of togetherness. It felt ironic to Rukmini, following this ritual when her consent was being blatantly violated. The crowd of guards around her also made the chances of her escape bleak. Rukmini shook her head, which soon filled up with despondent thoughts.

Perhaps, suicide was the only way out. If not Krishna, it would be Yama, the God of Death, who she would choose over that Shishupala. *But how could she even find the means to kill herself? Why was even the God of Death deserting her like that man she loved did?* Rukmini fought back tears for a while and then let them flow, mindless of the other women interpreting them as characteristic of a bride who was leaving her parental home. Except that Rukmini could not wait to leave it.

The privacy of the palanquin gave her sometime for quiet grief. Alighting at the steps of the temple, Rukmini saw the majestic statue of the Supreme Mother of the universe. Decorated with turmeric and flowers, the Goddess looked like an eternal bride to her husband, a compassionate giver of boons to those who sought her refuge. Rukmini saw no other friend beyond her. When her gaze dropped to the feet of the Goddess, the mist in her eyes cleared, showing the freshly sharpened copper scimitar, gleaming at the edges. *That,* Rukmini thought, *was her way of escape.* She would give up her life as the bride of the man she loved, at the feet of the Goddess. Mechanically following the lead of the priest who led the ritual, Rukmini concluded the pooja and prostrated before the Goddess, with a final thought of gratitude for letting her even know a man like Krishna in this life. The moments with him were enough. Rukmini prepared herself as she discretely reached out to the scimitar, detaching herself from the world.

If there is a life after this,
May my ears hear only his soothing words
May my youth blossom with his embrace
May my eyes rest on his breathtaking form
May my tongue taste the love from his lips
May my nostrils be delighted by the fragrance of his chandana
May my life be his, so that we are one and the same!

Rukmini opened her eyes, about to grip the hilt of the scimitar when a movement caught her eye. The movement reflected on the reddish surface of the gleaming scimitar—it was the one whom her eyes had thirsted to see this whole year!

Springing to her feet, Rukmini turned around and saw Krishna. A Krishna who she had never seen before! Her gaze stopped at his round face, those compassionate eyes and the well-contrasting jawline that proclaimed his will to take her away. His shoulders covered by leather arm guards with bronze plates holding them in place were a sight of assurance, as were the strong arms that held the whip and the reins of the four horses of superior breed that pulled his chariot. The armour made of bronze, and the aesthetically carved jewellery were covered with dust, an indicator of the swiftness with which he had ridden all the way to reach her. *Just as per her plan, following her lead to the letter.*

Her bosom heaving with anticipation, Rukmini stared at him, and then at the long lines of Brahmin men and women that had gathered at the entrance of the temple. Rukmini had not noticed, but they had made their way close to her, separating her from the ring of the guards. In the rear of the rows of Brahmins, she saw Agnidyotana raise his right hand to bless her. Offering a hurried salutation in gratitude to the acharya, Rukmini raced towards the chariot, reaching out to Krishna's outstretched hand. Her heart paced like a horse in full gallop when he caught her hand and hauled her into the chariot. In full view of the commonfolk of Vidarbha, Rukmini threw her hands around Krishna's neck, burying her face against his shoulder. A year of no communication had left a lot to be said. But the moment melted the words into one meeting of gazes. His triumphant grin making her beam, she turned to face the commoners of Vidarbha, the only 'family' from who she could take leave before leaving for her marital home. From the entrance of the temple, Agnidyotana led the rest of the brahmins to chant auspicious hymns, invoking the Vedic Gods to bless the couple. The commonfolk on the streets took the lead and cheered them, some of them rushing to block the guards from reaching them.

Rukmini joined her hands in respect for those who saw what she saw in Krishna. Her eyes suggesting a warm farewell, she turned to Krishna, determined for the next course of action. Grasping the whip and reins, she set the chariot into motion.

'Watch my back.'

'As you wish,' Krishna grinned, picking up a bow and they left for their new home, Dwaraka, the flourishing coastal city at the western end of Saurashtra.

Facing Rukma in Battle

Rukmini had chosen the temple of Gauri as the spot to elope after a lot of thought. The location being on the western outskirts of Kundina, was closer to a lesser-used trade route that would go north till the southern borders of Avanti and then access the highway towards the coastline, from where she expected the ride to Dwaraka to be smooth. She had explained the same to Agnidyotana who conveyed it to Krishna. With Shishupala and his retinue, along with Jarasandha, arriving from the northeastern direction, she expected the chances of a clash to be lesser. But she realized the loopholes in her speculation as three rows of Magadhan soldiers encircled the outer ring path around Kundina. She turned to Krishna who seemed to sense her worry. Unperturbed, he took up the bow. Before stringing it, Rukmini saw him blow into his conch, Panchajanya.

'Set them to a full gallop,' he said, nocking multiple arrows onto the bow. Rukmini nodded and cracked the whip. The four horses of Krishna's chariot were of superior breed and seemed to know what their master wanted them to do. They broke into a gallop that Rukmini had not been prepared for. Forced to lean forward to hold on to the ends of the reins, she almost lost her balance when Krishna let the arrows go. She let go of the whip and held onto the flag post, seeing Krishna let another set of arrows amidst the closing enemy lines. The arrows helped in creating an opening as the foot soldiers ducked for cover. At that moment, Krishna retrieved the whip and cracked it again. The horses picked up speed. Rukmini felt his hand gripping her waist. Pressed against his heavy armour, she heard him say when to duck, when to hold on to the reins and when to let go of the support, and so on, totally unaffected by the number of enemy soldiers.

Within moments, they had broken free of the three enemy rings. Rukmini let out a sigh; the adventure she had faced still sinking in. Dust had covered her face and limbs as it covered Krishna's too. His curls were askew and the condition of her braid was no better. The flowers from her hair had scattered around on the chariot, on her clothes and his...

At that very moment they glanced at each other and shared a laugh. The enemy had now recovered and started to pursue them. Rukmini again grasped the reins to help Krishna focus on driving the pursuing soldiers away. But he smiled and pointed at the cloud of dust on the horizon. The chariot kept its speed till Rukmini saw Balarama emerge out of the cloud, leading the armies of Dwaraka. He waved at them before the Yadava soldiers gave them the cover, ready to take on the hostile armies. Krishna then took back the reins and slowed down their pace. Rukmini squeezed his arm that still held her by her waist, trying to absorb the moment. She had succeeded in defying Jarasandha. She had frustrated the most dreaded man of Bharatavarsha and won the man she loved for her groom. The unwritten doctrines of Jarasandha that bound Bharatavarsha were shattered today. She leaned against Krishna, balancing herself on the speeding chariot, imagining the blow it would deal Jarasandha as she would be savouring the wedding bliss with Krishna. Tomorrow, would see a new Bharata that would stand up to Jarasandha. Or so she hoped.

But her idyllic thoughts came to an abrupt stop when a familiar voice called out to them from behind. Turning around, she saw Rukma pursuing them. From the abuse he hurled at Krishna for eloping with her, she could make out that her brother was in a fit of anger that she too had never seen. Pursing her lips, her jaw clenched, she turned to Krishna. 'Enough of this. Defeat him Krishna!' Krishna slowed the chariot but looked at her in askance. 'You heard me. Defeat him. Let him and the world know that I went with a deserving, valiant man who shamed three armies. Defeat my brother, Krishna.'

Without a word, Krishna took up the bow again and twanged it as Rukmini pulled the reins of his chariot. Her brother was more than happy to shoot the first arrow, which was cut up by Krishna's. His next arrow whizzed past Rukma's ears and Rukmini knew that it was not a missed aim. She had learnt basic archery and it was supposed to be a greeting. Perhaps a call to step back from hostility. But the gesture only incensed Rukma further and he hurled a javelin at Krishna. It met the same fate as his first arrow. The exchange continued and to her frustration, Krishna did not seem interested in stepping up the attack. Rukma's tongue seemed to have assumed its most venomous form, which only made her feel embarrassed.

'Do you seriously expect him to use his brains now? Rukma understands only one language, Krishna. The language of power. Show him who the better warrior is!'

'Rukmini!' Krishna looked only amused at her annoyance. 'He is my brother-in-law.' There was a whizzing noise that very moment and Krishna pulled her away from the path of Rukma's arrow.

'That is your brother-in-law. He does not care if his sister dies, but wants to defend some non-existent "family honour"!' Rukmini glared at Krishna who shot another arrow in a trice, which cut up Rukma's bow. His next arrow wounded Rukma's charioteer on his shoulder, making him faint. Even that failed to deter the Crown Prince of Vidarbha. He challenged Krishna to a sword duel. With a dismissive shake of his head, Krishna obliged. Rukmini cursed Rukma's foolishness and turned away from the scene of the duel. Watching Krishna with the sword was a delight, if only the opponent was worth his steel. But Rukma, with his temper out of control, made the duel very predictable. Not after long, the sound of blades clanging against each other stopped and she turned to find Krishna holding his sword to Rukma's neck after disarming him. Alighting from the chariot, Rukmini went up to them. 'Accept it Rukma, I chose him. And I chose well. Stop embarrassing me now, will you?'

Rukma refused to meet her eye.

Rukmini continued to look at him, hoping for sense to prevail, hoping for a farewell that would at least have her brother assuming the grace to accept his defeat and her right to choose. But Rukma avoided her gaze and turned away. His shame of defeat apparently bothered him more than any amount of pride that his sister had chosen better. She bit her lip when Krishna backed away and gently patted her arm, motioning her to get back to their chariot. 'This may not be the time, Rukmini.'

Rukmini pursed her lips. If Rukma did not change his mind, she could not return to Vidarbha at all. And her brother was not in a frame of mind to even comprehend that. Rukmini suppressed what she feared was a sob and followed Krishna. She badly wished there was a way to knock some sense into her brother. *Some way.* The thought made her hopefully turn around, but to her horror, she saw Rukma aiming a dagger at Krishna.

'No Rukma!'

It all happened in a moment. Rukmini rushed to put herself in the way of the dagger. The whizzing in the air made Krishna turn around and pull her closer. They both ducked just as the dagger was about to pierce her in the back. Krishna left her and leapt at Rukma, knocking him down to the ground. She felt her limbs freeze, along with the blood in her veins. *How was she going to face Krishna after this heinous act of her brother? Even after being defeated in an honourable way?* Tears blurred her vision and it was only when Balarama's hand patted her head that she came back to her senses.

'Brother, Balarama,' Rukmini's voice was shaken, something that had never happened to her. She saw Balarama nod at her, with a mix of affection and assurance and walk up to Krishna and

Rukma. It was then that she saw that Rukma had been tied up with a rope by Krishna.

'Krishna, wait!' Balarama hurried towards his brother. 'He is the brother of your bride!'

Rukmini realized that Balarama had misinterpreted Krishna holding his sword to Rukma's neck and hurried to Krishna's side. Balarama continued, 'It is you who always preached restraint to me even in the toughest moment, Krishna. How could you forget that the celebrations of your wedding at Dwaraka would give no joy to your bride if she sees her husband kill her own brother?'

'Brother Balarama?' Rukmini cleared her throat to explain but felt Krishna nudge her and squeeze her hand, like he did not want her to recount what had happened. She looked at Krishna and he shook his head and let Balarama continue.

'Well, at times, I do have to remember that I am older,' Balarama chuckled, in a visible bid to lighten up the atmosphere. 'Both of us cannot forget how Rukmini helped us in the past. The least you owe her is to not make her shed tears when she should be celebrating.' He smiled, patting Krishna's arm. 'Now set course, you both. But go slow and give us a lead of two days. Someone needs to prepare Dwaraka for the grand welcome!'

Krishna nodded with a smile and lead Rukmini back to their chariot. The horses broke into a gentle trot. For the first time, she did not feel like seeing Rukma's face. And in the name of the whole pantheon, she could not understand why Krishna stopped her from telling Balarama what her brother had done. He just let his older brother chastise him, smiling in return. She looked at Krishna, who now held the reins. A wave of mixed emotions swept her. His eyes were still on the path and his arm enveloped her. She rested her head on his shoulder.

It was only when Krishna stopped the chariot by a rivulet that Rukmini realized the distance they had covered. They were past the borders of Vidarbha.

'I am not thirsty,' she managed to say.

'But we should wash your wounds,' he pointed at her palms, bruised by the rough pulling of reins she had to do earlier during the day. The turn of events had made her oblivious to her own pain. But he had not failed to notice.

'Why did you not tell brother Balarama what Rukma did?' she asked Krishna as he wiped off the streaks of blood from her hands.

'Balarama would have killed Rukma if he knew that my life hung in the balance even for a moment.'

'And you still care for Rukma's life after all that?'

'Rukmini, why does your brother hate me so much?' Krishna looked at her. 'There is no enmity that I harbour towards him.'

'When does he use his own brain?' Rukmini's characteristic annoyance against Rukma surfaced. 'He is just a pawn in the hands of that Jarasandha!'

'How can we nurse anger against someone who is not even capable of his own thought, Rukmini? The least that my brother-in-law deserves from me is a hope that he would be himself, someday.'

'And you let your brother misinterpret you ...' Rukmini thought aloud.

'A lot of people think I did things I actually did not. And that I did not do things I actually did.' Krishna waved her concerns away. 'A pittance to pay for the greater good, isn't it?'

'Stop that! I am already in love with you!' Rukmini grinned. 'How much more helpless do you want to render me, love?'

Krishna's smile made her heart stop. In the rays of the setting sun, he did look like the god that many thought of him as. 'Enough to put up with my eccentricities for this life ...' He cupped her face with his hands and lifted it, bringing his lips close to hers, 'And beyond.'

Part Two

After the Wedding

The first day as a newly wedded wife was expected to be full of surprises, but what Rukmini had not expected was to face a corridor full of women grinning and chuckling with suggestive nods, early in the morning. Not all of them looked like palace maids. Clearly, the family or the extended version of it at Dwaraka was much larger and Krishna waking up earlier and leaving their room did not help.

'Where is he?' she asked the nearest woman.

'Where is who?' another giggled. Rukmini remembered her from the wedding ceremony as one of the noblewomen in the Yadava clan.

'The one who brought me to this,' Rukmini narrowed her eyes faking helplessness.

More giggles followed.

'Don't you know his name?'

'How heartless of him to leave you alone when you need him the most?'

'We are here for you, sister…'

'Now, ladies…' Rukmini raised her hands, regretting the attempt to humour them. 'If you came for the joy of seeing a coy bride after her nuptial night, you are in for a good deal of disappointment. Coyness and I don't go together. I am looking for Krishna. And what I actually need now is a bath.'

There was another gasp from her right. 'You need a bath and need your husband to accompany you?'

'Now, now, ladies…God of gods, this is an ambush! A few more of you and you can surprise a whole army to their deaths!'

Rukmini sighed seeing Revathi emerge from the other side of

the corridor. The women eventually left.

'Had a good sleep?' Revathi asked with a mischievous glint in her eye.

'You too?' Rukmini protested as Revathi laughed and turned to the two women attendants behind her. 'Help the Princess with her bath.'

Patting Rukmini on her arm, she added, 'The boys are early risers, sometimes even going entire nights with no sleep. But take your time to catch up with Krishna's routine. I haven't caught up with Balarama's yet. Even after all the ashram training.'

Rukmini grinned and walked towards the bath. By the time she came back to her chamber, she noticed the jewellery spread out. The maid assigned to her had a really good understanding of what suited her. Dismissing the two maids of Revathi, Rukmini sat before the silver surface that served as a mirror.

Malathi.

A stab of guilt struck her. Her faithful maid had stood by her, by even spurning her own lover. And Rukmini had not been able to reciprocate it. Absent-mindedly, she began to wear the jewellery and let her long hair down. Malathi was an orphan and Rukmini was all she had. Rukmini chided herself for not charting out an escape route for her friend. She wondered if Dwaraka too had a spy network in Vidarbha through whom she could contact and convince her companion to join her. As she struggled to hook a large string of emeralds behind her neck, she felt Krishna's hands close in on hers. Through his reflection on the silver mirror, she saw him smile, and she smiled back. 'Liked the jewellery I picked for you?'

She turned around in disbelief and obvious admiration. 'I could not have chosen better!' She smiled in gratitude.

Her guilt multiplied. She was now the bride of a man who took care of the minutest of issues, and who never forsook those who trusted him, at any cost. *How could she enter his life, abandoning Malathi?* Tears blurred her eyes. She averted her gaze and turned to face the mirror.

Before she spoke anything, Krishna reached out for the comb and brushed her long hair. Quickly wiping her tears, she stared at his reflection in the mirror, smiling sheepishly.

'Mother Devaki and Mother Rohini helped me do my hair during the marital rites. I... I need help doing it and was wondering who I could ask today. And you seem to be doing it with remarkable ease!' she exclaimed in obvious admiration, noticing that Krishna had already braided her hair half way even as she fumbled for words. 'Where and when did you learn this?'

'I... had a lot of practice. And I am not going to risk revealing the details!' Krishna grinned with a mischievous glint in his eyes. 'Can't afford to anger my new bride, no.'

'If it is any consolation...' Rukmini narrowed her eyes, returning his smile, 'there is nothing of your past that I don't know of. Remember I used to have you tracked down even in the remotest corner of Bharata. Would I leave out finding about your life at Vrindavan?'

Krishna mocked a sigh of relief. 'Nothing like a wife to whom a man can bare everything. Let me thank all those who gave me enough experience to braid their hair—Lalita, Vishakha, Chitra, Champaka, Sudevi, Indu...'

'Stop showing off!' Rukmini nudged him and examined her plait. Her smile faded as she thought of broaching the topic. 'Krishna, it does feel painful when you remember your childhood friends. You do miss them, don't you?'

Krishna's smile turned inscrutable. 'It also feels assuring when I know that the distance from me keeps them safe.'

'There would be a day when Jarasandha's shadow shall stop lurking over the northern plains, Krishna. You shall make it happen.

I am sure you will.'

'And I shall take you to Vrindavan that day if you promise me to not feel jealous.'

Rukmini nodded laughing and pursed her lips for a while. 'You remember Malathi at Vidarbha, don't you?'

Krishna frowned, trying to remember, and Rukmini was almost sure even the deliberation was an act. 'Is that her?' Krishna pointed at the door.

Rukmini stared at Malathi who waited there, rooted to the spot for the moment and turned to Krishna, who beamed. 'Just confirmed with the priest about the auspicious time for her wedding with Vasantaka.'

Rukmini rushed forward and took Malathi in her arms. From the corner of her eye, she saw Krishna leave the room signalling her to join him in the dining chamber in a while.

'Whoever has done this puts my job in jeopardy!' Malathi exclaimed, examining Rukmini's plait.

'Don't fear that, Malathi. He has a lot more to do for me.'

They laughed aloud, the sound of waves outside accompanying their voices.

Dwaraka, now, felt like home. A home where they could bring in the much-awaited new chapters of their lives.

Life at Dwaraka

It was late afternoon when Rukmini reached the mansion of Devaki and Vasudeva. Devaki was immersed in her prayers, a bit untimely according to what Rukmini knew about them.

'Her ways are indeed different.' Vasudeva smiled, leading her to the eastern portico, which oversaw a brief expanse of the coastline that ended in a cosy cove. 'Hope your first day as a lady of the household is going well.'

Rukmini nodded with a smile. 'I was wondering why mother and you did not join us for the midday meal, Father. And Revathi …'

Vasudeva waved her concern away. 'Devaki doesn't leave home, my child. And I can't leave her alone.'

'We could have come here—'

'No, no no… Revathi, I know, has taken a lot of pains to decorate your mansion for the first midday meal, and I hope it went well?'

Rukmini nodded, grinning, as she remembered the playful banter she had had with Krishna, Revathi, Balarama and mother Rohini at the dining hall. It felt unusual not to have Vasudeva and Devaki with them. But it looked like others were used to the older couple's solitude and left them alone, out of respect.

'While we wait for Devaki, I wanted to know if I can speak about a role we would all like you to assume. Rohini was unsure, as you, being a princess, and we functioning as a republic …'

'I respect this form of governance!' Rukmini interjected. 'Father, it has always fascinated me, working in a system where no one person is put on a pedestal and everyone has a voice. It must be far better than the monarchical...'

'Trust me, it is not as ideal as you put it!' Vasudeva laughed. 'But your enthusiasm is heartening, Rukmini. For the Shoora household lacks a strong female voice in the Sudharma,' Vasudeva explained. 'Rohini is great with internal affairs. Revathi, the rightful owner of this land, consciously keeps away as she, in her noble heart, does not want to remind the Yadavas in any way that they made a home out of *her* rightful inheritance. Well, I strongly feel she had to have taken birth in another era and not ours! Subhadra is still a child...and you have seen your mother-in-law, Devaki, and her reclusivity.' Vasudeva shrugged.

Rukmini was yet to see the famed sabha of the Yadavas in function—Sudharma, as they called it. She had briefly been there with Krishna when they formally welcomed her to Dwaraka, but that was all. The mezzanine floor of the sabha that served as an upper platform, was the section where the ladies had been seated. Rukmini was not aware that their presence in daily affairs was mandatory. 'I am sure the Yadavas respect the Shoora household a lot. The scions of this family saved them from Jarasandha's wrath.'

'After being the very reason why Jarasandha became wrathful in the first place, according to many people,' Vasudeva remarked. 'And as I said before, there is a lot about the Yadava republican council that is less ideal than it should be...much like a lot of monarchies of today.'

'Any concerns that need my immediate attention, Father?' Rukmini asked, a part of her full of enthusiasm to enter the sabha as a functionary and not as an upstart princess who used to eavesdrop stealthily or force her way into the court of Vidarbha, only to be sidelined by Rukma. Dwaraka seemed to be a place where her voice would be welcomed and valued.

'Well, you shall know in time. We have seen a lot, child Rukmini. Don't want my old eyes to blur your vision and any fresh ideas you might bring in, given your experience. Krishna values it a lot!'

'My experience? I…' Rukmini checked herself before the words 'hardly have any' stumbled out of her mouth. If Krishna valued what her brother called 'eavesdropping', 'backdoor meddling' and a lot more as 'experience', there was a lot to live up to. Especially if they expected her to obtain intelligence about Jarasandha's future plans when she almost had no access to her natal home. Probably her friend, Mitravinda, could fill in for her from Avanti. Rukmini's frown deepened as she furiously thought about avenues to gain access to any information that would help the Yadavas gain an edge over Jarasandha.

'By Mahadeva, what am I doing?' Vasudeva exclaimed. 'Enjoy your phase of rightful pampering as the new bride before these affairs start wrinkling that beautiful forehead of yours and rob your sleep, child.'

'Not to worry, Father,' Rukmini beamed. 'I am actually excited. What is life without a few intrigues and surprises round the next corner?'

Vasudeva smiled and began to explain about the influential families and households whose patriarchs and the noblewomen formed the members of Sudharma, their level of influence over others, the armies each of them commanded, the wealth and other details when Devaki finally concluded her pooja and came out.

'Mother Devaki.'

Rukmini had lost her mother in her early years, being the youngest of six children. Though extremely pampered by her father and maids in her childhood, it was a different surge of emotion when Devaki enquired about her well-being and other issues like settling down in Dwaraka, the food and about any inconvenience due to the sea winds. She also took care to ask about her indulgences and hobbies.

'If horses and chariots interest you then you have indeed chosen your marital home well. The sea-faring trade enables us to procure superior breed horses much before any other kingdoms of Bharata can get them. In fact, horses also may serve as great gifts to any of your princess friends. I heard that the princesses of Avanti and Panchala are your friends.'

Rukmini nodded, almost wonderstruck at Devaki's keen interest in her. The pleasantries went on for a while before Devaki slowly rose to her feet. 'The sunset is a beautiful spectacle to watch. I should let you get back to your mansion before that.' The smile on Devaki's lips made Rukmini grin. 'But before you leave…' Devaki signalled her to follow her towards her garden where she kept a Tulasi plant. 'Keep Her in your garden, Rukmini. She will give you the strength when you need it.'

Rukmini nodded. She touched the plant in reverence, but looked at her in askance. Having a Tulasi plant in the backyard and worshipping her as a Goddess who protected the women was a common convention across the households of Bharata, but Devaki's keenness suggested something beyond common beliefs. The older woman called a maid to take the plant and carefully consecrate it in Rukmini's garden.

'You know that when Krishna was born, Vasudeva and I were prisoners at Mathura. We smuggled him out of Mathura as soon as he was born and, in his place, came the daughter of Krishna's foster parents.'

'I also heard that she manifested into a Goddess when your brother, Kamsa, tried to attack her.'

Devaki nodded thoughtfully. 'I was hopeful that Kamsa would think before he harmed a girl child. But he did not. Stricken with guilt about how I would face Nanda and Yashoda, I tried to keep her away, but failed. The effort made me faint. Your father-in-law was also in shock when he saw that monster throw the infant against the wall. But he also saw Kamsa behave as if he had seen a ghost. It was like he saw and heard something that made him tremble with fear. He then tried to make amends for what he did to us and behaved in an absurd manner. The girl was no ordinary child, Rukmini. She was indeed a Goddess. This is the Tulasi plant that sprouted where we had buried her mortal remains. Even during the long journey from Mathura to here, this plant did not whither. It beats me how.'

Rukmini looked at her, trying to imagine how the woman had survived all this.

'It is not easy being Krishna's mother,' Devaki spoke as if she had read Rukmini's thoughts. 'And I can bet it is going to be much harder being his wife; with the sheer number of kings he managed to scare, my Krishna. The Goddess shall protect you, strengthen you when you feel weak and calm you when you feel anxious. She shall be the friend you need.'

It was hard for Rukmini to shake away the effect of the story she had heard. Walking back to her mansion, she saw the maids plant the Tulasi into an aesthetically carved pot, placed on a raised platform that was intricately carved and resembled a miniature fortress. What kind of a man her husband had to be to have a Goddess throw herself in the fray to protect him? *If not a God himself.*

The Swayamvara at Panchala

The early months of wedded bliss flew by. The political affairs, internal and external to Dwaraka, made Krishna busier each day, and with him, Rukmini too. The Sudharma welcomed her with open arms, and kept her mornings occupied. She enjoyed slow horse rides around the city with Revathi in the afternoons. Young Subhadra endeared herself to her and Rukmini gradually became acquainted with many friends and cousins of Krishna who swore by him. To some, she also became the woman to go to if they needed a favour from Krishna. She also made a regular practice of meeting the younger ones when they engaged in their military practice. The practice sessions in the recent days had intensified after the news of Draupadi's swayamvara was announced.

In one of her early morning rounds, something unusual happened. Rukmini saw Satyaki miss his aim as he practised on stationary targets, thrice in a row. She stopped in her track. Satyaki was foremost among the archers that the Yadava clan could boast of. He had even fought in major battles.

'Satyaki.'

The warrior turned and acknowledged her with a polite smile and turned to his practice. *Unusual again!* Like brother Balarama, Satyaki too was a hearty young man, offering sharp quips and a delight to have conversations with. Rukmini sensed that something was wrong. She decided to draw Satyaki's problem out with a quip herself.

'Did the Princess of Panchala start distracting you from your aim?'

Rukmini expected a sheepish grin, but instead saw disappointment loom large in his otherwise sparkling eyes.

'Her thoughts better not distract me, sister-in-law.' He averted his gaze. 'Lest I commit the sin of desiring someone who will soon be an equivalent of a mother.'

'What?'

Satyaki's lips parted for a moment and then pursed. 'I shall not be participating in the swayamvara.'

'What? Satyaki, you are the best hope of the Yadava clan! You are our best archer!'

'There are people better than me. And some of them, I love too much to disregard when they personally come up to me and tell me to stay away.'

'That is so not fair, Satyaki. Who was that? And who is a better archer than you?'

Satyaki turned again to meet her gaze. His eyes showed a visible struggle. 'Princess Rukmini, haven't you ever seen your husband in action with his bow and arrows?'

Rukmini froze. *Krishna desires Draupadi?*

Satyaki turned away to focus on his practice leaving her reeling. *He desires her so much to openly ask Satyaki not to participate!*

The early months of pregnancy had already turned her mornings uncomfortable. The bitter taste that had brutally set in upon her tongue, slowly pervading her body and soul, made the world go dark. Rukmini staggered towards the fence of the large community garden, drawing the attention of a few female attendants.

'Relax, Lady Rukmini. It is not unusual for the head to reel during this phase,' the older of them consoled her.

Like it was the physical discomfort that was consuming her. If only...

A slew of emotions made her bosom heave. Panchala was a powerful kingdom. Their alliance would indeed strengthen Dwaraka's chances with her enemies.

And Draupadi.

Rukmini remembered the Princess of Panchala. Majestic. Large-hearted. Always in control.

'Learn some grace from Princess Draupadi and stop being the annoying spitfire that you are!' Rukma's words had not hurt her then. Now, they did. Especially when her husband seemed to agree with her brother. The husband for who she had abandoned everything at her natal home.

Rukmini suppressed a sob with some effort and demanded to be left alone as soon as they reached her chamber.

What chances did she have against Draupadi, who brought with her the most powerful ally of the Yadavas while all she had to offer was...only that foetus taking shape in her womb? The sob racked her body when she felt a hand upon her shoulder. She looked into those eyes that had always given her hope, soon to mirror someone else's image.

'Malathi told me you almost fainted.'

The warmth of his palm over her cheek felt surreal. Like a dream that would fade away. Only Rukmini knew how she managed the stoic expression.

'Rukmini, are you eating well?'

'She missed her morning meal,' Malathi intervened, earning Rukmini's angry glare.

Krishna smiled with a slight shake of his head. 'Bring the meal here, Malathi.'

'I am not hungry. My tongue feels—'

'With an extra serving of the sour meat,' Krishna promptly added.

This show of love! When his heart was clearly set upon that... No, I shall not break down and make a greater fool of myself!

It was impossible to deny Krishna's love. But if it were true, why would he go to those lengths to secure Draupadi's hand. Draupadi, her dear friend, who considered her a sister!

'I want you to get better soon, Rukmini. I want you to come to Panchala with me. We cannot miss Draupadi's swayamvara.'

'I am sure she shall wed the best of men, Krishna,' Rukmini managed to say. *How could he ask of her to come and see him marrying another woman? And not just any other woman, but Draupadi!* 'But I am afraid I cannot travel in this phase.' She almost bit her lip for saying that.

'We shall be back long before your third trimester begins,' Krishna laughed. 'Come on, you are someone who raced on chariots till yesterday. I can't leave you here. Nor can I miss the swayamvara!'

Is it so easy for men? Rukmini had half the mind to lash out. But something in his eyes stopped her.

'We have charted out the journey and the places to halt. It is going to be a pleasure trip filled with newer joys. Trust me, Rukmini.'

It was the first time she had seen him this persistent, almost like a young boy. It was hard to resist that charm in spite of knowing that she would lose him to another woman. The lump in her throat got heavier as Rukmini forced herself to nod. Arguing anymore would make her break down, an indignity she did not want to subject herself to. She felt relieved when Malathi again interrupted their conversation.

'Pardon me, but you have guests—' Malathi had hardly completed her sentence when two chirpy voices followed her.

'We are hardly guests!' Mitravinda walked in, followed by a giggling Bhadra. 'Rukmini!'

Even as her long lost friend embraced her, Rukmini saw Bhadra hug Krishna. Well, the girls of Kekaya, Madra and the surrounding kingdoms were known to be forward. Besides they both were Krishna's cousins. And honestly, Rukmini knew they weren't a threat to her even if they married him.

'And our girl time starts,' Bhadra declared, almost egging Krishna to leave them all alone. 'I literally smuggled Mitravinda to Dwaraka and we don't have much time to stay here. Just wanted to wish Rukmini.'

As much as her forwardness seemed odd, this cousin of Krishna had an aura of warmth around her. Rukmini had first met her during her wedding with Krishna and had immediately liked her. And yes, as much as it seemed strange, she too could do with some distance from Krishna right now.

'We shall take care of this too!' Mitravinda chipped in when Malathi brought the midday meal.

With an affectionate pat on her cheek, Krishna left the room. Rukmini's eyes welled up the very next moment.

Rukmini's Insecurities

The rest of the day was eventless. Mitravinda and Bhadra managed to cheer Rukmini up, even if briefly. She learnt that Mitravinda had badly wanted to visit her after her wedding and could not openly do so, given her sour relationship with her brothers Vinda and Anuvinda. They too had a rivalry with Krishna. So, she visited her cousin Bhadra at Kekaya instead and the girls made a secret trip to Dwaraka to celebrate her pregnancy.

'What's wrong, Rukmini?' Bhadra asked her after a while. 'Something is surely bothering you.'

Rukmini shook her head, forcing a smile on her lips. But Mitravinda was a dear friend and Bhadra was no less. She almost considered unburdening herself to them when she saw them exchange a meaningful glance with each other. Bhadra wanted to tell her something and Mitravinda was signalling Bhadra not to.

'You girls have wanted to tell me something since the afternoon. Don't hold it back, it is bothering me,' Rukmini said, deciding against sharing her insecurities. 'Now, stop hesitating and tell me everything.'

'Now may not be the right time.' Mitravinda shook her head.

'We want to marry Krishna,' Bhadra blurted out, earning a glare from Mitravinda. 'Rukmini, please don't hate us, I beg you.'

This came from out of the blue. And strangely, Rukmini did not feel as pained as she did when she imagined Draupadi as the co-wife. In fact, she felt no pain at all. Krishna's affection for both his cousins was known. It was almost like she was sure that they hardly had it in them to compete with her.

'Pray, hear me out, Rukmini. This happened long ago. Our mothers Shrutakirti and Rajadhi, you know, are sisters of Uncle Vasudeva. They underwent limitless misery when they heard of the torture Vasudeva and aunt Devaki underwent at the hands of Kamsa.'

'They could do nothing to help their brother as their own husbands were too afraid to anger Jarasandha by antagonizing Kamsa. They prayed to the Gods to let at least one of Uncle Vasudeva's sons survive and if that happened, they vowed to get their daughters wedded to that son,' Mitravinda explained.

'Since we were born, they told us that we were meant to be Krishna's brides. We can now not even dream of someone else as our groom, Rukmini.'

Seeing those anxious faces, Rukmini could not feel any pang of anger. *Had the news of Draupadi's swayamvara made her feel that disillusioned?*

'I told you, we could not have chosen a more inappropriate moment!' Mitravinda looked at Bhadra, who was on the verge of breaking down.

'Calm down,' Rukmini replied with a serenity that surprised herself. 'Have you checked with Krishna first?'

They shook their heads. 'How can we ask him without your consent, Rukmini?' Bhadra asked.

'He may even reject us if he even feels you have the slightest doubt about this! We would not know how to handle that. It may be better to not ask him at all and remain devoted to him all our lives!' Mitravinda added. 'What we ask of you is not a small favour, Rukmini. We shall not even hold it against you if you reject us. But we had to let you know of our situation.'

'You hold a sway over Krishna that no woman can, Rukmini. We know that. We can only hope to be blessed with a miniscule portion of the love you enjoy,' Bhadra pleaded.

Rukmini wanted to laugh at their gross overestimation of her supposed 'control' over Krishna. *Like who could actually control him. Could she tell him to forget all about Draupadi's swayamvara? Could she be the compassionate elder sister to Bhadra and Mitravinda and convince Krishna to marry them as well?* Rukmini sighed to herself. Truth was that she did not know Krishna enough to predict him. It had just hit her. She did not know him!

'We have made our case.' Mitravinda shrugged. 'Take your time, Rukmini. We shall not press you further.'

Rukmini bade them a warm and unaffected farewell when they wanted to meet other members of the family before leaving for Kekaya, and chose to retire early. The day had brought with it some rude jolts and unexpected discoveries. She had lost her mind over Krishna making such a huge decision without as much as giving her a clue. And here she was again, perceived as someone who controlled his decisions. *What could she have told Krishna had he discussed the swayamvara of Draupadi with her?* Rukmini did not have an answer. She remembered those historical times when there were kings faithful to one wife, a practice that eroded as marriages became more of a political move to gain and consolidate power. *Wasn't Draupadi's swayamvara the same thing? What was her Krishna trying to do? Setting right this rotting civilization; was it even a possibility? If he was prepared to devote himself to the cause, would she not support him?* All said and done, she knew she was not ready to receive and make space for a powerful co-wife like Draupadi.

But by nightfall, Rukmini decided to accompany Krishna to Panchala. Independent of what happened there, Draupadi was a friend who helped her during her time of need. Their friendship had to be preserved and protected from the political upheaval.

Rukmini pretended to have fallen asleep when Krishna came in the night. His arm gently went around her belly, yet to show signs of the life it bore. She felt his breath tingling her neck. And involuntarily moved closer. She thought she knew him. She did not. *Was it ever possible to fully know the man?*

The Pandavas

Panchala

The travel to Panchala was indeed planned with a meticulousness that only Krishna could have done. Had it not been for the uncertainty of losing Krishna to another woman, Rukmini might even have enjoyed every bit of it. Every moment of Krishna's company was now even more precious, given the inevitable moment when he would no longer be exclusively hers! *Was he ever?* Rukmini lost the count of how many times she had pondered over the question.

The retinue of Dwaraka arrived at Panchala a couple of days earlier and Drupada's hospitality left nothing to be desired. Rukmini felt surreal on meeting Draupadi. There was a time when she promised herself that she would be at the forefront of Draupadi's wedding preparations and celebrations. Here she was, as per that promise, and yet, with that nagging mixture of envy, guilt and loss. Most annoyingly, Krishna and Draupadi did not look one bit like the to-be groom and bride, with their open banter and exchange of quips. Rukmini watched them, trying to detach herself from what she had childishly thought of as hers alone. There was this might of Panchala that could become an asset to the Yadavas. She had to admit the security that Dwaraka would have, given such an ally would stand by them. Except that she now did not understand even the need for the swayamvara? *What was the point?*

Her sleeplessness persisted even the night before the swayamvara. It was hard, especially when Krishna asked her umpteen times what he could do to make her sleep. *Like he would be there by her side the next night!* Rukmini finally faked sleep and by sunrise, she was too tired to even get ready for the big event. Others did not bother her, considering her pregnancy. But Rukmini finally managed to reach the palace to give her best wishes to Draupadi.

'Pity, we could hardly spend time together, Rukmini! And the day has come,' Draupadi seemed to experience the typical jitters of the uncertainty that loomed large.

'I have a feeling we will get closer, Draupadi,' Rukmini managed to smile, embracing her as a friend and trying to keep all the feelings at bay. Proceeding to the arena of the swayamvara with other women of Drupada's family, she saw the next-to-impossible task that the suitors had to perform to win Draupadi's hand—shooting at the eye of a rotating mechanical fish by looking at its reflection! It needed not just a superior archer, but also a warrior who could keep himself together—limbs, mind and spirit. He had to be the best of the best. To her initial cheer, Rukmini saw Shishupala, one of the early participants, fail to accomplish the task. To her horror of horrors, even the ageing Jarasandha tried, as she and other women looked upon with sheer disgust. Thankfully, he failed. It was the turn of the Kurus next. Rukmini could feel the anticipation rise among the crowd when the Kuru Prince, Duryodhana, tried. But he missed the target by the distance of a bean seed. His dear friend Karna was next. Rukmini turned and saw Draupadi's forehead perspire. Even before Karna could shoot, a sense of uneasiness came over her and Malathi had to support her. The wife of the Panchala prince came to her and ordered her maids to take her to the royal palace.

As she was led away, Rukmini heard about Karna failing to shoot the target. *That sealed it. Krishna would return to Dwaraka with two of his wives.* Rukmini was glad to be led away. She needed this time for herself, to face the inevitable with dignity. To not allow envy to scar her mind. Malathi had hardly got her settled in Draupadi's chambers when they could hear a loud cheer from the arena.

'Looks like someone succeeded!' Malathi exclaimed. Rukmini sent Malathi to find out and closed her eyes, invoking every God and Goddess she could remember to give her the strength to bear the reality. In less than an hour, Malathi's voice broke her solitude. 'It is some brahmin! Some poor brahmin!'

Rukmini's eyes shot open. She was almost sure that it was just a dream.

'Can you even imagine, my Princess? A maiden born and brought up in luxury like Draupadi, garlanding a poor brahmin. His clothes were dusty and tattered at places! He looks like he survives on alms!'

'Stop blabbering, Malathi! Who was that?'

'Some unnamed brahmin. If I were in your place, I would rush there and urge Princess Draupadi to reject him.'

Rukmini rushed towards the arena but her own weakness prevented her and Malathi rushed to help her, cursing herself. 'I was being a fool. How could I tell you to rush, my Princess! The daughter of King Drupada can handle her future. You must rest.'

'For the sake of Mahadeva! I am fine!' Rukmini protested and tried to walk towards the arena. But a crowd had collected before the palace. Women were rushing to arrange for the ceremonial welcome of the groom. Before Rukmini could step out, a guard stopped her.

'The situation in the arena is tense, Devi. It may not be wise for you to rush there. We fear a riot.'

Rukmini stood by the entrance, watching a battalion of guards moving in to take their positions and another moving towards the arena. She gathered from the other women that the kings present there rebelled against the fact that a poor nameless brahmin had won the swayamvara.

Did she not even think before she garlanded a nameless brahmin?

Wait, a nameless brahmin achieved this feat? And Krishna had not even participated. He had in fact, stopped the Yadavas from taking part? Like he knew there was someone up for the task beforehand!

Rukmini felt incapable of even thinking beyond that. She had passed through hell in the last couple of months, thinking that Krishna desired Draupadi's hand. While he, on the other hand, had entertained no such desire, like a true friend.

Rukmini shrank within herself, realizing how petty were the thoughts she had had all these days. The women of the palace were on the verge of mourning the outcome of the swayamvara and nobody noticed Rukmini's tears. It was a good couple of hours before Krishna came to the palace.

'Rukmini, Drishtadyumna's wife had sent a message about you falling sick—'

Before he could say anything else, Rukmini threw herself upon him, breaking down.

'It's alright Rukmini—'

'No, it is not, Krishna. I have been such a petty woman who doubted you!'

'Sshhhh!' Krishna led her towards the inner chamber, away from everyone.

'Listen to me…you have to,' Rukmini insisted. 'I thought you wanted to win Draupadi's hand! I have been so...'

Krishna drew her close again, putting a finger on her lips. 'No, Rukmini. The culprit here is me. I wanted people to think that way too. It was the only way to keep everyone distracted till we were sure that…'

Rukmini stared at Krishna as he whispered, '... Arjuna and his brothers safely reached Panchala and Arjuna succeeded at the swayamvara.'

So, that nameless brahmin is Arjuna!

'I could not take any chances. Perhaps I was wrong in not

trusting you with this information and caused you misery all through.'

He knew what she went through! Rukmini froze for a moment, not knowing how to react. And he had lavished his love ever since she had entertained that doubt against him and suffered within herself.

'The issue was much beyond trusting you on this secret, Rukmini. Your sorrow was not just known to me, despite your efforts; brother Balarama, Revathi, Mother Devaki and even Subhadra noticed your aloofness, the dark circles under your eyes and your abrupt departures from family gatherings. If seasoned spies were keeping a watch on us, they would know exactly what to look for while observing a family. Every night, when you turned the other side to not let me see your tears, I felt the urge to share the truth with you. Then I would remember the risk that I would put the lives of the five brothers at.'

Rukmini listened in silence. A part of her was trying to comprehend the burden that Krishna bore. The rest of her was almost indignant at him for letting her suffer that way. Rukmini stood silently as these thoughts clashed with each other.

'You have the right to sulk and make me grovel all my life. I deserve that.' His smile was so disarming that Rukmini almost melted, but she checked herself and punched him on the chest.

'Krishna,' she turned solemn.

'I'll make it up to you.'

Rukmini shook her head. 'I need time to think. Let us talk perhaps when we retire.'

Krishna continued to look at her, alternating between various charming expressions in a visible bid to woo her.

'By Mahadeva! Talk to the royal family of Panchala first and help sort this out, Krishna! They are behaving like Draupadi died.' Rukmini pointed to the worrisome chatter building outside the chamber. 'And I need to talk to you at night.' But the intriguing developments that followed the swayamvara kept coming in the way of their conversation. The first shocking development was that Draupadi had agreed to marry all the five brothers, a practice that was restricted to very remote pockets of Bharatavarsha and completely unheard of in the present day Kshatriya world. Rukmini could not believe her ears when she heard of it. But Krishna's grave nod told her that the decision had been taken and it was final.

'How...how and why did Draupadi even agree?'

'She saw much beyond what many could see,' Krishna's cryptic reply told her he was at peace with Draupadi's decision as well. Rukmini did not speak for a long time before Krishna himself took the initiative. 'You want to talk, Rukmini?'

She wanted to. Just that she was still making sense of all these huge developments and Krishna's responses to them. 'Till today, you had behaved like Draupadi's swayamvara meant everything to you. And in the face of the most shocking development, this stoic acceptance of yours... it is unnerving, Krishna. Did you even try talking her out of it? Or try and understand if she was under some pressure? By Mahadeva, Draupadi is not like me. Her forbearance should not be taken advantage of!'

Krishna smiled like he knew her worries were futile. 'She is alright, Rukmini. I am more concerned about *you*.'

Rukmini sighed and let him lead her towards the couch. 'I fear I don't understand you, Krishna. What do you want? What do you seek?'

Krishna smiled cheekily, which exasperated her. 'A boat ride along the waters of Ganga for now. Come with me.'

Her first instinct was to hit back at his arm, but Rukmini also felt that some cool breeze could relax her and help to gather thoughts. The realization that life with Krishna was going to be filled with not just political intrigues but also uncertain emotional ones had already dawned on her. But it was not the fears that made Rukmini uncomfortable; it was being unfairly blocked out from Krishna's plans that bothered her. Like he thought she was not capable of protecting a simple secret.

Thoughts of this kind rushed through her mind as they walked past the long corridors of the guest mansion of Panchala. Rukmini was unmindful of the slew of guards, male and female, greeting them with reverence, asking them if they needed something, till they came upon a woman. Rukmini's eyes halted on her for a moment and a sense of discomfort gripped her. The female guard was voluptuous with chiselled features. Something about her was different, unusual from the scores of other women who guarded the palace. Even from her bowed head, Rukmini saw the woman's gaze follow them to towards the corner of the corridor. She looked at Krishna, who she knew to be perceptive about the unusual. But he looked calm.

Rukmini halted in her steps. 'Krishna!'

He turned back to look at her. 'Something is not right about her.' She pointed her thumb in the direction of the woman. Seeing Krishna's raised brow, she turned around and did not find the woman. The place where she had stood was empty. 'The last female guard that we passed by; did you not notice her?'

'Rukmini, we passed a score of them.' Krishna smiled, patting her arm.

Rukmini gazed back at the empty corridor, trying to feel any movement in the shadows. But there was none. Like she had imagined it all. *But the face of the woman ...* Rukmini was sure she had seen her somewhere. The dark shadows of the night could create illusions but not with the clarity with which Rukmini remembered the face.

'Let us go.' Krishna pressed her arm. She followed him, still sure that she had not imagined the woman. They strolled across the garden where Daruka awaited them with Krishna's chariot. The hustle that was present on the eve of the swayamvara had died down and a good number of failed suitors too had left, save those wished well for the Pandavas. The route that led towards the river was full of empty encampments that had housed the retinues of the royal guests. A calm prevailed in the air, but not in the mind of Rukmini. However, her lips held all the troubling thoughts at bay. They got onto one of the boats where Krishna insisted that the boatman trust him with the oars. Rukmini welcomed the privacy. But invisible barriers kept clouding her mind.

'Why did you not confront me, Rukmini?'

She looked up, unprepared.

'When you felt that I desired Draupadi's hand and that hurt you, why did you not confront me?'

Rukmini averted her gaze, wondering why she did not do it. Her former self, the Princess of Vidarbha, left nothing for speculation when she did not like something. She had fought tooth and nail against Rukma and her other brothers even on trivial matters. *What had tied her tongue in this matter?*

'If it looked like your rights were going to be usurped, why did you not fight back, Rukmini?'

When Rukmini met his gaze again, she felt pain erupt in his eyes. 'Why did you not fight back?'

The gaze was surreal. Rukmini stared back till the intensity was too much for her and she shook his hand. 'Krishna!'

'What happened?'

'You… you looked like…' Rukmini paused sensing the calm and cheer surface back on his face. It was almost like Krishna had not been himself in those few moments. Rukmini shook her head to focus on their conversation. 'The day when I would have to fight with you for my rightful position, this marriage would cease to have any meaning, Krishna. I trusted you to have a good reason, for whatever you did. Not only that, I trusted you to tell me about whatever you believed in, whatever you sought out and whatever you strived for. But you blocked me out, Krishna! If charade is what was needed to be carried out for a strategic reason, I would have acted better than you!' Rukmini found herself heaving out of unexpected anger.

'Forgive me, Rukmini.'

'Leave that aside. I always assumed that you were a great friend of Draupadi's. And now you stay stoically out of the whole polyandry issue...like her future does not affect you at all? Krishna, realizing one fine day that I know nothing about the man I loved and eloped with, realizing that I have no idea about what my part in his life is and I am clueless about what he aims to achieve is unnerving.'

Krishna looked at Rukmini for a long time before leaving the oars and setting right the jewel that hung on her forehead. 'Rukmini, the struggle ahead may be far more unnerving. The uncertainty that looms upon not just the Yadavas but the whole of Bharata is...'

'And setting it right is just your job? With no role for me to play than being an ornament by your side?'

'Ornament!' Krishna chuckled, shaking his head. 'Rukmini, you already fought your battle, love. None can even gauge the defiance you single-handedly put up against Jarasandha when your own family did not lift even a finger for you and, worse, stood in your way. You fought relentlessly where even seasoned warriors succumbed to the might or lures of Jarasandha. You—'

'Escaping the wedding with Shishupala is the end of my battle? Is that the end of my story? Krishna, how can my battle be done when you are still fighting?'

'My battle, the battle to re-establish dharma, is at multiple fronts, Rukmini. It is a tricky task to identify the right field for it. At times, it may be a clash between the near and dear. At times, it may involve a gruesome skirmish or facing an unforeseen ambush.

At times it would involve the ignominy of running away—'

'At times…' Rukmini interjected. 'Rather, at all times, it should involve taking the woman who loves you into confidence than blocking her out.' She had hardly finished the sentence when the boat hit against a rocky protrusion from the adjoining cove. Rukmini held on to the walls of the boat to steady herself and gasped when her lower garment turned moist. 'It is leaking!'

Cautiously, they made their way towards the other side, a rather desolated bank. The lake was fed by the perennial waters of Ganga and looked like a river by itself in full flow.

Rukmini felt fatigue catch up. 'Look for another boat, Krishna. I shall catch my breath.' In the moonlight, she saw Krishna frown, cocking his ears as if he felt something. He then nodded, unsmiling. 'Alright, stay alert, love.' His squeeze on her arm felt like he meant to say much more. Rukmini saw him turn around the corner of a rocky path. Her defences had been on an alert since she saw that elusive female guard who looked out of place at the Panchala guesthouse.

The chirping of the crickets and the gurgling of the flowing water were the only sounds she heard for a while. It felt like Krishna had been gone far longer than she had expected him to. Rukmini tried to rise to her feet, holding onto the creeper hanging from the tree trunk, when she felt the hair on her neck stand. Her hand closed upon the hilt of her dagger.

'Whoever it is, I can sense you!' Rukmini warned, turning around. She saw nobody. 'Krishna!' she called out again, turning towards the bank.

'Don't move!' Hostility oozed out of the voice behind her and that very moment Rukmini felt a sword at her neck. 'The edge is tipped with kalakuta and so are my nails. One wrong move and you may regret it. I understand there is an unborn life you may want to care about if not yours.' It was a woman.

Rukmini pursed her lips. It was the guard that she had seen at the guesthouse! She was an assassin. 'Who sent you?' Rukmini stood her ground. 'Whoever it is, they have doom coming upon them!'

'Don't you worry about my employer! Just tell me where Krishna is.'

Rukmini held her breath, but said nothing.

'Where is he?'

'Why? You lost your heart to him?' Rukmini scoffed. 'But too bad, he is taken.'

'I am a Kritya, you silly woman!' the assassin grunted. 'Too bad if you believe our kind have hearts to lose. Now tell me where your husband is and you can go unharmed.'

'Princess of Vidarbha! What a surprise!' Rukmini turned to her right and found a man in royal garments with a thick dark shawl over his torso, which spoke of his opulence.

'Sudakshina, Prince of Kashi!'

'Must say you have done your job a tad better than I expected, Kritya. I can now forget the sorrow of losing in the swayamvara.'

'Stay away!' Rukmini held out her dagger when he tried to approach closer.

'Take her to the camp,' Sudakshina ordered Kritya.

'Not a part of our bargain,' Kritya defied him, much to Rukmini's surprise. 'The deal was to kill Krishna Vaasudeva. And you stay away from my job.'

'Your job, Kritya,' Sudakshina turned scathingly, 'is to obey my orders. Leave the woman in my camp and that son of a slave will come grovelling for his unborn child!'

'Not when the mother of the child is capable of finishing off her husband's enemies, you lowly rat!' Rukmini shoved Kritya away and attacked Sudakshina. Though taken by surprise, Sudakshina ducked in time to escape her dagger and took out his sword. Rukmini held her weapon close to hold his blow when she saw Kritya stopping him with her own sword.

'You seem to have forgotten our understanding, Sudakshina. When you hire a Kritya, no woman, no child, no brahmin and certainly no pregnant woman is to be harmed!'

Sudakshina seemed consumed by rage. His bulky build was enough to intimidate strong warriors. It was worse when he had the wife of his arch enemy within his reach and an assassin hired by him stood in his way. An assassin who had poison literally at her fingertips.

'You commit a felony, lowly woman! Don't you dare forget that your family is under my protection! And I can crush you like a fly,' Sudakshina grunted menacingly.

Rukmini's lips parted in concern for the Kritya. Even in the face of threat, she admitted her growing fascination for the mystical assassin who had no qualms in turning against her own employer if he violated the code.

'If you had a tenth of the courage to actually do what you threaten, you would not have needed to hire me, you fool!' Kritya kicked Sudakshina, relieving herself of the deadlock. As the Prince of Kashi steadied himself, she blocked his way again. 'If you knew us Krityas well enough, you would know that family always comes *after* our pledge to stand by the code!'

As interesting as the face-off seemed, Rukmini remembered that they were in a potentially hostile zone and she had to make her way back to safety. The next offence by Sudakshina almost succeeded in upsetting the Kritya's balance and he wasted no time in assaulting Rukmini, though she ducked out of his reach just in time.

'Run!' the assassin shouted, looking at her. 'I shall hold him off!'

The moment of distraction proved costly to the Kritya when Sudakshina used it to throw a well-aimed knife. Though the woman ducked, it pierced her arm. Rukmini rushed to her in concern.

'You must stay away!' the Kritya warned her, staggering back by a yard. Suppressing the agony of the wound, she launched herself at Sudakshina. The blood that her wound oozed seemed to have unleashed a feral instinct that caught the prince of Kashi by surprise. The leap made Rukmini wait for the impact with bated breath. Sudakshina instinctively raised his sword.

'Watch out!' Rukmini warned as she saw it piercing the Kritya's belly. But with one move of her twin daggers, the assassin had made Sudakshina's head roll to the ground, blood sputtering from both their wounds.

Rukmini backed away by instinct when she felt Krishna's arm steady her from behind. She looked at him, partly shocked at finding no traces of surprise in his eyes. 'You alright?' She nodded and both turned to the Kritya lying on the ground.

'The wound needs to be bandaged,' Krishna stepped forward.

'The poison…' the Kritya tried to warn as she weakly sat up.

'I shall be mindful. Just stay still.'

Rukmini watched him tend to the assassin's wounds. The woman who had wanted to kill him a while ago… he was helping *her*.

The Kritya was finally up on her feet.

'Thank you,' Rukmini smiled. 'And your family is welcome at Dwaraka. They will be protected there.'

For the first time, the assassin smiled. 'What you said about losing my heart… I think I may have found it.' She turned to leave, but looked back. 'No wonder half the kings gathered here want you dead. You have something about you that threatens the heartless, Krishna.'

Rukmini sighed in relief, throwing her arms around Krishna. But the whole adventure left her more excited than tired. 'You were close by, weren't you?' she asked Krishna when he held her close.

He nodded, not speaking for a long time, as he walked with her around the lake. 'I had noticed the Kritya shadowing us the very day we arrived at Panchala. She had another opportunity on the night of the swayamvara. But you were with me, Rukmini. And she did not risk it.'

'And you drew her out in the open, hoping to find who hired her. And you knew that he did not share her principles and played her against him...' Rukmini completed.

Krishna nodded. 'Go on, say, risking your life and our child's.'

'I know you, Krishna. You would not have done it if the stakes were high.' Rukmini paused in her steps, making him turn to her. 'And I knew the risks when I chose you over anyone else, Krishna. I want to be in this battle by your side. Wherever is the battlefield. Wherever.'

'It is not going to stop at such small adventures, Rukmini.' He looked at her tenderly.

'I don't expect it to,' Rukmini agreed. 'But how long shall we be in this reactive and defensive mode, Krishna? This Prince of Kashi, Shishupala and a whole lot of kings that are against you, it is because of Jarasandha. Is it not time to go on the offensive and end his hegemony?'

Krishna beamed. 'It is. And we need an alternative before we can end Jarasandha.'

'And the five brothers and Draupadi are your alternative.'

'What is with completing my sentences today?' Krishna laughed.

'I thought that was a part of the marital vows. Wasn't it?' Rukmini chuckled, walking ahead. It felt strange as to how much at ease she felt even after such a close shave with death, which had endangered her life and that of her unborn child's. A part of Rukmini wondered how that was possible. Perhaps it was because of the presence of the man who had the strength to show compassion even to an assassin. But how was that possible with a person who has been hounded by death even before he was born? Staring at Krishna, Rukmini picturised his childhood at the secluded settlement of Vrindavan, fighting against one danger after another till he came face to face with his murderous uncle Kamsa who he overcame. And then he risked his life multiple times to save the citizens of Mathura from the vengeful Jarasandha. How can a man persecuted every day of his life possess that serenity? Perhaps it was his strength, his core, that enabled him to win over every threat, every opponent and every intrigue.

'Krishna …' Rukmini reached out to caress his curls. 'What made you marry me? What is it about me that convinced you that I deserved a place in your life?'

Krishna's knitted his brows, merriment springing from his eyes. 'I smell a trap.'

'You know your way around traps, don't you?' Rukmini winked, 'And no, you can't get away with flattery or clichéd lines about love transcending lives and all.'

Krishna pursed his lips, pretending to be thoughtful. 'How does one define love, Rukmini?'

'Your love, or the way this world perceives love?'

'Is my love different?'

Rukmini nodded. 'Your love strengthens you and those fortunate to be loved by you. Wait, your love has something infinite about it. Like you feel one with anything and everything around. You aren't capable of hatred, Krishna.' Rukmini paused, remembering Mitravinda and Bhadra. 'I realized this is impossible with any other man in this universe. Any other woman in your life does not make you belong any less to me.'

Satyabhama

Dwaraka

Sudharma bustled with the full attendance of its members. Overseeing the men below from her mezzanine portico, Rukmini tried to capture the mood of the sabha. Even as they were returning from Panchala, she had sensed some discontentment in some of the leaders. It seemed like they too had their hopes pinned on Krishna winning the hand of Draupadi and were slightly unimpressed when he let the alliance with the powerful Panchalas slip towards his cousins, the Pandavas. Krishna had stayed back at Khandava, the new capital of the five brothers while Rukmini had returned to Dwaraka with the others. She would have loved to stay back and help out Draupadi with setting up her new home. But it was Krishna's wish that she returned to Dwaraka and handle the aftermath of Bharatavarsha's biggest swayamvara. When they would get to know that Krishna had willingly stopped the Yadavas from trying their luck for the sake of the Pandavas, there were bound to be questions. Rukmini leaned against her seat, a hand upon her belly, now bulging with life, and watched the men below having a discussion among themselves.

The sabha greeted the arrival of Ugrasena, the aged father of Devaki, who had remained the token chief of the Yadava federation. Ugrasena addressed the gathering.

'Haven't the past months been kind to the Yadavas? Thank Mahadeva for that. Our daughter Pritha, or Kunti as is her adopted name, and her five valiant sons have escaped the dreadful fire at Varanavata and have won the hand of Princess Draupadi at

Panchala. Our own predicament in the past did not allow us to go to the aid of our daughter in the hour of her need.'

'Neither did her family aid us in the hour of our need, Chief Ugrasena,' the interruption came from Satrajit, a Yadava noble who made a name for himself by acquiring a fortune through his entrepreneurial endeavours. Rukmini remembered hearing mixed opinions about him. Some of the Yadava leaders looked down upon Satrajit for failing kshatradharma and becoming a full-time merchant while others like Akrura and Kritavarma encouraged him and became partners in his businesses to lay their hands on some of that fortune. Nonetheless, the meteoric rise in Satrajit's wealth had considerably increased his influence in Sudharma.

'We both went through some trying times. The reunion at Panchala and the happy occasion that followed it were but a boon from the Gods above,' noble Akrura added and looked at Ugrasena to continue.

'There may be some of us who feel that the alliance with the Panchalas has been wasted in favour of a family that is just starting out,' Satrajit blurted out.

'Pray, leave some things like familial bonds out of your business calculations, Satrajit,' Satyaka, the elderly patriarch of Shaineya clan interjected.

Satrajit wasted no time in taking offence. 'I agree, the sabha has little tolerance when it comes to numbers and facts that disagree with the pompous ideals we have been brought up with. Pardon me for wasting your time, noblemen. Pardon my interruption, Chief Ugrasena, do please go ahead with what is to be discussed after the heart-warming reunion.'

Ugrasena sighed at the jibe and shook his head to continue. 'The sons of our Kunti are yet to set up their capital city at Khandava. There can't be a better time for us to improvise our relationship with the Pandu family by extending monetary assistance in building their capital.'

The sabha fell quiet for a while, each of the noblemen pondering over the money they would need to give up to match this proposal.

'Wouldn't it be good to help a flourishing city close to our erstwhile Mathura?' Akrura added.

Rukmini glanced at Satrajit who looked unimpressed. She cleared her throat and rose, inching towards the parapet wall. 'Salutations Chief Ugrasena and other elders. I laud the suggestion by grand uncle Ugrasena. Throwing in our lot with the Pandavas will not only help Dwaraka with a strategic political partner in the northern Bharata, but shall also win the affections of all those close to them, like the powerful Panchalas. I am just stating tangible benefits for those who want to look beyond familial reasons.' Rukmini pointedly glanced at Satrajit who frowned for a moment before acknowledging with a calculated smile.

'Optimistic strategization. Nice to hear someone who has her feet on the ground. Your nobility shows, Princess Rukmini,' Satrajit replied.

There has got to be a 'but' coming. Rukmini thought, keenly observing the nobleman's face. Satrajit was profuse with praise in the following sentences, a strategy he always used to pre-empt silence from the supporters of the one he opposed.

'However, Princess of Vidarbha, marital relationships cannot ensure a trustworthy ally always, especially in the case of royal families. Who knows it better than you, a princess yourself?' He paused, looking pointedly at her.

He was hinting at the fact that the relationship of Dwaraka with Vidarbha showed no improvement after Krishna married her. Rukmini felt Revathi's comforting hand upon her knee and discretely nodded.

'Relationships, whether marital or otherwise, are never

undervalued in families where dharma reigns, noble Satrajit,' she replied with an unaffected smile. 'The five Pandu brothers and the family of Panchala stand for that. Senior noblemen in the Sabha, I am sure, can see that, given their infinite wisdom.' She looked around, briefly catching the gazes of Ugrasena, Akrura, Satyaka and others, some of who approvingly nodded. 'Gratitude is the one quality that the sons of aunt Kunti possess in abundance. Our wealth shall find a worthy recipient who will value it and flourish the empire.'

'Moreover,' Rukmini continued, 'it is time we learnt some lessons from our arch-enemies too. Don't the illustrious noblemen who adorn Sudharma remember how Jarasandha neutralized the Yadava federal spirit using his son-in-law Kamsa? I learnt it all from Krishna and brother Balarama. The king of Magadha not only held the erstwhile Mathura to ransom, but also had a potential military base in Mathura to keep his other rivals, the Kurus, under check. Had it not been for the presence of mind of father Vasudeva and mother Devaki, had it not been for the sacrifices of the blessed couple Nanda and Yashoda of Vrindavan who gave up their daughter in the process, had it not been for Krishna and everything he risked and faced, Jarasandha would have gained control over all of the northern Bharata today. This time, we keep him in check by propelling the progress of another formidable force that could bring him down—the five Pandava brothers whose power is now on the rise. We help rebuild a city, much bigger and majestic, close to where our Mathura was razed to the ground. We take the battle to Magadha.'

'Saaho!' Satyaka and Akrura rose to their feet.

Satrajit leaned back against his seat, letting the cheer rise and ebb away. Inadvertently, the debate was between him, the wealthiest Yadava, and Rukmini, who seemed to be more than making up for Krishna's absence, especially today. His wealth,

Satrajit knew, had been a stroke of luck. The long unused ports of Saurashtra, which had sprung to activity after Dwaraka was established, found an early player in him and the risk paid off well. And Satrajit knew that this rise in his wealth would hit a plateau some time or the other. 'We barely managed to escape Jarasandha's wrath, Princess Rukmini. I thank all Gods that you, my child, got to enter the Yadava fold at Dwaraka. You were spared the sight of our homes burning in Mathura. We had retreated from our beloved city just the night before it was burnt down. The burning stench of what had been our home haunted us for days. I am afraid, your advice to use all our wealth to propel some probable ruler, who would possibly be a force to keep Jarasandha possibly under check is, I must say to my regret, far-fetched. The Yadava treasury, my Princess, is not in a position to undertake such a huge risk, that too as a gift.'

'Why are we arguing without even getting into numbers?' a new voice chirped into the silence that followed. Rukmini's gaze went up from Satrajit to the smaller portico above him. She saw a girl, barely over fifteen autumns, craning her neck to be visible to everyone below. 'I mean to say, why can't each of us volunteer the wealth we can send to Khandava Prastha and see if that makes up for the investment needed to build a city. Let us openly ask for estimates from the treasurer of the Pandu family.'

'Satyabhama,' Satrajit called out with a slight frown and looked around, slightly embarrassed.

'Is that your daughter, noble Satrajit?' Ugrasena asked with a warm smile. 'I thought she was too young...'

'Pardon me chief, Ugrasena,' Satrajit replied in a hurry. 'My daughter still has a good couple of months to go before she attains the eligibility to speak in Sudharma. I had brought her along so that she could observe the proceedings and learn. Satya, child, you can't speak out of turn.'

'I did not mean to, Father. But it is so obvious, why can't you all just—'

'Sshhhh!' Satrajit raised a finger.

'Well, let her complete what she has to say,' Rukmini beamed. 'If Satyabhama has a valid argument to add, can't we overlook those couple of months she has to go?'

The whole of Sudharma had their eyes fixed on this maiden who was now conscious of the attention she had. Rukmini noticed Satyabhama swallow and attempt to speak but words did not come out of her mouth.

'Go on, Satya. Forget the fearsome noblemen here.' Ugrasena smiled. 'Consider this as a question your acharya would ask you during your schooling. How would you, as a Yadava noblewoman, see the situation and what would your solution be?'

'I mean… I think the need to gift and invest wealth to set up the Pandava kingdom is already established. What we now need is only the estimate. Even if the numbers are beyond us for the moment, the wealth can go in instalments. The time would also be congenial to negotiate trade agreements that would be mutually beneficial. I can wager that Krishna would be thinking on the same lines!' The last sentence came out in an unabashedly loud manner that raised many brows. Satyabhama gasping and biting her lip only lent emphasis to what Rukmini guessed.

'Err… Ever since Dwaraka was secured as a new home… rather ever since Kamsa's death, I hear a lot of young men and women speculate on what Krishna Vaasudeva thinks or wants,' Satrajit tried to cover up and then turned to Satyabhama. 'And for the moment, forget that I am your father, Satya. You lost me at the "need to gift and invest already being established". Explain that?'

'From what Princess Rukmini explained and advised,' Satyabhama briefly glanced at Rukmini, 'while many of us have practically become vaishyas, we should remember that a province needs all the varnas in spirit. The wealth should be invested in such a way as to serve all the purposes. Quick-turnaround investments fill up our treasury. The impact, too, is short-lived, but we need them. We, the population, have divided our tasks and professions into varnas. Our investments should follow the structure as well, and in consonance with the purusharthas assigned to each varna. Like a profession fulfilling the purushartha, kama is classified as shudra, the task of vaishya is to secure artha, kshatriya to establish dharma and that of a brahmin is to secure moksha to all of the society. The wealth should be invested in these four categories too. The shudra segment of our wealth is an investment into purushartha, kama. The risks are low, and turnarounds are quick. Then, there are investments that have a longer turnaround. The risks are relatively high. But even the impact on the treasury is stronger. The vaishya investment, or the investment fulfilling the purpose of artha.' Satyabhama paused for breath.

'A new twist to varnas! Interesting!' Rukmini could not locate who made the comment, but it had indulgence and amusement. Both of which she shared.

'Then, there are investments we make to secure the society, the land, from dangers, be they from nature, criminals or enemies. The return on this investment is the safety of the common citizen. This infuses the courage within the common man and woman to go about their lives with no fear. It is the investment into dharma—kshatra dharma. While the three purusharthas secure this life, the fourth is an investment beyond the bounds of this life. To keep our progeny in this fold, but with a focus on the impermanence of the world around us. To remember fulfilling the dharma that our bodies have inherited, but also realize the dharma of ourself beyond our body. The investment into Moksha. The so-called returns cannot be judged by the rules of commerce.

But we shall surely be judged by our descendants and our future births.

'Father, Princess Rukmini's sound advice is for us to graduate some of our wealth by channelizing it into building dharma. And dharma will protect our interests in return.'

The speech arrested Rukmini's attention. The maiden looked simple in her demeanour, pampered with gaudy jewellery, but had her heart in the right place. Her teacher, whoever it was, needed to be appreciated.

'May I say, if there is a calamity that requires all the men to leave the place, I am afraid to say our women will outdo us in administration!' Akrura grinned and a congenial cheer arose among the noblemen.

'Satya, my child,' Ugrasena addressed her. 'That was an impressive understanding. I would like it if you assist Princess Rukmini in putting that vision into practice. Will you?'

Satyabhama looked at Rukmini and nodded eagerly. Rukmini nodded and smiled back. She remembered Krishna's words of encouragement—that her words were capable of finding allies even in the direst of situations. *Did he mean Satyabhama?*

Rukmini's attention then got drawn towards Ugrasena's voice. 'We have also received an invitation from Madra. For the swayamvara of Princess Lakshana. And also, a message from the King of Kekaya, regarding the wedding of Princess Bhadra.' Ugrasena paused and looked at Rukmini as if to ask something. Rukmini nodded.

'Mahadeva willing, celebrations await Dwaraka.' He smiled and concluded the Sabha as the rest of the noblemen cheered.

❦

'A temple!'

Rukmini looked up in between examining the scrolls of trade

agreements. Satyabhama looked visibly excited.

'A temple, elder sister. The temples of Saurashtra have wealth deposited by generations of devotees. But obviously that wealth cannot go into administrative purposes.'

'Of course, using temple wealth, the wealth given by devotees out of faith, for administrative purposes shows the imbecility of the ruling establishment in managing their treasury.'

'But that temple wealth can go into building new temples. One at Khandavaprastha! Once a temple is built, it will be easier to develop land around it. Please, elder sister, sound it off to Krishna, I am sure he would agree!'

In the past six months of working together, Rukmini had noticed that Satyabhama could hardly hide her infatuation for Krishna. Perhaps that was what made Satyabhama assist Rukmini, even if it meant some uncomfortable confrontations with her father Satrajit. In the past couple of months, she had practically become a member of the Shoora household, sharing at least one meal with them every other day. *But where would this innocent love take the girl?* Rukmini, for a moment, felt protective about her, given Satyabhama's sense of abandon. Her thoughts galloped in various directions till Satya waved her hand. Rukmini shook her head and smiled. 'Just a bit drowsy,' she chuckled. 'This Pradyumna is quite a handful in the night.' Her four-month-old son was a perfect excuse to explain her absent-mindedness. 'And coming to the temple idea, I heard some news of a different kind, Satya. Something of concern. Hopefully the building of this new city at Khandava does not get stalled due to that.'

'What's wrong with Khandava, sister Rukmini?'

'A large part of Khandavaprastha is a treacherous forest with scattered tribes and villages. In the last six months, the Pandavas managed to unite them, convinced them to live together and expand their means of living. But they now face a new challenge. A certain

Naga faction under the leadership of Takshaka. Basically looters, robbers, abductors and... all sorts. The last I heard was that they tried looting the grain sent from Kekaya to Khandavaprastha. The eldest Pandava, Yudhishtira, expressed his wish to handle that menace before he accepts any more investments.'

Satyabhama narrowed her eyes and shook her head. 'The "crime" of doing something good never goes unpunished. What is with this Naga faction now? Hope they find a solution soon.'

'So, for now, we can go back to focussing on the port trade of Saurashtra.' Rukmini smiled, tying up the bundle of palm scrolls.

'That wristlet, it suits you so well!' Satyabhama pointed at the jewel studded with large rubies and pearls around Rukmini's right wrist.

'Thank you!' Rukmini replied, partly amused at the sudden change of topic. 'It is Krishna's by the way. Raided his collection as I got bored of mine.'

'Instead of getting newer jewellery made so that you could send the wealth to Khandavaprastha?' Satyabhama looked directly into Rukmini's eyes. When Rukmini tried to wave her away, Satyabhama caught her hand. 'Heed me, elder sister. As a merchant's daughter, I studied risks and returns all my life. There is a limit to what you can give away.'

Rukmini was about to dismiss Satyabhama's advice when the young woman almost surprised her. 'I have another of this kind. It's a pair actually, which I never wear. If you like it so much, Rukmini—'

'It's a pair?' Rukmini frowned.

'Sister Rukmini, I had gifted this bracelet to Krishna. Very long ago. He had come to Mathura and won this impossible wrestling bout against a monster of an opponent and I was just so relieved and overjoyed. I simply gifted it to him.'

'Sister Rukmini!' a voice interrupted them before Rukmini could reply. It was Bhadra, dressed in red. 'Satya, I knew I would find you here too. Are you both back to solving all of the problems of Saurashtra here in Rukmini's garden? What jobs do the men have left to do at Sudharma? Honestly, I am curious.'

The jingle of Bhadra's anklet accompanied her mirth as she hurried towards them. 'So, give it a break, ladies, it is the month of Kartika. It is picnic time, frolic time! Who is up for a trip to Prabhasa? Why am I even asking? Rukmini, you can't get out of this. Pradyumna will be fine with the nurses for a day. We start at dawn and will be back by sunset. Rukmini! You—need—a—break. Lakshana has already made all the arrangements.'

'Bhadra, I am not sure. Why don't you and Lakshana—'

'Krishna is going to cancel if you don't come. Please Rukmini, please. The trade of Saurashtra will not stop if you come away for a day.'

The only one way to stop Bhadra's persistence was to agree. Rukmini smiled and nodded. Bhadra turned to Satyabhama. 'And you will join us by dawn. Or better still, sleep here with Subhadra tonight. We can all start early.' She beamed.

Satyabhama smiled uncomfortably and rose to her feet. 'I would love to, Bhadra. But there is a limit to imposing myself on family occasions.' She stopped, seeing the expressions of Rukmini and Bhadra. 'I mean… maybe next time.'

'Silly girl! Did anyone say something?'

Satyabhama shook her head. 'I remembered something else. A shipment is waiting to be accounted for and my father is going to be wild at me if I don't finish the task by tomorrow. You ladies have a great time and bring me Lord Somanatha's prasad.'

It was evident to both the women that Satya was at the brink of tears.

'What's wrong with her?' Bhadra exclaimed.

'I think I know what it is,' Rukmini replied softly.

'Did I say something that hurt her?'

Rukmini shook her head and smiled, as if making her mind up for something. 'Let her be, Bhadra. She will join us during the next Kartika.'

Subhadra and Arjuna

'I am not interested. Does anyone even listen to me? Does my consent even matter? Nobody cares for a maiden's wish in this whole city of Dwaraka!'

'By Mahadeva! Someone stop her drama!' Bhadra exclaimed.

'Foolish girl! We know what is good for you,' Lakshana, the Princess of Madra laughed.

'I don't like jasmines. I hate them, I hate them, I hate them!' Subhadra threw back her head. 'How can you women take my braid under your control and violate my consent?'

'Subhadra! Arrgh!' Mitravinda grunted. 'You need to stay still for me to get the strands right.'

Rukmini absent-mindedly looked at her three co-wives pampering their sister-in-law. Her mind was actually on what lay in the southeastern corner of the room, close to the window. Subhadra, Rukmini knew, was learning archery, but these were the kind of arrows that seasoned warriors used. And they were neither of Krishna's or Balarama's. They were unused, newly sharpened and possibly forgotten by someone who had visited Subhadra. The visitor, whoever it was, had come after the maids had cleaned up Subhadra's chamber in the morning. Rukmini's eyes fell upon her own mansion, which the window overlooked. There was only one person who could access Subhadra's chamber—the guest who she and Krishna had been hosting since a fortnight. Her attention was suddenly drawn to an abrupt entry into the room.

She saw him stop shortly in his footsteps, looking at the room full of women.

Arjuna.

'Come on in, brother. You are no stranger!' Mitravinda waved.

'I... I thought I heard someone scream for help,' Arjuna looked around hesitantly. As Rukmini observed, he avoided looking at Subhadra till the very end, when he stole a quick glance and then smiled at Mitravinda.

'Here, this is your "damsel-in-distress."' Lakshana pointed at Subhadra. 'Throwing a tantrum for sheephalika flowers when not in season.'

'Poor Arjuna, he rushed all the way because of your screams!' Lakshana frowned. Subhadra made a face at her, but suddenly stopped, seeing Rukmini picking up the arrows.

'Well, Arjuna came just on time!'

Subhadra sprang up unmindful of the half-plaited braid, much to Mitravinda's exasperation. Hurrying to Rukmini, she almost snatched the arrows and showed them to Arjuna. 'How do they look now? I sharpened them just as you instructed brother Satyaki and me, yesterday.'

Rukmini observed Arjuna stare at Subhadra blankly till she went closer to him. She observed the discrete nudge she gave him that made him finally recover and he nodded vigorously. 'They... They look as good as mine. May—maybe better.'

'Brother Arjuna, don't start humouring and pampering Subhadra for Mahadeva's sake!' Bhadra warned. 'At least, the teacher has to be stern. Otherwise this girl is going to dance on your shoulders like she does on ours.'

'Don't listen to them!' Subhadra held Arjuna's arm. 'And I know it is time for practice and that I am late. Let's go.' Subhadra almost hurried out of the room, pulling Arjuna behind her.

'Your braid... by all Gods!'

'I am knotting my hair. Anyway it becomes messy during practice and I will have to redo it again!' Subhadra's voice trailed through the corridor as her sisters-in-law shook their heads at each other.

Rukmini stared at them. *How can they not notice something so obvious?*

'Sudharma may start anytime. I am already late,' she told them and walked away swiftly, hoping to catch Krishna before he left for Sudharma. But upon reaching her mansion, Rukmini found that Krishna had already left. When she hurried to the Yadava grand council, the day had already started. She apologized for the delay.

'It is perfectly understandable, my child,' Ugrasena beamed. 'You are hosting a very special guest who is training Satyaki and other Yadava youth in advanced archery. Taking care of him is the first priority. Anyways, there is not much to deliberate today, except that noble Kritavarma has an interesting suggestion.'

Rukmini nodded and took her seat, trying to catch Krishna's eye. He saw her and motioned her to be seated. There was an unusually blank expression on his face.

Kritavarma nodded. 'I was just thinking about fixing Subhadra's marriage with the eldest prince of Hastinapura,' he filled in.

Rukmini's eyes grew wider for a moment before she quickly masked it with a thoughtful expression. 'I... Subhadra is young.'

'Daughters always seem young to mothers, and sisters-in-law who are as loving as mothers,' Ugrasena grinned. 'Anyways, it is just a suggestion and we need due deliberation.'

Rukmini nodded with a straight expression and cleared her throat. 'May I know why particularly Duryodhana? I mean, our aunt Kunti has five capable sons.'

'That did not go unnoticed, Princess Rukmini,' the elderly Hridika, the father of Kritavarma replied. 'In fact, Bhima and Arjuna were the first ones who came to my mind. But my son Kritavarma had an observation to make. I thought the casual conversation we had yesterday should be deliberated upon by this sabha. It is not only a matter of our daughter's happiness, but also, of the Yadavas in general.'

Rukmini stole a glance at Krishna and shook her head, being as discrete as she could. But Kritavarma interrupted, making Krishna look at him.

'The Pandavas' marital alliance with the Princess of Panchala is complicated, sister-in-law Rukmini. Pardon my indiscretion, but Indraprastha can be considered a dominion of Panchala right now.'

'It's not fair to state so,' Rukmini protested. 'The five brothers haven't risen to power solely by their father-in-law's backing.'

'No, no, that's not what he meant,' Hridika joined in. 'We are friendly with Indraprastha. We are happy for the sons of our daughter Kunti. But we also need to consider the macro fallout, Princess Rukmini. Better not forget Jarasandha. He has been bested more than once in the recent years, starting from your brave stance, years back.'

Rukmini smiled at the praise but something told her to be alert. She nodded at Hridika to continue. 'We all know that Jarasandha tried to hijack Princess Draupadi's swayamvara too, but fortunately, that too did not go according to him. His next target through marital alliance would be the Kurus of Indraprastha.'

'We need to make a move before he does, sister-in-law,' Kritavarma added.

'I hope we should also deliberate on how it would be perceived, our attempt to score an alliance with the side that allegedly tried to murder our Kunti and her sons in cold blood,' the elderly Satyaka, who till now, was a silent spectator, entered the discussion.

Rukmini noticed Krishna exhale and smiled to herself. His silence suggested that he had a plan.

'My father is right,' Satyaki added. 'Noble Arjuna has been training the Yadava youth in archery almost every waking hour of his stay here. Aren't we bordering on, say, being ungrateful when we don't even consider him as a choice?'

'Think beyond the obvious, Satyaki,' Balarama pointed out. 'I love the five brothers like my own. But the noble Hridika's observations can't be wished away. Besides, I have observed Duryodhana as a student for a while. His darker side, as we fear, is the result of his company. That suta, Karna, and the Gandharan uncle, Shakuni. A worthy life partner can inspire her husband away from that undesirable company and make him walk the right path. If this alliance can settle the cold war between the house of Pandu and the Kurus, we would be aiding our aunt Kunti.'

Rukmini frowned. Balarama's intentions were always noble and large-hearted, like Krishna's. But somewhere somehow, he would miss out something very important in comparison to his younger brother's acute judgment. It was an observation Rukmini had made over time. Rukmini let the discussion go on for a while and then countered, 'Not to state the obvious, but what about Subhadra's choice? Shouldn't we talk to her about this?'

'Of course, we should and it is her choice that we shall honour at the end of the day,' Balarama declared. 'But as her family, we need to have our deliberations right and guide her in her decision-making. That is our duty too. Krishna, you have been quiet.'

Krishna finally smiled and nodded. 'Not much to add when you say it that way, brother Balarama. I wholeheartedly agree with you that it will be Subhadra's decision that will be honoured.'

The topic was about to reach its conclusion when a couple of guards hurried in. They looked at Ugrasena blankly and then at each other, obviously at a loss of words. 'Lord… Lord…'

'What is it?' Balarama asked, mildly irritated.

One of the guards swallowed thrice and looked at his senior. The older guard nodded and turned to Ugrasena, 'My Lords, we saw, noble Arjuna whisk Lady Subhadra onto his chariot and drive out of Dwaraka.'

The news stupefied everyone for a while as Rukmini recovered from her own surprise and sighed with relief.

'Do you even hear what you speak?' Satyaki shouted at the

guard. 'It is Arjuna about who you are talking.'

Balarama sprang to his feet and held the guard by his shoulder. 'Tell me correctly. Did Subhadra resist or cry for help?'

The guard blankly scratched his head.

'Speak out!'

'We...we were too far to notice, Lord Balarama.'

Balarama clenched his fists. 'How could he do this? How could they do this?'

Krishna rose and patted Balarama's shoulder, 'We just heard Subhadra's choice, brother.'

'How are we even sure, Krishna? And all of a sudden?'

Krishna walked up to the middle of the Sabha. 'Arjuna has stayed with us for just over a fortnight and the youth of Dwaraka are already sensing a difference in their archery skills. Satyaki is the testimony to that. He is aware that the Yadu home is the natal home of his beloved mother, our aunt Kunti. Chief Ugrasena and others, Arjuna had to just ask us for Subhadra's hand and we would have considered ourselves lucky. But…' Krishna's gaze paused at Balarama and at Kritavarma. 'Interestingly, Subhadra seemed to be in a hurry. Mahadeva knows what we did to arouse that sense of insecurity in her that she convinced Arjuna to take her away in this manner.'

Balarama still looked thoughtful. 'Still a speculation, Krishna. We can't say that for sure.'

'There is only one way to find out, brother. Let us all go, bring them back for a ceremonial wedding.'

'Yes, without further delay,' Rukmini spoke. 'Let our Subhadra not leave the borders of Saurashtra with a sense of guilt or loss. Let her leave with an assurance that her natal home is always ready to welcome her and her new family with open arms.' Rukmini's eyes blurred without her knowledge. She brushed her tears away, almost ashamed of letting the emotion show.

The men hurried to gather and leave before Arjuna and Subhadra got far.

'I never imagined it would happen so soon!' Rukmini collapsed on the couch after the excitement and the hurried wedding that followed Subhadra's elopement with Arjuna. 'Now, tell me how you had this planned.'

Krishna shrugged. 'I had a whiff of it a couple of months before, when brother Balarama started warming up to Duryodhana and started pinning the crimes of the Kuru prince on his friends and relatives. After that, you know what happened.'

Rukmini punched his arm. 'And here I was, thinking like I am the smartest person in Dwaraka for spotting the lovelorn couple.'

Krishna grinned and looked at her tenderly. 'The coming Kartika would be a special occasion at Prabhasa.'

Rukmini cringed. 'Don't remind me of the preparations for the next festival please! I am yet to recover from the superhuman hustle we managed for Subhadra's wedding!'

'I meant to say, if you want to invite Rukma…'

'No!' Rukmini shook her head. 'No! Stay away from all of them, Rukma, Vinda, Anuvinda, Shishupala… the whole lot.'

'Rukmini…'

'No, Krishna. If you meant this seeing my emotions get better of me that day at Sudharma, I beg you, let it go. Well, as a daughter and sister, it is natural for me to miss my home. But let us not forget that Jarasandha is still at large. We enjoyed small victories. But who knows what he has got planned ahead? After he is eliminated, perhaps we can consider reconciliation with some of our relatives. But I am not in any hurry for reunions, Krishna. Do something about Jarasandha. Go on the offensive.'

Part Three

Rajasuya

After Subhadra's wedding, Krishna visited Indraprastha much more frequently, as Rukmini along with Mitravinda and others focussed on the economic side of the Yadu confederacy. The activity in the northern plains seemed to happen at a feverish pace at the Pandava capital. But the spy network of Dwaraka could not gather much information about Jarasandha, which made Rukmini restless.

The growing number of toddlers in the household was a delight to every member of the Shoora family. However, the fear about their future and safety made Rukmini sleepless during the nights.

'Jarasandha is old now. Perhaps he has finally settled down, accepting the fact that he had his run and it is now the turn of others?' Revathi suggested as they discussed the matter one day.

'His dominion as the royal alliance-maker has definitely come to an end…' Rukmini remarked, still unsure why her heart failed to be at peace.

'If half the princesses of Bharata have reached Dwaraka, then…' Revathi shrugged, keenly observing Rukmini's face. 'Are you sure your stress is about Jarasandha and not about the… *growing* household?'

'Krishna's household… abnormalities have to be expected and accepted, elder sister,' Rukmini beamed. 'Let me admit, it has not been easy for me. But then the workload is so much that I am almost thankful for the extra pairs of hands and the brainstorming. It is strange… I just cannot explain how…'

'His constant throwing of surprises probably holds you all together! And by Mahadeva, I just noticed the new patch of floral creepers in your garden. They are managing well in this soil and despite the sea!'

But before the women could indulge in the deeper nuances of gardening, they were interrupted by Balarama. 'Forgive the interruption ladies, time to go to Sudharma.'

'Now? It will be sunset in a while!' Rukmini was surprised.

'We were just settling down for some ladies' time, Balarama,' Revathi protested. 'Try managing without us for once... Can't you?' she cooed naughtily.

'Love, how I wish I could excuse myself too,' Balarama responded, imitating her mirth, and making Rukmini laugh. 'But unfortunately, when a member of the Shoora family calls for a gathering, at least his family members need to be present. Did I mention, unfortunately?'

'Member of Shoora family? Who?'

'Your husband and my little brother,' Balarama rolled his eyes.

'Krishna has returned from Indraprastha? When?' Rukmini sprang to her feet, calling on Malathi to fetch her shawl.

'Not long before. He called for a gathering as soon as he alighted from his chariot.'

They hurried towards Sudharma. Rukmini saw Krishna wave at her. The fatigue of travel showed on his face but the eyes had the same spark that once used to make her heart flutter. Krishna shifted his gaze when Ugrasena asked him to brief the sabha.

'With a promise to allow everyone to go back to their afternoon siestas, let me come straight to the point,' Krishna started, bringing back the characteristic cheer. But what he mentioned next made everyone forget about any siesta for this afternoon, and many afternoons to come. 'We have often wondered about finding a permanent solution to Jarasandha's problem, especially in the face of his newly growing influence over our immediate neighbour, Shalva, and even a portion of Madra. The good news is that our cousin,

King Yudhishtira of Indraprastha, has willed upon something that, among others, will help us solve this problem once and for all. The Pandavas are contemplating Rajasuya.'

A quiet prevailed in Sudharma, as each of the leaders tried to comprehend the consequences.

'Rajasuya is a campaign that pronounces the yajamana of the yajna as the emperor of the land. It involves a subcontinent-wide digvijaya, or campaign,' the noble Akrura thought aloud in an attempt to make sense of the development. 'King Yudhishtira wants to perform Rajasuya?'

Krishna nodded. 'The august leaders of the Yadu confederacy would require no proof of Yudhishtira's worthiness to command the title of the Samrat of Bharatavarsha.'

The senior Yadava leaders looked at each other, most of them fearing to speak the next words. Some even hoped that none would speak up and the news could be treated as something that would not affect Dwaraka.

'When are the Yadava soldiers expected to join them as allies?' Satyaki braved the chiding stares from others. He stared back at a couple of them in disbelief. 'Or do we want the world of tomorrow to know that the Yadava valour was not an indispensable force behind the making of this new empire?'

'I am sure your enthusiasm is appreciated, son,' Hridika replied. 'But as the son of our Vasudeva once cautioned us to deliberate upon the battles we choose, we must deliberate over this too.'

'The opposition mostly boils down to Jarasandha of Magadha, if I am reading the political landscape right,' Rukmini observed aloud. 'There may be some enthusiastic regional war lords and clansmen who would prefer to not bend without a fight. While we cannot underestimate their resistance, it is obvious that eliminating Jarasandha more or less decides the result of the campaign. Doesn't it?' She looked at Krishna.

'A campaign planned without eliminating Jarasandha is bound to encounter a much stiffer resistance,' Krishna replied. 'If the Pandavas manage to subdue Jarasandha, then planning the rest of the campaign may start to make sense. With the combined forces of allies and their own valour, one can be reasonably sure that they would succeed. Each victory would add to the growing sentiment.'

Barring Satyaki, there was a non-committal silence across the Sudharma. Ugrasena leaned forward. 'Son Krishna, do you suggest that we pledge military assistance to the upcoming imperial campaign of Rajasuya?'

'Grandsire Ugrasena, Jarasandha still holds sway over a large confederation of kingdoms. They may not officially pay annual tributes to him, but their kingdoms are congenial bases to any initiatives taken by the King of Magadha. He practically controls their welfare. Kashi, Avanti, Chedi, Vidarbha, Koshala and now even Shalva are under his control. After long, we have an alternative to the power centre he commands. With the Yadavas, Kekaya, Madra, Matsya, Panchala and hopefully, the Kurus of Hastinapura supporting them, the sons of our aunt Kunti have an opportunity to solve this problem of Jarasandha once and for all, while also being ready to become the much-needed alternate power centre. A benevolent one too. An empire that Bharatavarsha has always deserved and needs to become.' Pausing to meet the eyes of every noble in the sabha, he continued, 'Don't we, the Yadavas, want to be proactive in supporting the establishment of this new empire and participate in the whole founding process? This is an opportunity, and an ideal one to protect dharma so that it can protect us.'

'Son Krishna, as inspiring as your words are, this Yadu confederacy is beginning to breathe easy after surviving a devastating number of attacks, fleeing our beloved motherland Mathura,' Hridika countered. 'Can we afford to again attract the wrath of Jarasandha? If by any chance the ageing lion is planning to let us off the hook over the recent developments, don't we risk incurring a fresh round of wrath if we support the formation of a rival empire?'

The fear of being hounded by Jarasandha was still afresh in every mind in the sabha.

'Is war on the battlefield the only way to—' Rukmini started aloud, but she paused as soon as she saw Krishna cautiously look up at her and discretely shake his head. This was the first time he was cautioning her from speaking her mind. Rukmini was sure he had a good reason for it.

'If the sons of Pandu manage to overcome Jarasandha by their own might?' Krishna asked as an alternative.

'If we don't join them, then the world can forget about the valour of the Yadus,' Satyaki rolled his eyes.

'Sounds reasonable to me,' Akrura nodded. 'Indraprastha does Dwaraka a favour by eliminating our arch rival and we pledge our allegiance to the new emperor-to-be in return. As practical as that.'

There was not much to counter after that.

'If Jarasandha is eliminated. A big "if"...' Hridika pointed out, 'we will be glad to be proven otherwise and would support this campaign too.'

Ugrasena ended the proceedings by pronouncing his hope that the sons of Pandu succeed in this mission of theirs.

'Why did you stop me at Sudharma?' Rukmini demanded of Krishna as soon as they had privacy. 'I thought I had a solution...'

'No, you had *the* solution, Rukmini,' Krishna explained. 'Overcoming Jarasandha on the battlefield is a gamble we would not like to play. You were thinking assassination and that would be the exact route we may need to take. Rather not be discussed in the sabhas.' Krishna arched his brows.

Rukmini pursed her lips and nodded. 'Right. And discussing beforehand with me could have helped instead of surprising us with the summon,' she remarked, unclasping the large necklace she had worn all day. 'Would you…like to have your evening meal with Mitravinda in private or—'

She paused when Krishna held both her arms, pulling her close. 'Rukmini, I need to leave for Indraprastha by dawn.'

'You…you just came.'

'Things need to happen soon. Before anyone gets wind of the upcoming military campaign,' Krishna replied, holding her tight. 'And I don't know how long I would be gone.'

Rukmini thought about Mitravinda, who was due for delivering her firstborn soon, about the new brides Satyabhama and Jambavati. About Charudeshna, her third son, who was less than a spring old, and who almost never got to sleep on his father's lap. And she, Rukmini, was to double up to play Krishna in his absence. The thoughts would have been enough to break her, given the stress of managing the affairs, but the hands that held her conveyed something of a higher need. 'You told me to go on the offensive to end this menace called Jarasandha, Rukmini. We cannot afford to lose time. After he is killed, the campaign needs to start before his allies can get over the surprise. That way, the digvijaya would be successful with minimum possible loss of lives.'

Rukmini nodded, closing her eyes for a moment. She had just begun to relax, assuming that Krishna would stay for a while. But it looked like he wanted her to be ready for something bigger while he was gone.

'Come with me.'

The boat ride used to be a frequent pastime in the early months after her wedding. Lately, even a night with Krishna had become a luxury. Indraprastha was the 'co-wife' that deserved all the blame rather than Mitravinda, Bhadra or the others. Rukmini noticed that it was not the rare joyride that Krishna seemed to be taking her on. She sat up when Krishna reached the end of the channel, almost near the open sea. He held on to a rock that seemed to work as a lever. *A secret waterway?*

'This channel goes through this hilly line of rocks and opens up in the direction of Prabhasa. A safe port that has the sturdiest of our ships. From there, one can escape to Kekaya, the most trustworthy of our allies.'

Rukmini observed the tunnel in the light of the flame Krishna had lit. 'Who else knows about this, Krishna?'

'Balarama and I discovered the tunnel during one of our first visits to Saurashtra. We waded through this too. The water is shallow enough. The closure of the mouth of this channel with a rocky camouflage was conceived to keep this a secret. He must have told Revathi.' He looked at Rukmini for a moment. 'In the course of the digvijaya, there would be phases when the best of our warriors would not be present at Dwaraka and if Dwaraka is attacked at its vulnerable point...'

'You want me to evacuate the city?' Rukmini's eyes grew wide.

'At least the children, the old and the weak. As many as you can save,' Krishna stated. Something in his voice sounded so prophetic that Rukmini shuddered. She mutely stared as Krishna showed her another channel, but something that passed in between two very close mountain ranges.

'This way is safe in the cover of the dark. During the day, if needed, this can also work as a diversion to mislead any enemy in pursuit.'

'I shall explore the length of both the channels sometime soon,' Rukmini thought aloud as they rowed back, in time to see the sunset. 'Every day, I see this setting sun and think of it as the end of another day where adharma still is alive, with a hope that a new day brings new strength to dharma. Krishna, the tour of these escape routes…do you expect anything unforeseen?'

Krishna looked at her. She knew that he knew her to be strong enough to face any onslaught without batting an eyelid. But expressing the fear of the unknown was something she could do only with him, a luxury she did not have with any other family member, because to them, she was the source of strength in his absence. He nodded, almost unwillingly. 'Just be prepared with a plan. If and when it happens, there won't be much time to prepare.'

Rukmini considered the number of boats required to ferry the vulnerable. The ships at Prabhasa, too, had to be readied for a journey if needed. There was time until the call would come for a full-fledged digvijaya. That was some consolation.

As soon as they reached the shore of Dwaraka, Rukmini smiled to see Krishna back to his cheery self. Pausing all thoughts about an attack on Dwaraka, she threw her arms around him. *Was she seeking to draw strength from him? Or was it to assure him that she was prepared to hold the fort in his absence?* Maybe it was both.

Shishupala's Attack

The sound of the waves seemed much louder than at Dwaraka. Or maybe because of the topography. Or possibly because a similar noise echoed inside of Rukmini. Deafening.

Prabhasa had always been a place of joy. A place where the Yadavas celebrated all their milestones. Be it a wedding, the birth of a child, a festival, or sometimes for no reason at all but to gather and add to each other's delight. The difference of opinions, the small-time rivalries and even the stress over intrigues were all forgotten during the precious time they all spent there.

Today's reason was something that surpassed every joy of the past. The enemy of the confederacy, the man who was the reason for them to flee to Dwaraka, the tyrant who had tormented them for decades—Jarasandha was no more. The Yadavas rejoiced at the news of the Pandava Bhima killing him in a wrestling match. It was a news that seemed too good to be true. And the Sudharma unanimously decided to take a break and go to Prabhasa to thank the God of gods, Somanatha, for this turn of events.

The Shoora household had another reason—the birth of Mitravinda's son, Sangramajit. Rukmini watched them rejoice with joyful abandon and smiled to herself.

Krishna deserved to see his people celebrating this way.

'Do the waves win or do the roars of our boys?' Revathi patted Rukmini's shoulder. 'And why do I feel like you still bear the burden of the world on your shoulders, little sister?' She handed over a goblet of wine to Rukmini.

'I shall have it a little later, sister Revathi. I am supposed to meet that old man who oversees our ships at Prabhasa.'

'Who needs wine when work is enough to keep your mind

off…wait, what work? That doesn't sound right!'

Rukmini chuckled. The wine had begun to show its effects on Revathi. But the wife of Balarama was right. Rukmini felt she needed to take that invisible load off herself.

'Greetings, Princess Rukmini.' It was Ratnasena, an old-time merchant who also excelled in his knowledge of ships. He had entrusted his business to his sons and was about to settle for a life of renunciation, but Krishna had sought his expertise in ship-building and made him the supervisor of the Shoora fleet, a role the old man happily agreed to do. 'You seem thoughtful.' He smiled pointing at the rest of the frolicking group.

Rukmini smiled back, trying to wave the remark away.

'It is hard when you have to let them all feel safe while facing the reality all by yourself,' he added. 'The ships are all in shape. You can check for yourself.'

'I would honour your judgment, uncle Ratnasena,' Rukmini nodded. 'Besides, trade may be off the priority list for a while. Family and other priorities beckon.'

Ratnasena nodded with a discrete smile. 'If it makes you feel better, I think I have a clue about why the ships need to be ready, my Princess. Better to be prepared for the unforeseen.'

Rukmini looked up as he handed over parchments containing the details about the ships, the ferrying capacity, the provisions, manpower at hand and other information. Rukmini thanked him and joined the rest of the family.

Perhaps, it was better to be paranoid than be caught unprepared.

'Take pity on the wine at least now, sister.' Bhadra pulled her towards a circle of women dancing to the tune of musicians. Lakshana was leading the singing. 'Even Mitravinda took some. She missed it all these months so badly. Rukmini nodded, finally tasting the drink.

'Bhadra, how is she doing after childbirth?'

'How does that look to you?' Bhadra pointed at Mitravinda

waving and hopping with Pradyumna and other children, taking part in their game.

'I mean...' Rukmini explained, 'it is common for a young mother to miss her natal home in this phase. You know it. But Mitra and I can't go to ours. I was thinking if she could go to yours, your mother being her mother's sister...'

'Why not! ' Bhadra squealed. 'In fact, we can all go to Kekaya! Rukmini, you have seen my parents and my brother. They would not differentiate between me and the rest of you. By Mahadeva, why did it not strike me when you gave birth to... Oh God of gods, you could have at least dropped me a clue...'

'Alright, Bhadra, I said relax! There is always a next time!' Rukmini laughed. 'For now, take Mitra and the children with you, and anyone else who want to join. I shall join later, perhaps after closing the trade temporarily and relieving the sailors.'

Bhadra nodded vigorously and went to discuss the impending travel with Mitravinda.

Rukmini turned around and found Satyabhama staring at her. 'What's the matter, elder sister?' Satyabhama asked in a cautious and low voice, though given the amount of noise and cheer around, she need not have bothered. Rukmini shook her head with a smile and a wave, trying to walk away casually. Satyabhama blocked her way. 'Rukmini.'

Rukmini crossed her arms. 'Nothing, Satya. I just feel the need to be sober and alert. But nothing says we can't dance and sing to our latest victory. Come on...'

'You know, I love Krishna more than you all do,' Satyabhama declared.

'Not now, please!' Rukmini groaned, as she knew that when Satyabhama started with this sentence, she would usually launch into a speech.

'I can make out his worry, his joy, his dilemma, his burden

and most of all, his valiant efforts to hide it all from us and behave like we, his wives, have the world at our feet. In those moments, the only thing I can do out of sheer respect and love is to humour him. Something all you princesses may think as a sign of being spoiled or pampered.'

'Satya, my dearest little sister, not now. I beg you this is not the—'

'No, Rukmini, this has to be the time. I am sober too. I have been seeing you since we arrived at Prabhasa. I can't let this go,' Satyabhama insisted, pulling Rukmini to a quieter place. 'You are so much like him, Rukmini. I have observed you both since you arrived at Dwaraka after your wedding. At times with admiration, at time with envy, and with a longing to be in the place where you are. I have seen you by his side. You are just like him. Except that your eyes cannot hide things as successfully as he does. And I cannot humour you like I do Krishna. Let me in on this, Rukmini. It is unfair of you not to. Let me in.'

Rukmini gave in with a shake of her head. 'By Mahadeva, you can be stubborn! Fine… it is actually nothing. Truly. You risk being disappointed at the end, Satya. But as you insist, let me share with you. A fortnight ago, we received the news of Jarasandha's death. The Yadavas are finally free of all their worries. Our armies have left to join the imperial campaign of King Yudhishtira in high spirits. But did it occur to you sister, that Dwaraka is at its most vulnerable right now?'

Satya stared at her and then inhaled deeply. She then replied in a softer voice, 'Not like this did not occur to me, Rukmini. Remember the day our armies left Dwaraka for Indraprastha, I warned about a probable increase in incidents of robbery and the preventive care to be taken. Grandsire Ugrasena simply waved it away with a token reminder to everyone to lock up their valuables in the secret underground vaults. I have spent sleepless nights ensuring everyone did that. I offered my vaults for safekeeping and there were women who looked at me like I was robbing them off their jewellery!'

'Satya, now you are a bride of Krishna Vaasudeva. You need to get used to taking blame for doing good to people. You know, it is part and parcel of our lives now.' Rukmini chuckled shrugging.

'Alright...but—'

'But…but, the bigger concern is not of robbery or any petty crime,' Rukmini explained. 'It is of a siege.'

'Siege?' Satyabhama exclaimed aloud, only to be shushed by Rukmini. 'Why on earth would anyone attack Dwaraka now? The kingdoms would still be reeling from the news of Jarasandha's death. When the campaign starts, they would want to keep their armies within their walls to defend their forts. This is *not* the time anyone would commit the foolish mistake of attacking another kingdom.'

'I would agree with your perception, Satya, except that there is a good chance we made enemies who may forget common sense at this moment. Krishna foresaw a possibility. That's why he showed me a couple of escape routes through the sea, from Dwaraka to Prabhasa, where the ships are ready to take us to the northern ports. Kekaya will be our safe haven in case of an attack like that.'

'Hmmm, that's why you are trying to send Bhadra and others away to Kekaya in advance, just in case… elder sister!' Satyabhama clutched Rukmini's arm suddenly. 'Can we both go tomorrow by dawn and survey those routes…I mean, just to make sure those escape routes don't have any surprises?'

Rukmini nodded. That had been in her agenda when she had come to Prabhasa. 'I would love some company, Satya. Just do me a favour. Don't start upon, for the three-thousandth time, about how you fell in love with Krishna at the age of five. The story makes me...well...jealous.'

Satyabhama giggled almost hysterically. 'Really? The great

Rukmini jealous of a "finally requited" love story of a simple Yadava maiden. Alright, I agree I have used the "humble origin" part to the maximum benefit. But still, you being jealous of me, that calls for at least two goblets of wine.'

'Careful!' Rukmini slapped Satyabhama's arm. 'We have to start very, very early tomorrow.'

❦

'So far, so good!' Satyabhama remarked. 'We can easily wade through the waters. Let me get on now.' She climbed up the boat they were on, groaning at the way the wet sand stuck to her lower garments. 'In case there is an attack, let it happen when the tide is low like today.'

They approached the opening from where Dwaraka could be visible. 'It has roughly taken us a prahara to reach here. The journey back may be quicker, given that the day would break soon. Here comes home!'

Satyabhama's attention was still on getting rid of the stubborn sand that stuck to her clothes. 'It would be bright by the time we reach Prabhasa and the other six are going to have a good laugh at two armoured women who went like they want to fight a war and returned with just sand on their clothes and a lasting scent of fishes!'

'Satya!' Rukmini barked, making her jump. Her attention was caught by the sight of lights in Dwaraka. 'Who lit up the city like it is a festival? No, by Mahadeva!' She and Satyabhama exchanged a look, as the reality dawned on them.

'Dwaraka is burning!'

❦

Before long, Rukmini and Satyabhama hurried to the shore and ran along the rocky path that led to the backyard of Devaki's mansion. Devaki and Vasudeva were at Prabhasa. A thudding noise came from the room, like someone was locked from inside. Satyabhama ran to the door and unbolted it.

Two old sentries who were supposed to be guarding the back gate through which Rukmini and Satyabhama had entered, came out looking beaten and scared.

'They...they were soldiers, Princess Rukmini!'

The younger sentry ran to the front yard and cried aloud. The fire was being spread by the strong sea winds. The residences of the common folk started to begun to come apart.

The next hour or two passed in quickly gathering, the remaining guards and sending them to bring every citizen in the city to safety. Thankfully, many had followed the noble families to Prabhasa. The guards at the front gates of the city had either been killed or knocked unconscious. It also took some time to convince the young mothers that getting out of the city was a safer bet for them and their children. Rukmini sent Satyabhama to check the vaults and led the remaining towards the private cove of the Shooras where there were about seven to eight boats ready. Satyabhama rushed back with three guards in her lead, carrying sacks of some money needed to negotiate their journey till Kekaya.

'The outer vaults were broken open and looted, Rukmini. I found this there!' She handed over a dagger. 'This was driven into a guard who was in charge of the vaults.' Satyabhama's voice was shaking. Rukmini guessed that the guard may have met a gruesome death trying to defend the Yadava wealth. Satyabhama steadied her breath as the survivors climbed on to the boats, with Rukmini shouting the instructions to those who knew how to row. 'I got the more valuable part of the wealth shifted to another hidden underground vault. It was intact,' she added, coming closer to Rukmini. But Rukmini was busy trying to examine the dagger.

'That low life! That imbecile rat!'

'Who?'

'Shishupala!' Rukmini exclaimed. 'He knew it! He knew the vulnerable state of Dwaraka. This was not a valiant campaign. This was just to mock at Krishna that while his enemy had been killed, Krishna would return to a burnt home. Where has this cowardly worm of Shishupala escaped to?'

'Rukmini!' Satyabhama pulled her arm. 'If it is a trained army, we must take these to safety soon!' Even upon multiple queries, the sentries and guards could not say anything more than the fact that it was a surprise attack and they were outnumbered. There was looting of cattle and horses as well as the burning of thatched residences and sheds. Thanks to Satyabhama's enforcement of locking the valuables in the state vaults, the loss to traders and the likes was minimal.

'Wait, Satyabhama. That man from Chedi, he did not come to conquer Dwaraka. He did not attack in the light of the day, like a true warrior does. Possibly he wanted to pass this off as a mass robbery that would hit the common citizens because that would cripple Dwaraka's economy, especially after its warriors had been drained out after a campaign. It is a crime that should not go unpunished!'

'I cannot agree more, elder sister. But how can we fight back or pursue them when we have to protect the vulnerable?'

Their attention was diverted when two guards brought an unconscious old woman and a boy of eight or nine springs who was wailing.

'Is that nobleman Babhru's mother? And this boy is his son for sure.'

'They carried away my mother!' The boy ran to Rukmini. 'And my baby sister too!'

Something inside Rukmini snapped. 'Follow me. We are going in pursuit of those imbeciles!' She thundered, calling out to the guards, 'Satya, take as many guards with you as you need to lead these towards the port of Prabhasa. Gather whatever warriors you can there and meet me on the highway towards Avanti. I bet that is the route this monster has taken. Where are the horses?'

'Most of the horses left behind by the army have been taken away, my Princess,' the sentries explained. Only Princess Revathi's stables are untouched as they were on the far end of—'

'Get me Revathi's chariot now.'

'My Princess!'

'Sister Rukmini!'

'Satyabhama, listen to me.' Rukmini held Satya's arms, now speaking in a much calmer tone. 'The road from Dwaraka meets the road from Prabhasa. If you can proceed on one of the faster boats and alert the rest of our guard there, we have a chance of stopping that Shishupala. I know he was here. I just know it.'

'That is just impossible!' Satyabhama protested. 'And definite—'

'You need to hurry!' Rukmini's tone had lost all traces of its usual form. 'The looters made away with the cattle. They won't be as fast as we think. Just leave. Light some torches along the tunnel so that the other boats catch up with you. But you must hurry! Babhru's wife and his infant daughter…we cannot give up on them.' She grunted in exasperation when Satyabhama stood unmoved, still unsure.

'Let me... let me come with—'

'Someone has to guide these people through the channel, Satya!'

'Then I can pursue Shishupala and you can—'

'You… you don't know Shishupala. I do.'

Rukmini did not wait any longer and strode towards Revathi's stables with just ten guards, already battered by the surprise attack in her lead. She did not turn back when Satyabhama called out her name twice or thrice and dearly hoped that the younger woman stuck to the plan. Rukmini knew it was a narrow chance. But they had to catch Shishupala and his henchmen before they made it across the borders of Avanti, carrying Babhru's wife and daughter with them.

❦

It was a hectic ride through the highway to Avanti. Rukmini realized that the horses yoked to Revathi's chariot were new and keeping them together was a challenge. The sentries who accompanied her found it as difficult. After a while, Rukmini let one of them drive, preserving her own strength for a possible skirmish. As the day brightened, the horses began to feel more comfortable. But there was no trace of the miscreants. Rukmini's patience was at its end when she reached the meeting point with the road to Prabhasa. Naturally, the time was short for Satyabhama to row towards there, gather the soldiers and meet her. After a while of resting the horses, Rukmini saw a cloud of dust on the far end of the road. She gave the order to proceed towards the border of Avanti. The ride towards the borders was eventless except for the fatigue of her guards. Letting a woman of Dwaraka be abducted under her watch was not something that would allow Rukmini to be at peace. Her heart sank at finding no traces of the miscreants.

Surely, they could not have escaped this soon!

Before long, Satyabhama and Lakshana caught up with her, additional guards in tow. They reached the borders of Avanti a little past midday. Rukmini felt her chest churn and was close to breaking down.

'Don't blame yourself, sister.'

'It could have been worse, who knows?' Lakshana tried to show her the brighter side but it was tough to accept it, knowing that Shishupala had a woman of Dwaraka under his mercy.

'Perhaps we should go further…' Rukmini thought aloud. But Lakshana and Satya disagreed.

'The news rattled everyone, Rukmini. We may have to leave

towards Kekaya from Prabhasa itself. Pursuing an enemy in a hostile land like Avanti…think of what Krishna would say.'

'What would Krishna do if a helpless woman is abducted by a miscreant? Certainly not leave her to fate,' Rukmini thought aloud. But there was a larger picture to consider. The safety of the elderly, children and women was her responsibility. But Rukmini's feet would simply not allow her to turn back.

She then heard it.

An infant's cry from the wilderness. Wasting no moment, Rukmini rushed in the direction along with the others. They found an abandoned carriage. It seemed the carriage was led that way with a purpose. The weeping infant and the unconscious woman in torn clothes told them what the purpose had been.

At Indraprastha

It was only when the bright rays of the midday sun fell through the window that Rukmini opened her eyes. She groaned at the numbness of her sore muscles and turned to her side when a maid asked for permission to make the bed. Most of Rukmini's days started early and the days that she woke up late somehow made her feel unproductive. But not today. It was after an eternity that she had slept for a night or perhaps a bit more than a whole night.

'I just feel burnt out,' she said, massaging her eyes.

'It is a miracle you did not drop down before we reached Indraprastha!' Malathi entered the room dismissing the other maids. 'My Princess, it feels so relieving to see you stretch after a night's good sleep.'

Rukmini remembered reaching Indraprastha the evening before and the grand dinner thrown at her arrival by the Pandava family. Given her fatigue and sleep deficit of the past months, she had barely managed to stay awake through it and went to sleep the moment she lay on the bed. 'Did anything unusual happen during the meal, yesterday?' she asked Malathi. 'I barely have any memory of even greeting the soon-to-be emperor.'

Malathi smiled and shook her head. 'You were not yourself and they perfectly understood that. The attention of everyone was on little Abhimanyu and Sangramajit.'

Rukmini sighed in relief before Malathi cleared her tone. 'Though I felt at one point...when Lady Subhadra told you about Lord Vaasudeva leaving on some urgent mission that was not the part of this campaign, you were strangely detached, like you were not even interested.'

Rukmini's eyes grew wider at the memory. 'Oh? Did it seem that bad?'

Malathi shook her head. 'Perhaps it was just me. I felt you may feel angry or annoyed or disappointed. You just looked...resigned, Rukmini. The past years have kept you both away from each other and I fear the distance is showing.'

'That's a silly thought, Malathi,' Rukmini frowned letting Malathi undo her braid and proceed to massage her head with fragrant oils. 'I remember Subhadra telling me about women being abducted from all parts of Bharatavarsha and Krishna going beyond Kashi to investigate. And yes, the details went beyond what I could process last night. I just needed a break or else, I fear even I was too weak to even put up a resistance if I was abducted.'

'Stop speaking thus! Like what you faced in the past months was not enough!' Malathi was alarmed at the thought.

It was late afternoon when Rukmini caught up with Subhadra and Draupadi, finally in her senses.

'You and Krishna, by all Gods and Goddesses!' Subhadra remarked. 'Even the most nail-biting love stories don't have so many fateful incidents of a couple missing each other by a hair's breadth!'

'Subhadra…' Draupadi nudged her.

'That's alright!' Rukmini laughed. 'Truth is always stranger than fiction. Krishna rushes to Dwaraka after the siege and I am well on the way to Kekaya. I go back to Dwaraka and he has already left for Indraprastha. I then make a whole journey, shifting the remaining people to Indraprastha and he has gone investigating some abduction racket. And no, I am not leaving Indraprastha without my husband now.' She paused, smiling, and let the dramatic effect of the last sentence sink in. 'Ohh, should I have emphasized a bit more on the "not leaving" part and lesser on the husband part for a more dramatic effect?'

They all laughed.

'Theatrics apart, I am not letting any of you go even for a short while till the completion of the yagna,' Draupadi declared. 'The attack on Dwaraka robbed my sleep. The uncertainties around Sahadeva and Bhima's campaigns are bad enough. I was just beginning to feel that this whole Rajasuya is—'

'Hold that there!' Rukmini stopped her. 'Everyone has so much stake in this now that you will be insulting them if you even doubt the mission now, Samragni Draupadi.'

Draupadi sighed. 'There were moments where it felt like all the troubles of humanity would end the moment Jarasandha was killed.'

'And then reality strikes,' Subhadra added. 'Now we feel like how on earth were we so fixated on that one man controlling all that was evil. There is so much to do. So, so much. Like accounting for the tributes that started flowing into the city from the campaign. I hate accounting and Samragni here is not so merciful.'

'Accounting? That is child's play for Satyabhama. Give her a day in the treasury, she will come back with the details of the inventory, the quality of metals and precious gems, future values of the wealth and possible plans of distributing it so that—in her words—the wealth doubles by some twenty or twenty-five months!'

The sudden wailing of a child made Subhadra jump, 'God of Gods, that is Abhimanyu! And he inherited his father's insomnia for sure!'

'Aren't you unusually quiet, Draupadi?' Rukmini asked her after Subhadra left. 'Or am I unusually chatty. Excuse that for today, because I am getting to chat like this after an eternity.'

Draupadi nodded. 'You make everyone around you so proud, Rukmini. The way you steered even the weakest man and woman out of danger. I just can't find words to show my pride.'

'Can't claim all the credit for myself, Draupadi. I had help. From all those seven.'

'Well, given the crisis, you deserve that and much more!'

'Much more? By Mahadeva, how many more co-wives do you want me to have?'

They laughed again. Moments of uneventful indulgence was such a rarity these days that Rukmini was determined to make the most of it. With Draupadi and the Pandavas around, it was like the burden was suddenly off her shoulders. It was a luxury Rukmini knew would be short-lived before the next intrigue came, political or otherwise. She knew it was just waiting to pounce on her life.

Rukmini's instincts were not wrong. She had hardly had a week's breathing time at Indraprastha when the next challenge came, its bearer being a rather flabbergasted Satyabhama, too shocked to even convey the news.

'Elder sister! I heard he is bringing all those women to Dwaraka!'

'Who? Krishna is returning from Pragjyotisha?'

Satya barely nodded, her face showing almost no traces of joy about their husband returning. 'I am hearing all kinds of rumours! I don't even… It is sheer stupidity. I thought our Krishna is wiser! This is a disaster!'

'Calm down, little sister. Let us welcome him back first and then—'

Satyabhama composed herself and then narrated in a low voice. 'My maid Nalini heard it from a traveller. Krishna defeated that Bhauma, who had been abducting women on the pretext of some Shakta religious ritual or something bizarre like that. And... and the trouble did not end with just killing Bhauma. The question was of restoring those former prisoners of his to a normal life and apparently the only way to do that was for him to marry them all and declare them as his wives.' She looked at Rukmini. 'Now tell me, elder sister, which part of this news should I dismiss?'

'You say he "married" them…' Rukmini thought aloud, betraying no expression.

Satya did not know whether to nod or deny what she had heard. 'He is bringing them all with him, till here. And they would come to Dwaraka, too. Rukmini—'

Before they say any more, a boy sought Rukmini's audience. Babhru's young son entered, visibly dazed at the opulent mansions of Indraprastha. 'Lady Rukmini, my mother is very ill. Can we get a vaidya to examine her?'

The boy was close to tears and broke down when Satyabhama patted his head.

'I was awake all night, trying to put my baby sister to sleep. Mother could not even get up from her bed,' he sobbed.

'Where is noble Babhru?' Satyabhama asked, wiping his tears.

'He...he left three days ago. Mother says he will come back. But... I heard him say he can't live with us.'

The boy apparently had no clue about the dynamics between his parents after the fateful attack on Dwaraka. Rukmini and Satyabhama found it hard to stop their own tears.

'Go back to your mother, son. I shall bring a royal doctor to the guesthouse soon,' Rukmini assured him.

'I'll go with him, while you bring the doctor, sister,' Satyabhama offered, and went with the boy.

Rukmini noticed Satya's sudden poise after hearing about Babhru's family. It was related to Krishna's rumoured decision of marrying those women rescued from Bhauma's prison. If it were true, there was not a lot to be argued against it.

❦

The soft bed of the carefully decorated guesthouse of Indraprastha gave her no sleep. There was, of course, nothing lacking in the hospitality of Empress Draupadi, or in her attention to detail when it came to hosting the family of the man who had championed their cause since the beginning. But Rukmini could not sleep that night. As much as Krishna's return from Pragjyotisha was a relief, his bid to marry the rescued women was something she could not digest. Worse, he gave her the power to veto. Rukmini heard the bell announcing the second quarter of the night. Krishna lay by her side, making no move to explain further. Like he understood that she needed the time and space to comprehend the gravity of the situation. His eyes were closed but Rukmini was sure sleep deserted him as it deserted her. It was not a small decision to rehabilitate all those women, that too as his wives. The decision had made Satyabhama lash out at what she called 'sheer stupidity.' Rukmini knew that Mitravinda and the others shared Satyabhama's sentiment, though they made up for the outspokenness of Satyabhama with their stoic silence.

Rukmini sat up and turned to look at Krishna. 'Awake?'

Eyes still closed, he responded with a nod.

'No decision of yours is made without due deliberation, Krishna. I trust your wisdom. But this beats me. I can't stand against you or let you do this without understanding what made you do this. I need to talk to you.'

Krishna's hand closed upon her wrist and he rose to a sitting position. 'They were misled, some abducted, some lured with religion, some with better lives, some with an illusion of serving a higher purpose. All of them, victims of their insecurities caused by the rigid aspects of our social code, misguided by the greed and lust of a zealot like Bhauma who exploited the combination. You know that simply killing Bhauma was not a complete solution, Rukmini.'

'You want those women to lead a dignified life again. Krishna, as a woman myself, as someone who saw the plight of Babhru's wife after that monster Shishupala molested her, I could not agree more with your intention. What makes me uncertain is the fact that you have taken it all on your shoulders. It is a terrifying burden, Krishna. Even for Gods.'

'Burden?' Krishna softly countered.

'Everyone, including our dearest ones at Dwaraka and Indraprastha, is going to be shocked at your decision. Not to mention some who would take it out of context in every other interaction with a single-minded intention to humiliate you. I am not even worried about social censure, Krishna. But haven't you examined your own past? You saved the citizens of Mathura from Kamsa, only to earn their censure when Jarasandha attacked them. You gave them a hundred times more prosperous city and I still hear stories about how they were uprooted from their home. You are leaving no stone unturned in ensuring a whole empire of dharma, a rule under which they can finally sleep without fear, and still, there is a continuous tirade of ire and rebuke. Krishna, would these women be any different? And let me tell you, pleasing them all is a job impossible even for the Gods! The whole pantheon of them!'

'By Mahadeva, you can be unkind to your own kind!' Krishna chuckled. Knowing that humour did not really help when Rukmini was in her mode of furious analysis, he reached out to set her hair right. 'Any woman in your place with the power to overturn such a decision of her husband's would have invoked it that very moment. The fact that you did not, says you know the gravity of the problem, Rukmini. There is no point celebrating the killing of a monster if the wrongs done by him cannot be corrected. If any one of them is driven to suicide because she does not find a home outside that prison, we are all going to become Bhaumas too. Or worse—it would be a very hypocritical position to start the work on an empire of dharma that this Rajasuya promises.'

Rukmini considered the impossible situation. 'Even as I battle the million questions in my mind, Krishna, where do we start? I mean, with making them a home. Housing them with due honour would require a huge portion of the city.'

'We have thought of some solutions there. Perhaps, Abhaya can run them by you when you are...ready?'

'Abhaya?'

The breeze of the Yamuna blew over the palatial gardens of Indraprastha. Rukmini walked up to the rest house and spotted a woman waiting. Dismissing the maids to have the necessary privacy for a free conversation, she nodded at Abhaya. The daughter of a local chieftain near the borders of Saurashtra, she was one of the first to find out about the abduction of the women by Bhauma. Rukmini could not help a tinge of admiration when she heard from Krishna that this brave maiden had risked investigating the whole racket by herself. And the fact that she, like many other royal maidens, had a soft corner for Krishna was also not surprising.

'Greetings, Princess Rukmini. I am Abhaya Dhaarmaseni.' There was a sense of calm determination in the younger woman's voice that appealed to Rukmini.

'Let me begin by... now where do I find words to appreciate your courage, sister.' Rukmini beamed.

'Means a lot coming from someone like you, sister Rukmini.'

Rukmini nodded through the pleasantries and broached the subject. 'Krishna told me that you planned to rebuild your fortress that was destroyed in a border conflict and house the women from Kamarupa there.'

Abhaya nodded.

'He told me that you all would be treated as his wives too.'

'I was kind of hoping you would influence him to rethink, sister,' Abhaya replied without batting an eyelid. 'Vaasudeva's intentions are noble... far nobler than the vision of an average human being. But this...' Abhaya shook her head.

'I can see where he comes from, Abhaya,' Rukmini replied,

remembering her night-long conversation with Krishna. 'One may see marrying so many women as ridiculous, others may see it as patronizing. But he only means to be with you all and ensure your return to the society.'

'I may be younger than you, Princess Rukmini, but even a cursory observation of the society is enough to say the chance of them ridiculing him is more than the chance of them accepting us.'

'Of course, they would!' Rukmini nodded. 'They would ridicule and meet a silent resistance from him, and then from all those who love him, for that is what he does—compel all of us to grow out of the superfluous codes and structures to actually see and realize what dharma is. Before what you call "society" will gradually taper down its ridicule, if only we persist.' Rukmini saw Abhaya look up and smile through her tears. 'Trust me, before everyone would be able to come to terms with what he just did, he would have done something much more ridiculous!'

'Elder sister, I can never forgive myself if anything from this came in the way of his...aim or well-being.'

Rukmini rose and walked up to her. There was something endearing about every woman who loved Krishna. She almost saw a part of herself in them. But then there was something that she would find them missing when it came to understanding him. Rukmini herself was cautious to not be too sure of her own understanding. At this moment, she prayed to all the Gods and Goddesses that she was right. 'Little sister, pardon me for saying this, but it would be way too much of vanity on your part to think that you have it in you to come in his way. Nobody has had it till now. Not even Jarasandha.' She grinned and saw Abhaya smile with gratitude.

'Greetings, Princess Rukmini.'

Rukmini turned and frowned. It was the Yadava nobleman, Babhru. Rukmini had almost developed a hatred for him on seeing the way he treated his wife after Shishupala molested her.

'Noble Vaasudeva has entrusted me with the task of building the residences of the ladies from Kamarupa.'

Rukmini smiled internally, realizing why Krishna would have sent Babhru of all people. Nothing could escape his attention, and Krishna always had a way out.

Shishupala at Indraprastha

It had been a strange couple of years for Rukmini, when the Rajasuya campaign was in progress. After the attack on Dwaraka by Shishupala, she and the other women of Dwaraka were hosted by the kings of Madra and Kekaya for a long while before she got to Indraprastha. The following year also had the Pandava Nakula campaign running westward, when a bigger portion of the Yadava armies returned home to Saurashtra, completing their committed participation in the campaign. Rukmini travelled back and forth, ensuring the rehabilitation of those whose homes had been destroyed in the raid by Shishupala.

Meanwhile, Krishna's resolve to marry all the captive women freed from Bhauma did not meet with as much ridicule from the Yadava leaders as she had expected, much to her relief. It was the imperial campaign that occupied everyone's attention. She came back to Indraprastha upon the return of Bhima whose eastward campaign successfully completed the Rajasuya. The women of Indraprastha began to ready themselves for the grand finale of the yajna. Rukmini was happy to be a part of a hectic yet eventless hustle leading to the grand gathering. Guests began to trickle into the city of Indraprastha, which had undergone a world of transformation over the years. In size, grandeur and even population, it surpassed its eastern Kuru counterpart, Hastinapura.

For a change, it felt good to not play a central role in a gathering like this. Rukmini watched the proceedings from the sidelines, enjoying the hospitality. In the evenings, she would excuse herself from the other women to ride her chariot along the outer roads of Indraprastha. There was so much of architectural beauty to explore. Rukmini did not expect the idyllic ride of this phase to come to a sudden halt much before the Rajasuya finale even took place. Her hands instinctively pulled at the reins when she heard the words come out of the heralds by the southern entrance of the city.

'Welcome, Lord of Chedi.'

Shishupala! The rat had the courage to come to this event as a guest? Rukmini could not decide what was worse—Shishupala coming here or him getting this warm welcome from the Pandavas like he was someone near and dear. While she, a witness to the destruction he wrought on Dwaraka, was present at Indraprastha itself!

Wheeling the chariot around, Rukmini made her way back to the palace. A good part of her wanted to confront Draupadi. *Did the monster who destroyed the city of the very Krishna who gave them a new lease of life now become an honoured guest of the Pandavas? Was it just because he was a relative or some absurd reason like that?* Then Rukmini remembered that people like Duryodhana and the other sons of Dhritarashtra of Hastinapura, alleged to have attempted their assassination too, were guests at Indraprastha now.

What on earth was Emperor Yudhishtira thinking? Did the allies who pledged their lives and wealth and the enemies who tried to take their lives mean the same on this occasion of his ultimate rise to power? She and Krishna had convinced the almost reluctant Sudharma to throw the Yadava lot behind the Pandava side, only to have their enemy honoured? Where had the famed gratitude of the sons of Pandu gone?

Lost in this whirl of thoughts, Rukmini almost failed to take notice of Mitravinda and Subhadra calling out her name as she absent-mindedly passed by the entrance of their guesthouse.

'Elder Sister?'

'Sister-in-law?'

'Rukmini!'

It was Krishna's voice that finally made her halt. Rukmini turned around and stared at him till he had climbed the chariot to shake her by her arm. 'You look like you have seen an apparition!'

'Much worse, Krishna,' Rukmini said hoarsely, and then cleared her throat. 'I saw Shishupala, Krishna.'

Krishna looked at her and patted her arm. 'Let us talk inside, love.'

Rukmini stared at him in disbelief. 'I said I saw Shishupala. He has arrived amid pomp and show like some honoured guest! And your cousins are welcoming him too!'

'Rukmini.' Krishna held her arm and looked at the guards around. She saw Subhadra and Mitravinda go back into the palace, apparently sensing the tension between her and Krishna. 'Now is not the time.'

Rukmini found it hard to believe her ears. Her Krishna had many traits, but this mindless restraint was not one of them. Following Krishna to a more secluded part of the garden, she stood away from him when he motioned her towards a giant swing. 'Shishupala played it shrewd, Rukmini. This time, we need to calculate our response.'

'Calculate our response—no. He deserves to be killed for what he did to—'

'Shishupala announced his support to the Rajasuya and the terms of this campaign say that the supporters deserve the protection of the yajamana of this yagna. He is technically under Yudhishtira's protection, Rukmini.'

Rukmini collapsed onto the seat beside him. *What was the use of assuming power or being close to those in power if a criminal like Shishupala could so easily escape the consequences of his actions by just being a 'supporter!'* Her gaze was fiery when she turned to Krishna. 'So, what do we do now, Krishna. Surely you would not be thinking of letting him go, not after what he did to Dwaraka!'

'Wait till the crowning ceremony is done without any hassle,' Krishna said, betraying no emotion. 'We can press the charge against Shishupala right after that.'

'And we do nothing about him being honoured as some

esteemed guest till then?'

Krishna shook his head. 'Not unless he does a terrible mistake all by himself.'

Rukmini pursed her lips, still digesting the surge of dismay within her. She stared at Krishna for long, hoping for some other idea to strike him. 'Krishna, say you have something planned out, even if you don't want to share it with me. Just say you are not going to keep quiet about this. I swear on Pradyumna, I shall not press you for details. I only want to see Shishupala punished!'

Krishna shook his head and his eyes betrayed a stoic unaffectedness that Rukmini had never seen. 'Rukmini, the kingdom of Chedi was a part of brother Bhima's campaign. He was not aware of what Shishupala did at Dwaraka before he assured protection to him. And Shishupala on his part, left no stone unturned in his profuse hospitality to Bhima, who almost felt that it would even be an end to the rivalry between Shishupala and myself. Bhima was beyond disturbed when he got to know the truth. He wanted to kill Shishupala that very moment. We restrained him with great difficulty. The Rajasuya is a crucial step to a higher goal, Rukmini.'

'You restrained brother Bhima when he was ready to correct a mistake,' Rukmini almost whispered, her eyes full of an emotion she had never felt in recent years. She stepped back when Krishna tried to hold her arm.

'Rukmini.'

'Leave me alone, Krishna.' She walked away towards the mansion and sensed him following her. Turning around, she raised a forbidding finger. 'No, Krishna. Allow me to digest a disappointment. You are human, after all. Can't expect you to play a god every time. Just...just leave me alone.'

The dawn of the final yajna of the Rajasuya was a tough one for Rukmini. The bustle and celebrations around her reached a peak. Even Satyabhama and others gave in to the celebrations. Draupadi's attendants took utmost care in arranging for special silks and jewellery for Krishna's wives and other women of his family. Even after the resonance of the vedic mantras being chanted in the sabha reached their pinnacle, Rukmini found it hard to appreciate the spectacle around her. It took her a superhuman effort to let herself be adorned for the poornahuti rites of the yagna followed by the crowning ceremony of Emperor Yudhishtira. From her balcony, she saw Krishna seated in the front row among the guests flanked by King Drupada of Panchala and the Kuru Patriarch Bhishma. The extended family members from other kingdoms sat behind them. She saw rishis revered in all corners of Bharata, and chieftains of all tribes and clans.

Then she saw Rukma, his gaze, too, scanned all the balconies where the women sat, and finally paused when he saw her. For a moment, she thought her brother's eyes spoke of genuine affection, but before she could be certain of it, she saw Shishupala sitting beside Rukma. Her eyes flamed and she turned away, training her gaze on the rising flames of the yagna. Every ladle of ghee poured into the flame seemed to increase her discomfort and a sense of foreboding. For a moment, she sought Krishna's eyes and he looked at her as if he knew what ran in her mind. He smiled at her, as if to appreciate the efforts she put to come, despite Shishupala's presence. Rukmini nodded but broke the gaze on the pretext to talk to Revathi. There were jovial conversations all around her. But try as she did, Rukmini found no solace in the banter.

What was the use of this Rajasuya, this consolidation of power, this empire touted as the realm of dharma if a heinous man like Shishupala sat on the same pedestal as Krishna did?

It was time for the agrapooja, the felicitation of the highest order to be offered to a person, who the yajamana of the yajna, Yudhishtira, considered as foremost among his well-wishers. Rukmini heard the women around her break into speculations.

'It may be the old patriarch Bhishma. The man has waited long enough to see a capable king crowned.'

'Is King Drupada any less? It was his might that brought the sons of Pandu out of their misery and poverty. It was his daughter's entry into their lives that transformed them into what they are today.'

'It is a tricky decision. Selecting one is bound to offend the others. I think the Emperor will play it safe by honouring Bhagavan Veda Vyasa. He is an ancestor as well as a rishi who commands everyone's reverence.'

Most of the women seemed to concur with that, while the men below seemed to still deliberate. Rukmini saw Sahadeva, the youngest of the Pandavas, rise to make his suggestion. She strained her ears to hear the arguments he put forth, but the noise around her was too loud to comprehend. But she heard his final words.

'... Krishna Vaasudeva.'

A cheer erupted in the Yadava camp and she saw Krishna look up with a slight curve on his lips. Drupada and Bhishma graciously nodded their approval. The joy on the faces of Yudhishtira and Draupadi was palpable and the cheer was louder. Satyabhama threw her arms around Rukmini and the women sitting around the wives of Krishna came closer to congratulate them. For some reason, Rukmini's gaze went towards Rukma, who seemed to be surprisingly happy. But beside him, Shishupala sat clenching his fists. By a coincidence, his eyes shot up towards Rukmini. Her nostrils flaring with a combination of contempt and vindication, Rukmini threw a scornful smirk at him and turned to watch the proceedings. The Pandavas had led Krishna towards the high throne as a part of the agrapooja. She saw Yudhishtira rise to wash

Krishna's feet. Tears blurred her vision, a momentary sense of pride overriding all other emotions. But the joy was not uninterrupted. She heard a familiar voice laugh out aloud, in open contempt.

'A great start to this empire of dharma indeed! By washing the feet of the son of a slave?'

Shishupala!

Rukmini was not the only one to be shocked at the interruption. She saw Rukma try and restrain Shishupala but in vain. The King of Chedi was beyond himself, his hatred for Krishna getting the better of him every moment. She saw Draupadi and Yudhishtira exchange a rather disturbed look while abuse after abuse was heaped by Shishupala. Many others tried talking sense to him but things only turned from bad to worse. The only thing that hurt Rukmini more was the silence of Krishna who seemed unaffected by the uncouth behaviour. To her dismay, she now saw some of the kings emboldened to take Shishupala's side—Dantavaktra of Karusha and even Vinda and Anuvinda of Avanti. At that moment, Rukmini saw Mitravinda stand and rush inside in apparent distress. Gathering herself, Rukmini rose to console and bring Mitravinda back. What her brothers did was not the fault of the Princess of Avanti.

Just as she rose, Rukmini saw Krishna shoot a glance at her but she did not wait to respond and rushed after Mitravinda instead. Jambavati, Bhadra and Lakshana followed her.

It took them some time to console Mitravinda, and Rukmini reminded them all to get back to the sabha. The wives of Krishna could not exit the scene when he was being accorded the highest honour, just because some fools tried to disrupt the event. As they hurried back through the corridor behind the grand court room, Rukmini saw a shaken Satyabhama meet them midway.

'He killed Shishupala.'

'What?'

'It was just getting beyond control. Shishupala then tried

attacking even the grandsire Bhishma. Then Krishna, he stood up like one possessed, gave a rather cold account of all of Shishupala's wrongs... which made the king of Chedi only angrier and then... Krishna beheaded Shishupala!'

They rushed back to their balcony, which was now crowded with all the women, including the attendants craning their heads to see what followed the unforeseen event. Rukmini could hear the rishis chanting swasti mantras to ward off the evil forces, and there were voices that were trying to bring things back to normalcy. A battalion of guards, too, made their way through the corridor as a precautionary measure and the women had to step back. Rukmini told the other wives of Krishna to wait and tried to make her way towards the parapet wall but there were many women who told her it was not wise to expose herself in case anyone else had some mischief planned. More guards joined in and their leader announced his task of escorting the women of Dwaraka to a safer location. Rukmini nodded and complied, but she could not wait to meet Krishna.

How could someone with so much restraint, lose it all of a sudden that way?

Reconciliation with Rukma

She had wanted Shishupala dead all along. But this was not what she had expected Krishna to do. Rukmini was at her wits' end when Krishna did not return all night. Mitravinda and Satyabhama too denied seeing him and she now headed towards the mansion of Draupadi, passing through the vast expanse of lush gardens. The ornate seats under the cool shade of trees were relatively empty today as compared to the last few days when the inner palatial complex of Indraprastha was bustling with allies and relatives. But Rukmini was in no mood to look at the aesthetics at the moment.

'Aunt Rukmini.'

It was a lisp so irresistible that Rukmini felt compelled to turn around. A girl of six or seven springs stared at her, eyes wide with uncertainty. Rukmini could not help but smile. The girl seemed of royal birth and also familiar. 'You are?'

'Rukmavati,' a third voice interjected.

Rukmini backed away, frowning. 'Not now, Your Highness.' She was about to turn around without even meeting his eye.

'Rukmini…' The voice seemed to plead with her. Something uncharacteristic of who she knew as Rukma. She met his gaze and he seemed to falter for words. After some visible effort, he could muster the courage to say, 'He told me that he was only visiting Prabhasa on a pilgrimage.'

Rukmini frowned.

'Shishupala… I had no idea he wanted to attack Dwaraka.'

'I don't hold you responsible for what Shishupala did. Happy?' Rukmini retorted and turned to go.

'You made the right choice, little sister.'

Rukmini halted.

'It took me to father a daughter before I could really understand what you went through. Pray, talk to me, Rukmini.'

Rukmini turned around again, this time staring at little Rukmavati. Her niece. She called the girl closer and lifted her in her arms. Rukma again approached her, this time, patting her head. 'Talk to me Rukmini.'

Wordlessly, Rukmini walked over to the nearest garden bench, still carrying Rukmavati in her arms. Seating the girl beside her, Rukmini took out the golden necklace around her neck, studded with rubies shaped into small crocodiles, and tried to put it around Rukmavati.

'No,' Rukma protested. 'Rukmavati, we still owe your aunt her streedhan. Don't increase our debt, my child.'

'Rukmavati, tell him that streedhan has nothing to do between what I gift my dear niece,' Rukmini retorted. 'Nor did I ever need it or see the need of it in the future.'

Rukma sighed and sat on the other end of the bench, seeing her play with Rukmavati. 'At least visit Bhojakataka or Kundina for a while. Let me make amends.'

It was Rukmini's turn to stay quiet. There were times when she had felt somewhat envious of Bhadra and Draupadi, seeing the love of their brothers. But reconciliation with Rukma was not something she had seen coming. Now that he had pressed for peace, she was unwilling to believe it.

'At least for a while, till the ripples of what happened yesterday die down,' Rukma persisted. Rukmini looked at him. Her brother seemed visibly troubled, and his concern was genuine.

'Thank you, brother Rukma,' she replied softly. 'But I am better off being with Krishna at this juncture.'

'He seems to disagree with you though.' Seeing Rukmini's surprise, he continued, 'Shishupala's tirade yesterday was a surprise to me. Our friendship did not last long after your wedding. Even the polite communication became less frequent after Jarasandha's death. When I heard of his attack on Dwaraka, I wanted to confront him. But he had already secured peace with the Pandavas during their Rajasuya campaign and I did not want to create an unpleasant scene at Indraprastha. But tell me Rukmini, if Shishupala was so afraid of the repercussions of his attack that he meekly surrendered to the campaign, what gave him the courage to raise his voice yesterday, that too in such an uncourtly manner?'

Rukmini needed no proof that Krishna had met Rukma the previous day. The lucid analysis that came from her brother's mouth was not his area of strength. 'You mean to say Shishupala was backed by someone?'

'Someone who used him to spur dissent but did not have the courage to support him in the open yesterday. Someone with sinister plans, I am afraid for you both, Rukmini. I invited Vaasudeva to come to Vidarbha and wait this uncertainty out. But he politely declined and asked me to take you to your natal home for a while. Don't trust my word. Ask him.'

Rukmini did not know how to react at this surprise. *Why did Krishna want her away from him? And why did he want her away so strongly that he struck a truce with Rukma of all the people?* Leaning against the backrest of the seat, Rukmini gently placed Rukmavati upon the bench. 'I trust you, brother.' She saw him smile with an affection she had never seen in Rukma before. 'But forgive me, eldest. I need to be with Krishna now. Trust me, we shall look after ourselves. Perhaps, come to Vidarbha later.'

Rukma nodded with difficulty. 'I will do everything to make it up to you. I saw your Pradyumna during the ceremony yesterday. He is well on his way to prove worthy in every aspect.' He paused pointing at Rukmavati. 'Rukmini, consider it my request for your pardon but if I offer—'

'Eldest!' Rukmini interrupted. 'Don't commit the same

mistake.' She smiled, brushing Rukmavati's hair. 'If that is going to be Rukmavati's choice after she grows up, I shall be the happiest person.' She saw Rukma nod, a mixture of emotions showing in his eyes. A part of her felt grateful to Krishna for initiating this truce. But unfortunately, this was not the time to celebrate the reunion. 'I need to join him, Rukma.'

'Remember my invitation...' Rukma's words trailed after her. Rukmini hurried towards Draupadi's mansion, hopeful of finding Krishna there.

Climbing up the spiralling staircase that led to the private chambers of Draupadi, Rukmini found Krishna and Draupadi emerge from there. She found Draupadi's eyes moist, but upon seeing Rukmini, the new empress of Bharatavarsha quickly wore a warm smile on her lips. 'See who arrives just as I was thinking of her. Come with me, Rukmini.' Draupadi pulled Rukmini, barely giving her a moment to meet Krishna's eyes, which were inscrutable as usual.

Draupadi's customary farewell had an elaborate tradition of honouring all the women of Dwaraka. By midday, the Pandavas too joined them as they were about to leave for Dwaraka when a row of men and maids of the palace came, carrying large plates full of expensive gifts, gold and silver bars and jewellery, and bowed to Rukmini in particular. Rukmini saw Draupadi and the five brothers grin. 'Something that ought to have been done long before,' Draupadi announced. 'Years before, I threatened this man to dare not let you shed a single tear.' She nudged Krishna. 'I considered you a younger sister, and now, you are officially the daughter of the Pandu household. And this is your streedhan.'

'Draupadi, I... I can't...' Rukmini found herself in a fix, neither willing to accept the wealth, nor refuse the love of the Pandu household. She turned to look at Krishna just as Arjuna blocked her view.

'Don't look at him. He will only confuse you with this…' He imitated Krishna's characteristic inscrutable expression. 'And while we have a whole life to figure out what in the name of Mahadeva that means, this can't wait.'

'And if he troubles you for accepting what's rightfully yours, tell me,' Bhima added, with a look of mock threat at Krishna.

'And if there is any more uncertainty, this is an order of the Emperor,' Yudhishtira beamed.

There was no way she could respond to the flood of love except by accepting the gifts. Rukmini saw Krishna smile but for a brief moment. Draupadi embraced her. 'Take care, sister.'

Before long, they were all on the highway that led to the western part of the new empire. Krishna remained aloof despite her multiple attempts to start a conversation. It was only when one evening they reached the confluence of routes that he spoke, not just to her, but to all his wives.

'Shishupala was not a stray incident. What started at Indraprastha may continue for a while before dying down. We shall now proceed in smaller groups. Balarama and Pradyumna shall lead the first segment towards Dwaraka, while Satyaki will lead the second. I shall lead the remaining. However, I want you all to take a detour to Kekaya and go with Brihadkshatra, Bhadra's brother. Stay there for a while and wait for my message before you start for Dwaraka.'

The sheer concern in his tone made them all agree.

Except her. Rukmini waited till he was done with the briefing and they saw Balarama and Pradyumna lead a segment of their retinue westward. Rukmini walked up to Krishna before he found another group to brief the next plan of action. 'I am coming with you.'

'I would not advise that, Rukmini.'

There was something infuriating about that response. Rukmini had to clench her fists to stop herself from punching his chest. It was like he was totally oblivious to the painful distance that had grown between them, since the night before Rajasuya. Pursing her lips to arrest the knee jerk response, she narrowed her gaze. 'I am staying with you. I am coming with you.'

Krishna's response was an inaudible sigh and a slight shrug before he walked away. Rukmini became more determined than ever. *Whatever was bothering him, she had to know it. Whatever was coming between them, she had to destroy it.*

Dantavaktra

'It may not be one of your wisest decisions.'

This was all that Krishna said to her when she insisted on accompanying him. Their retinue had reached the western borders of Kuru when spies reported about possible attempts to ambush them by some supporters of Shishupala. The news that Dantavaktra of Karusha had also taken a mysterious detour after he left Indraprastha added to this uncertainty. Krishna had insisted that all his wives proceed to Kekaya instead, on the pretext of a casual visit to Bhadra's natal home. Everyone agreed except Rukmini.

The killing of Shishupala on the auspicious occasion, an act quite uncharacteristic of Krishna, could have been due to her—her continuous pressure upon him to do away with the King of Chedi ever since she saw him as a guest at Indraprastha. She had seen what Krishna could turn into when his apparently never-ending restraint broke. *Had she unleashed something dark within her godly husband?* Rukmini hoped not. And there was no way she was going to let him face any ambush while she enjoyed Brihadkshatra's hospitality at Kekaya.

'You have been a source of courage and wisdom, Rukmini. Try and understand. At times, it is braver to stay away from conflict. Krishna would not have suggested this otherwise,' Bhadra had made one last attempt to change her mind.

'I love Krishna too much to disregard his insight. I am sure you do too. Don't do anything that you will regret later, Rukmini,' Mitravinda had warned.

'We may feel better if you are with us,' Satyabhama and the others tried in various ways, but in vain.

Rukmini waited alone in her tent. The journey through what

might be hostile territory was about to begin. Something hurt her deeper when Krishna chose to ride alone in his chariot with the eagle banner, leaving her another one, driven by Daruka's chirpy sister, Padmini. It was like something cruel and cold had taken over him. But Rukmini did not protest. He could tell her if she had been the root cause of whatever they faced now. It was as if he knew that his silence and distance would hurt her and deliberately chose them. But Rukmini was not the one to relent. If silence was his weapon, so was it hers.

After two or three days into the journey through Avanti, even Padmini had stopped with her chatter. Hence, Rukmini took over, adding her own mirth, much to Padmini's surprise. She laughed aloud to the silliest of jokes, humoured the horsemen who flanked her chariot and had almost created a mini camp of her own.

The journey through Avanti passed uneventfully. The guard heaved a sigh of relief. This was the last place where they could expect trouble. The lands of Saurashtra, divided between the Lords of the Yadava council would begin from now on. They would have lesser issues to lose their sleep over.

But Rukmini was far from relaxing. Her veil of nonchalance at Krishna's continued distance was threatening to break. But she did not want that to happen before the guard. She had to reach Dwaraka as soon as possible and busy herself with her routine, spend more time with her children, tend to her long untended garden with the newer botanical insights she had gained from Draupadi, update herself with the new positions of the council—the list was endless. If she had some free time, Rukmini could unburden herself to her dearest friend—the Tulasi plant in her backyard.

The night passed but sleep would not come to her. Rukmini suppressed a sob and got out of bed. The position of the stars told her that it was a good two hours before dawn. She entered Krishna's tent and saw him asleep. And she was losing hers! A part of her ached to punch him awake, probably just push him off the bed or do something much more shocking that would rob him off his sleep. But something beside him caught her eye. The eagle banner! A sight that had been the first source of consolation when she was on the brink of committing suicide. Rukmini smiled as a lone tear flowed out of her eye. She instantly knew what to do to punish him back. Taking the banner, she quietly left the tent and walked towards his chariot. Daruka too was fast asleep and she had no heart to wake up Padmini. And Krishna's horses were no strangers to her. They listened to her. She needed no charioteer to ride back home.

When she goaded the stallions to a quiet trot, she could see that they knew their way home. She could trust the four of them and even doze off in the chariot to wake up right in front of the gates of Dwaraka. She imagined the surprise people would feel seeing her alone on Krishna's chariot. She decided to respond with a practised smile. *Devaki and Vasudeva would sense something was wrong and chide Krishna upon his return. Perhaps her quiet departure would earn him some censure from brother Balarama. Well, he deserved all that and more. He deserved to feel the hurt she felt.* The thoughts added to the force of her whip and the loud neigh of Sugriva brought her back to this world. She immediately felt guilty of hurting the horse and halted the chariot to pacify the faithful animal.

The day was about to break. Caressing Sugriva's mane, she was about to mount the chariot again when she felt the horses stiffen. Like they had sensed the presence of something they did not like. Rukmini felt the hair on her own neck stand.

Her grip over her sword tightened.

'A little lost, my Princess?' The voice was steely.

Rukmini turned around to see her path blocked by several

soldiers, armoured and armed for a battle. She tried to rush back to the terrace of the chariot but a menacing horseman blocked her way.

'Allow me to lead you to where you truly belong.' The speaker came forward, goading his horse to step ahead of his band.

'Dantavaktra,' Rukmini mouthed. She had seen this king of the small-time principality Karusha play a fiddle to Shishupala in their younger days. He was never an object of her attention.

'Neither am I lost, nor do I need you to "lead" me anywhere. I am almost home.' Rukmini met his gaze. The horses of Krishna's chariot behind her neighed uncomfortably. They had sensed the hostile presence. But they could not bolt, leaving their beloved mistress. But something in Rukmini steeled her against fleeing. She lifted her sword to her face. 'Perhaps it is you who lost your sense of direction here, Dantavaktra.'

Dantavaktra frowned with a slight shake of his head. 'My sense of direction is not your concern, Rukmini. I lay in wait here, for that cowardly husband of yours. But then, destiny gave me this opportunity to reunite you with your true lord, my dear friend Shishupala.'

Rukmini needed no more provocation and launched herself upon Dantavaktra who turned his horse with a violent jerk, narrowly missing her offence. Rukmini landed on the ground but retained her balance. She could have driven her weapon onto his mount, but chose not to. Daylight was yet to break, and as his horsemen closed in upon her, the dust arising from the trotting clouded her vision further. Rukmini kept her gaze upon Dantavaktra who circled around her, brandishing his sword.

'But you look like a prize worthy of keeping!' He smirked. 'Though I don't share the same soft corner that my good friend had for you in his heart. Do I leave your limbs scattered on the road as a surprise gift for that scum of a Yadava, or do I keep you alive long enough to make him see me take you apart, limb by limb.'

'What a tragic dilemma, Dantavaktra! Why don't I solve it by severing that head of yours! It will save your hard skull some thinking!' Rukmini gritted her jaw. She was about to leap onto Dantavaktra again but sensed one of his minions close behind her and backed by a yard to get a vantage point.

'In case you think numbers can daunt me…' She left the sentence midway to leap at the unsuspecting soldier and slashed his neck. The severed head landed at her feet. Taking advantage of the daze it had caused, Rukmini broke out of the menacing circle of horsemen, but not before wresting a spear away from the last one she passed. She hurled it at Dantavaktra. But he blocked it with his long sword. Rukmini expected him to react with an offence of his own but his menacing calm made her frown. Then she caught it, the discrete signal, a flick of his fingers, and she straightened herself to face the next couple of swordsmen.

It proved to be a miscalculation. Rukmini realized it the moment she heard the twang of a bow behind Dantavaktra. But before she could move, the arrow pierced her right shoulder. Pursing her lips to not let the painful scream escape her mouth, Rukmini almost knelt on the ground as Dantavaktra came upon her. Shifting her sword to her left hand, Rukmini rolled away, frustrating his blow. She managed to slash his arm and draw blood, but he had the advantage of being mounted on a horse that moved quick enough to escape with just a wound. Another horseman attacked Rukmini but she dodged him to face the next one, locking her sword with his. A deadlock was not advisable when numbers weren't in her favour so Rukmini jerked the weapon off, causing him to fall off the horse, and whirled around. But the arrow lodged in her shoulder allowed her limited movement while inflicting pain beyond her imagination.

Just then, Dantavaktra's sword drove into her back. Rukmini knew this wound was fatal and struggled to retain her balance. But she would not let him have the pleasure of seeing her pain. Not as long as life allowed her.

'A long trail of your blood. That would be a beautiful sight to greet your imbecile of a husband!' Dantavaktra laughed, drawing back the sword with a twist. Rukmini almost felt the world go dark, except for another piercing war cry. *Of another woman. The woman who swooped in between her and Dantavaktra, upsetting him off his steed as his soldiers rushed to form a protective ring around him.* Rukmini recognized her saviour as another ring of women surrounded her.

'Abhaya!'

And the world went dark.

❦

When she gained consciousness, Rukmini found herself on Krishna's chariot, with Abhaya holding the reins and driving it into the fortified settlement that was the home of the women Krishna had rescued from Pragjyotisha.

'Quick! They need reinforcements!' she heard Abhaya shout instructions at the guards who rushed to them.

'Abhaya…' Rukmini managed to groan through her pain. Abhaya caught her by both arms.

'Stay with us, elder sister!'

'What…'

'We need to extricate the arrowhead from her shoulder!' Abhaya shouted at the nearest soldier and Rukmini's eyes closed again.

It was past midday when she gained consciousness again. Rukmini's heart leapt at the first voice she heard.

'How many?'

Krishna! He was there in the very adjoining room! Rukmini realized she had been resting in Abhaya's chamber. *And Krishna had reached there!*

'Abhaya, tell me how many we lost?'

Rukmini gasped. She felt her rage increasing.

'About...six...' She heard Abhaya's voice breaking. 'We rushed the reinforcements but he had numbers to his favour for that period... Krishna!'

'Krishna!' Rukmini gasped, trying to get up.

'She is conscious!' a maid behind her shouted, rushing to support Rukmini. The next moment, she saw Krishna rush into the room, followed by Abhaya. The blood shooting from his eyes made Rukmini's heart stop.

None of this would have happened had she listened to him and left for Kekaya like the rest!

The stitches along her shoulder and neck gave way when she tried to get up and blood spurted down her arm. This made Krishna halt in his steps, hardly a yard away from her. She saw him narrow his eyes and turn around. 'Krishna wait...Krish...' Rukmini rose to her feet but the effort had drained whatever little energy was left within her. But more painful was the sight of him retreat from her when they were this close. Her heart shattered.

'Abhaya, don't leave her side!'

Abhaya rushed to her side just when Rukmini was about to collapse. 'Call him back, please.'

'You need to rest, Rukmini. You need to rest, my sister.'

Consciousness was an intermittent visitor in the next couple of hours. Abhaya did everything within her reach to nurse her wounds. But there was something beyond the loss of blood that was tearing Rukmini apart from within. The physical agony too increased with what seared her mind and the doctors tending to her had to resort to sedating Rukmini to make her rest. She lost count of the days.

'How long has it been?' she managed to mumble when she regained her consciousness after what she felt like an aeon.

'Five days, sister. You are healing. But you need to rest till this fever subsides.' Abhaya felt her forehead.

'What happened Abhaya? Where is Krishna?' Rukmini sat up with superhuman effort. Abhaya tried to coax her to lie down, but finally gave up.

'He killed Dantavaktra,' Abhaya narrated. 'The battle was gruesome. It was a Krishna I never imagined to see. Even for a long time after he had smashed Dantavaktra's head with his club, it was a Krishna I felt scared to approach.'

'He fought with his club?' Rukmini asked. The club or mace had always been Balarama's favourite. Krishna had preferred weapons that ensured a quick death to opponents. It was a compassionate side of his warrior self that Rukmini had treasured. 'Where is he now?'

'Dwaraka, sister. He had to leave yesterday as Shalva besieged the fortress.'

'Shalva?' Rukmini exclaimed. 'When? What on earth is happening, Abhaya?'

'He told me to tell you...to not return to Dwaraka until he sends a message or comes personally. The same was to be conveyed to Bhadra and others at Kekaya. The messengers left this morning.'

Rukmini felt the same sense of foreboding she had felt when she had seen Shishupala abuse Krishna in the sabha. Beneath the glorious facade of the Rajasuya was a shaky empire! An empire where even the Emperor's closest allies and champions were not safe.

Adharma had become so deep-rooted! Jarasandha was just what was visible of a deeply entrenched rot. The physical agony stopped being a concern. 'Abhaya, I need to reach him.'

'Elder sister...' Abhaya paused. 'Krishna told me to tell you that he needs you to heed his words this one time.'

Rukmini collapsed against the headrest of the cot. 'How safe are we here? If, say, Avanti decides to attack us tomorrow, we would need to move to a safer place. Possibly to Kekaya or even back to Indraprastha.'

'We have had issues with Avanti in the past. But trust me, we need not fear them for a while,' Abhaya assured. 'Pray, rest and get well soon, sister. Your condition has changed Krishna into something else. Get well, and things shall settle back to normalcy.'

'Are you sure about it, Abhaya?'

'I mean, things can be brought back to normalcy if Krishna is his normal self. Otherwise…you are a wise lady, Rukmini. Continue to be the same inspiration to people like me as you always have been. Rest now.'

Days passed in frustrating uncertainty. There were stray messages about a long-drawn battle between the forces of Dwaraka and the forces of Shalva. Dwaraka had been devastated beyond everyone's imagination. There were rumours of notable Yadava leaders being held captive and the list included Krishna's father Vasudeva.

Rukmini even considered reaching out to Rukma to send some of the Vidarbha forces for help, but finally decided against it. Krishna would have surely sent her a message if he wanted it.

Come back, Krishna. Come back victorious and joyful like you always do.

Part Four

The Fateful Game of Dice

Victory did indeed favour Dwaraka but not without claiming its cost. With her wounds taking longer to heal than expected, there was little Rukmini could do about the rehabilitation efforts. After a troublesome fortnight, Rukmini finally had a messenger from Dwaraka.

'Satyaki!'

'Glad to see you on your feet, sister-in-law,' Satyaki bowed. 'There was not a day Krishna did not think about you and your sacrifice of putting yourself in the way of danger before Dantavaktra attacked your camp.'

Is that how he is telling you all about it when I am on the verge of believing that it was almost foolhardy?

Rukmini sighed. 'How is Dwaraka recovering, Satyaki? You look so weary and—'

'Dwaraka too is healing, Rukmini. But there is disturbing news from Indraprastha.' Satyaki rose from his seat looking more troubled than ever. 'Emperor Yudhishtira... he lost all of his empire to Duryodhana of Hastinapura in a game of dice.'

'Lost his empire in a game of dice?' Rukmini spoke no further, staring at Satyaki, and expecting something that would negate the sheer ridiculous nature of the news. 'Satyaki! This losing and winning in dice... we have heard the story of the Nishadha king, Nala, in the distant past, but now, people play this game just for the laughs, right? This cannot be true!'

'This game was true, sister. He was challenged in an official capacity. The game had the sanction of that blind king of Hastinapura.'

'There has to be some deceit here! Some foul play! How could the eldest not see through it?'

'The same question has been bothering me ever since I heard about this. There are more painful details, sister-in-law.' Satyaki sighed, cringing. 'The first game, I heard, resulted in Yudhishtira losing their treasury, armies, empire…his own brothers, himself and Empress Draupadi too!'

'What!'

'She was dragged into the sabha in front of all the elders and humiliated like no woman has been in the history of mankind!'

Rukmini cupped her mouth, words drying up in her throat.

'Draupadi's entry though turned things around and she compelled the blind king to annul the game. But then there was a second game where the Pandavas lost and have to fulfil an exile period of thirteen years.'

'There has got to be a conspiracy, Satyaki. Shalva's attack and this game all at once. What does Krishna say?'

'We are all leaving for Kurujangala, where the five brothers and their queen are temporarily camped before they go deeper into the jungles. Krishna is on the way. I shall accompany you if you wish to join us.'

'Of course, I am coming!'

After bidding a quick farewell to Abhaya, Rukmini and Satyaki set out to meet Krishna, Balarama and the Yadava entourage on their way to Kurujangala.

The dark circles under Krishna's eyes told Rukmini how disturbed he was after his best friend's humiliation. Joining him on his chariot with the eagle banner, Rukmini wordlessly held his arm for a long time. She could sense the partial relief on his face on seeing that she was better. But the uncertainty of the future of Bharatavarsha was disturbing. And nobody was prepared to face the consequences.

'Do you feel you miss Jarasandha? At least his attacks were

not from the rear and he always kept us on alert,' Rukmini asked in a bid to engage him in a conversation.

'I also think he being touted as the face of adharma was overrated. For all his reputation about treating women as pawns in forging alliances, I cannot imagine him doing to any woman what was done to Draupadi.'

Rukmini shrugged, unable to disagree. The news of Draupadi's humiliation had sent her into a daze of disbelief, much in contrast to her younger self who would have cursed and lashed out till she saw the perpetrators meet their destined fate. But no, plain shock seems to have consumed her. The Yadava camp was calling for a war against Hastinapura. Emissaries from Panchala too had come to draw a strategy and the thirst for war increased by the hour even as they proceeded to meet the Pandavas. Krishna's was the only inscrutable silence amidst the heated debate that took place among them.

The journey to Kurujangala was otherwise eventless. Rukmini saw Krishna rush straight into the hut where Draupadi was. The sight of the humble dwelling made her heart skip a beat as the image of the opulent mansion of the erstwhile empress played in her mind.

'I can't understand why Eldest does not accept everyone's suggestion to challenge the sons of Dhritarashtra in the battlefield!' Rukmini exclaimed when she finally got to meet Draupadi. 'Satyaki and the others are frustrated and disappointed.'

Draupadi, though bereft of the dazzling jewellery, silks and well made-up hair, still looked regal as she shook her head. 'It was to avoid the bloodshed.'

'You are wiser than this, Draupadi. The futures of each of those kingdoms that pledged their allegiance to the sons of Pandu lie in the balance now. Don't you all have a responsibility towards them?'

Draupadi sigh. 'How can the one who staked their future take up the role of leading them in war, Rukmini? Unless he atoned for what he did. That is exactly why Yudhishtira is keen upon completing the stipulated exile. As ridiculous as it sounds.'

'Of course, it is ridiculous!' Rukmini protested. 'Thirteen years is a long period, Draupadi. The sympathy and camaraderie that the kings of Bharata have towards you and your husbands could fizzle down to nothing then. Do you trust that the sons of Dhritarashtra would do nothing to turn the tide?'

'They will do everything in their power to wear down this "wave of sympathy", Rukmini, of course, they will.' Draupadi smiled. 'They know that the kingdom they won by deceit stands on a loose foundation. They are bound to be insecure. But sympathy is not what we need right now, my friend. This is a test that we chose to undergo to gain the strength that no army can give us—the strength of dharma. Completing this exile is important. My own self disagrees with me even as I say this aloud. But I know that this is the wiser thing to do, in order to not become objects of sympathy, an unreliable trait.'

Rukmini leaned against the rock boulder by which they sat, away from the men whose discussions too seemed to dwell on the same topic. 'You are as stubborn as your husband.'

She saw Draupadi's lips curve even if for a brief moment and could not help but admire the strength of the woman. 'Have you confronted Yudhishtira as to why—'

Draupadi shook her head. 'I need time.'

Rukmini squeezed Draupadi's arm. 'Take as much time… And if I know you well, it would be futile asking you to come with me to Dwaraka. Won't it? Even if for a short while?'

Draupadi nodded and they looked at each other in silent

camaraderie. Finally, Draupadi spoke. 'What is going on between you and Krishna?'

It took all of Rukmini's presence of mind to not show how the topic alarmed her. 'Nothing.' She shrugged after a pause. 'We are just preoccupied with the turn of events—Dantavaktra, Shalva, the game.'

'Now, Rukmini, if I know you well, this had started even before Rajasuya. I brushed it aside thinking I was mistaken. But it seems to have lingered and ...' Draupadi paused as a tear fell from Rukmini's eyes.

'Alright. I really don't know. He has blocked me out.'

'Your husband, left to him, can block the whole world out, my sister. But you, who found your way into his life, would surely know better.' Draupadi patted Rukmini's arm. 'Hold your ground. You need to protect the other seven and those from Kamarupa too.'

Rukmini needed to hear just that. Nothing more. Nothing less. Casting a sideward glance at Krishna who seemed deeply engrossed in a conversation with Yudhishtira, she promised herself to not let him block her out. Whatever was his plan for the future, she had to be a part of it.

'Choosing Me Was a Mistake'

Kritavarma and Bhangakara seemed to be unstoppable in the day's proceedings at Sudharma. The Pandava camp supporters found themselves in a fix. Rukmini saw Satyaki fervently staring at Krishna to stop the Yadava council from shifting its allegiance to Hastinapura. But Kritavarma pressed that aligning with the exiled made no sense to the future of the Yadu confederacy. An argument that most had to concur with. Bhangakara only saw the opportunity to strengthen Kritavarma's claim. Rukmini saw Satyabhama argue furiously with Bhangakara and intervened only when things got personal.

'Our daughters, Kunti and Subhadra—anyone remembers them? Or is it a new Yadava convention to abandon their sisters and daughters when their households face a crisis?' Satyabhama's jibe was loaded when she pointedly looked at Bhangakara.

'Fight for the freedom to choose, and then fight for this "convention to stand by sisters and daughters at the time of crisis". You think shifting the tenets conveniently does the job?' Bhangakara retorted.

'Shifting alliances for pure greed without an ethical stance will surely do the job for some people as I clearly see it,' Satyabhama's voice turned shriller. 'Look at Magadha and Chedi. The kings Sahadeva and Drishtaketu haven't budged from their stance though their relationship with the Pandu household is marred with personal tragedies.'

'Of course, both of them have benefitted from their fathers' deaths, little sister. The spineless rats will of course show their gratitude to those who coronated them.'

'Gratitude is the keyword, brother Bhangakara. Even the

so-called "spineless rats" seem to possess it while it appears to be scarce in the council of civilized nobility like this. We are still struggling to make place in our homes for the multitude of gifts given away by Emperor Yudhishtira and we already talk about changing allegiances!'

'The sons of Vasudeva have offloaded the job of speaking in the sabha to their women.'

Rukmini turned to her left to spot the source of the unsolicited comment.

'Now, now. I urge you all to listen.' Ugrasena rose to his feet seeking Akrura's support. 'It cannot be denied that our Yadu confederacy faces a crisis right now. We shall need some easy trade understanding with the powerful kingdoms. But we can also see ways to negotiate it without pledging a military alliance to Hastinapura.'

'Hard, but not impossible, Grandsire,' nobleman Babhru agreed. 'As Lady Satyabhama points out, we cannot ignore the self-respect as well as the well-being of our daughters, their families and their children.'

'Before we all get into heated arguments, let us remember that the military allegiance was not officially sought by the King of Hastinapura. It was just an indication by his brother-in-law, Shakuni,' Satyaka pointed out.

Rukmini saw Krishna's detached eyes stare into a vacuum, as if looking into a grim future, no matter what steps were taken. After some thought, she stepped forward, closer to the parapet of the balcony.

'Seconding the nobles Babhru and Satyaka, our immediate need should be to protect our trade and commerce. I suggest our trade guilds operate through their contacts in the trade guilds from those kingdoms that would benefit from Hastinapura's... unexpected rise to power. I suggest our merchants make the move before Hastinapura sees any way to throttle us economically. Additionally, we should explore increased trade with our allies, too...'

'I am beginning to see the wisdom in what Kritavarma and Bhangakara suggest.' The voice came from the most unexpected quarter.

'Brother Balarama!' Satyabhama gasped, but stopped herself from saying anything.

Rukmini saw Revathi hurry towards the wall, her eyes expressing the same disbelief.

'While I also appreciate Princess Rukmini's forethought, let the interested Yadava nobles explore ways to warm up to Hastinapura. Just hold back any large-scale commitment till it is discussed in this gathering. We are a confederacy and not a monarchy. We should not attempt to curtail the freedom of any Yadava noble. Nor should we forget that the well-being of this whole confederacy is paramount.'

Rukmini shared an unsure glance with Revathi and Subhadra, as Ugrasena concluded the sabha. She saw Kritavarma walk up to Balarama to exchange a word with him as Krishna wordlessly exited the sabha.

'Krishna!' Rukmini exclaimed, seeing him seated on the swing that adorned the front part of her mansion. It had been a while since they had even spent an evening together, given their punishing schedules after the recent developments.

'Rukmini,' he acknowledged her and walked towards the inner chamber.

'I was held up at Satyaki's place and partook my evening meal there. Did you have yours?'

Krishna nodded, staring into the distant sea waves visible from the window. Rukmini walked up to him, enveloping him in her arms from behind. She felt his hand hold hers for a while, before he let go. Despite the gloom around them, this proximity was what she needed the most at this moment. It was comforting, his presence. Or so Rukmini felt till Krishna spoke again.

'Love, you made a mistake choosing me.'

'What?'

Krishna turned around, extricating himself from her arms. 'Rukmini…' He shook his head. 'Choosing me, as a husband, and Dwaraka as your home, was a mistake.'

'Krishna, whatever makes you…'

Before she completed the sentence, Rukmini saw Krishna walk away and halt at the head of their cot, staring at the garden.

'It beats me how you cannot see the wisdom in leaving this relationship, Rukmini. The Yadavas walk towards their doom, this way or the other. This is no place for you. And there are worthy grooms in the land of Bharata who would treat you with the honour and grandeur due to you.'

Rukmini would have laughed if not for the melancholy in his tone and the darkness circles under his eyes. She vehemently shook her head trying to figure out what made him say the unthinkable.

'Cutting all ties with your natal home, working inhuman hours to see the rise of Indraprastha, braving attempts on your life and now facing everyone's contempt at Sudharma—don't tell me you aren't seeing the sheer futility of your husband. No woman deserves this, Rukmini. I urge you, leave me and find a man worthy of you!' An elusive Krishna was bearable, though he tested her patience at times. So was the inscrutable Krishna whose response was so counter intuitive that she had almost reconciled with the impossibility of understanding him. But this looked like a defeated Krishna. Rukmini prayed hard it was a prank like he used to play in their younger days. In all practicality, when Rukmini had begun to receive proposals for Pradyumna, Krishna's suggestion about her remarriage was little more than a joke. And an unkind one at that.

If he felt defeated and was crumbling from within, Rukmini was at a loss about how to hold him together. It was he who held everything together always, at the risk of his life, reputation and loved ones. She had fallen in love with him for that, for seeing himself in the world and the world as one with him. Rooted to the spot, she looked into his eyes, the grimness giving way to the heavy realization that he meant what he said. Suppressing the anguish, Rukmini looked away. It was like her own limbs and mind had torn away from each other. Speaking out a coherent sentence seemed like a superhuman task.

'Krishna!' she exclaimed. 'I have to meet Subhadra. I promised her I would meet her now. We have to talk about this later.' Walking towards the exit, she turned around. 'Don't leave. We do need to talk. And you need rest.'

To her partial relief, Rukmini saw him walk to their bed. A sob threatened to break out of her chest and Rukmini hurried out. Meeting Subhadra was only a ruse. Rukmini needed to get away from this side of Krishna she never knew even existed. *Unkind. Pessimistic. Defeatist. Like all the struggle they had undergone till now could just be thrown away.* Rukmini felt her head grow heavy with each thought, walking about her mansion wherever her feet took her. Reaching her backyard, she collapsed in front of the Tulasi plant. Even the Goddess did not seem to have answers for the tumult in her mind today.

What did he even mean? How did he even say what he said? What had happened between them that even Draupadi, in the depths of her own ordeals, noticed and she had not? Remembering Draupadi's advice to stay her ground, Rukmini wondered what could even be saved if he, who was everyone's hope, lost hope. Anger consumed her from within, directed at the man who dared think that another man could become her husband. If there was a life without Krishna, Rukmini was sure it was in the wilderness of some forest, dedicated to tapasya, seeking to be his bride in the lives to come and beyond. *Had she lost out on the merits of her past lives that this journey with him threatened to come to such an abrupt and heartless end?*

If Krishna had proposed separation with her, what were his plans for the other seven? And for those women from Kamarupa? Rukmini realized she held their future, too, in her hands! And she was clueless about how to react, how to protect them all. *How exactly did Krishna think the eventuality would pan out on Subhadra and her son Abhimanyu? On the sons of Draupadi who were due to arrive at Dwaraka any day? What was Krishna even up to that made him suggest such ridiculous stuff?*

He had been her hope, ever since she had met him at the ashrama of Sandipani. It was that inexplicable bond that formed between them that had given her the strength to fight Rukma and Jarasandha's stranglehold upon her life and bring the Magadha King's unchallenged race to power to a halt. Since then, Krishna has driven every sense of purpose in her life.

Was it not a tapasya in its own right? Decades of standing by him? Did everything to happen only to come to a naught?

'Are you just thinking about the last couple of decades, Rukmini?'

Rukmini looked up, the moment capturing the rest of her body in a sense of surreal stillness. Perched upon the ornately carved platform of her Tulasi plant, she saw Her.

The Shakti that reigned over consciousness
She who held the power to cloud the mind
Or illuminate the self with the ultimate viveka
The one capable of instilling unspeakable terror
The very life breath of every divine force

The source of this very existence,
The primordial aum
Beyond all the finiteness
The Goddess born to Nanda and Yashoda

Tears streamed down Rukmini's eyes, but she could not blink, awestruck at the spellbinding resplendence that stood before her. 'Yogamaya!' the name escaped her lips. 'It needs a Goddess to become the bride of a God...and…'

'Saying you aren't one is akin to denying Me, Rukmini,' Yogamaya smiled. 'Remember the lives before, some in the memory of the seers, some even beyond. You are more than what you think you are, Rukmini.'

The stillness around her seemed to stir into what seemed like the eternal string of lives she shared with him, her Krishna. A togetherness in spirit that did not know separation.

'You've always held the power of defining his purpose. You choose it for him—when to continue and when to give up.'

'What can I do now?'

'You know.' The smile dissolved into the orb that had begun to envelop Rukmini. It was a glimpse of infinity, which for a moment, made the world she knew seem insignificant. Rukmini's eyes closed and her head bowed low enough to touch the ground.

'Hold on and he will be compelled to. Give up and he would follow too.'

'He cannot give up. Not now, right in the middle of this near impossible mission! Nor can I! But everything seems to be loaded against us, Mother!'

'Then, hold on, Rukmini. Fight on by his side.'

'It is beyond me, to keep fighting on. Grant me the strength, Yogamaya!'

'You have it within you. Just make your choice, Rukmini.'

The words melted into a silence that made Rukmini feel the world around her reel. The sense of direction melted into nothingness, so much so that she could not even bear to open her eyes. She was almost sure that it was the end...her threshold to the worlds not known to mankind. Except for the voice that called out and the hands that shook hers.

'Rukmini!'

It was like a fervent tug that brought her back. She heard her name again and again, every successive call more frantic than the last. So frantic that her senses could not but relent. The warmth of an embrace covered her; Rukmini felt consciousness nudge her back within the lines of existence. Cool air, filled with fragrance greeted her nostrils. Her parched lips parted and felt the coolness of the droplets of water that flowed in.

'Rukmini.'

She opened her eyes and looked into his, reminiscent of the infiniteness she had just experienced, except for the moistness that quickly filled them when he held her to his chest.

'Krishna!'

'I crossed a line I should not have,' Krishna whispered. She could feel his voice choke.

'What happened?' she asked, realizing then that she was on their bed.

'You fainted at the threshold.' The concern in Krishna's voice was still high. 'All because of my silly humour. Rukmini, now you know me enough to see through when I joke just for the small joy of seeing you sulk or even hit back. The moment I thought I could grab you into my arms and...'

Krishna's lips locked with hers. Warmth gradually returned to her limbs, which were still numb with faint. Rukmini wholeheartedly let herself get lost in the moment, unmindful of even the tears that flowed out of her eyes, onto his hands that had cupped her cheeks.

Her heart had begun to race before it calmed down, enough for words to find her. Rukmini tried to speak but could only sigh at first and then chuckle. 'Like I would commit the mistake of thinking that I know you again.'

Krishna let Rukmini go, allowing her to sit up, still leaning to the swan-shaped backrest. 'You say you don't know me?' He beamed, the husband wrought with worry, in a moment, morphing into the enigma he always was.

'Perhaps…' Rukmini smiled. 'A little. Just enough to expect you to throw a surprise the moment I feel that I know you.'

'You deserve more credit than that, love,' Krishna replied with a slight shake of his head, now, laying by her side.

Rukmini nestled back into his arms. 'I thought I had walked up to the garden till the Tulasi.'

'Trust me, Rukmini, had you crossed the threshold in the influence of whatever I blabbered, I would have fainted.'

'Enough!' Rukmini nudged him, laughing, and kissed him again. The sheer delight of the moment made it feel like the whole ordeal was worth it. Especially when it granted her a glimpse of what she needed to know. It had changed everything between her and Krishna. And for the better. Rukmini cleared her throat, trying to fit into the normalcy that had returned. 'When are the sons of Draupadi expected to arrive?'

'About that, we still have the whole night to talk.' His eyes pleaded a postponement of the topic and his hands wandered in search of the knot behind her back.

Durvasa

The temporary absence of Krishna during his travels was never a reason to discontinue the routine that he followed in his household. Rukmini saw to it. Especially an activity such as feeding peripatetic rishis, brahmacharis, seers and bards the morning meal. Apart from fulfilling the duty of a grihastha, this was something that helped Rukmini gather information about what happened across Bharatavarsha. This need to stay updated had only increased after the fateful dice game. Rukmini paid extra attention to the preparation of the morning meal, which she personally served to the guests, as she asked about their welfare and that of their families.

Rukmini's hair stood up on end on seeing a certain rishi, short and potbellied, but eyes dazzling with what they called the power of tapasya. Handing over the container of payasanna to the maid behind her, she brought her hands together.

Raising both his hands in a blessing, the rishi introduced himself, his very name causing everyone in the room to hold their breath.

'Maharishi Durvasa.'

No sooner had the name come out of his lips, Rukmini heard a clang from her side. She glared at the maid who had dropped the container of payasanna in fear.

'Is my reputation so scary that a container full of such a delicious payasanna has to be wasted?' Durvasa guffawed aloud.

Unknown to those around her, even Rukmini heaved a sigh of relief. The rishi's reputation as a short-tempered man with a powerful tongue and a legendary power to curse was strong. 'Forgive us, Maharishi. It has to be the good fortune of the Shoora household to host you.' Rukmini smiled and added, 'When you visited a member of our family the last time, five heroes, sons of Gods, were born as a result, who could change the course of Bharatavarsha.' Rukmini chose not to add the next sentence in her mind. *Until fate proved that it still holds the reins of this land.*

'And our fight against this mysterious fate continues.' Durvasa beamed as if reading her mind. Rukmini nodded and led him inside the inner dining chamber, partly to make up for the maid's clumsiness and partly in cognizance that the visit by such an exalted rishi would not be a casual one. Durvasa partook of the meal she served herself.

'The sons of those five heroes are indeed under the care of another loving mother. Your payasanna would turn anyone into a glutton, Princess Rukmini!' His compliment was warm, almost making Rukmini doubt if the tales and legends around his short temper were exaggerated. 'How are the boys doing?'

'Training in a gurukula set up for them a little away from the city, Maharishi. Empress Draupadi as well as the royal family of Panchala have entrusted us with the education of their sons. Acharya Punardatta, the son of Guru Sandipani himself, has established a temporary ashrama to focus on their education. Brothers Satyaki and Chekitana as well as my Pradyumna regularly train them in the combative arts.'

'A separate ashram away from the city would also shield them from any unwanted gossip-mongering among the Yadava populace.' Durvasa looked her in the eye.

'Your perceptibility cannot be faulted with, Maharishi,' Rukmini nodded, genuinely wonderstruck about his awareness of the Yadava factions and the dynamics of Sudharma sabha.

'Every small thing taken care of and yet, you don't seem to enjoy a night's sleep, Rukmini,' Durvasa remarked. 'All because you chose to wed a man against your parent's wishes, your shoulders have to now bear the responsibility of his destiny.'

'Between sharing his burden and being his burden, the choice is obvious, Maharishi.'

'Rukmini, take me to the boys now.' Durvasa rose to his feet with a sudden change in his mood. Rukmini's limbs froze for a moment sensing the transformation but she gathered herself and led Durvasa to a chariot, which she chose to drive herself.

'Faster, Rukmini,' Durvasa urged even before she cracked the whip. Rukmini nodded but could not hasten the horses beyond a certain speed before they crossed the busy streets of Dwaraka. But Durvasa seemed to be possessed with an unreasonable sense of urgency.

'Is this what your famed horses are capable of, woman?' Durvasa shoved her, almost upsetting Rukmini's balance. 'I can probably run faster if I am on my feet.'

Had this been any other man, Rukmini would have showed her angry side and lashed back furiously. But the past hour of interacting with Durvasa helped her keep her anger in check. And she strongly hoped that her speculation about his strange behaviour had a good reason. But even the horses galloping at their swiftest did not seem to calm the Maharishi down and his taunts continued despite Rukmini's efforts.

'Halt here!' Durvasa snapped and jumped down the moment Rukmini pulled the reins. They had not yet reached the ashrama where the Upapandavas were living. He raced along an inconspicuous detour, which she knew led towards a humble fishing hamlet. Rukmini hurried behind him and met with a sight that almost made her heart stop. All the sons of Draupadi—Prativindhya, Sutasoma, Satanika, Shrutasena and Shrutakarma—were there before her eyes. The youngest, Shrutakarma, was unconscious while the other four frantically tried to revive him.

'Aunt Rukmini!' Prativindhya called out.

Before she could rush to the boy, Durvasa lifted the limp

Shrutakarma in his arms and rushed into the adjoining wilderness. Rukmini and the other four boys followed him to see the rishi crush a fistful of grass he had plucked and pour the juice into Shrutakarma's throat. After a tense while where none spoke, they saw Shrutakarma cough out aloud and vomit. The blue colour that had enveloped his skin had begun to recede.

'What happened here?'

'We came to fish and left him on the shore as the tide seemed treacherous, aunt Rukmini,' Sutasoma explained. 'It was a short while, but Mahadeva knows what he ate!'

The youngest among the five was still weak to answer their questions. 'Take the boy back to the ashrama. I am sure Acharya Punardatta has the medicine to fully cure him of any remnants,' Durvasa said, his voice back to its gentle tone.

'Maharishi…' Rukmini turned to express her gratitude once they reached the ashrama and entrusted Shrutakarma to Punardatta. Words failed her when she imagined what could have happened had Durvasa not hurried her.

'I was a recipient of Empress Draupadi's hospitality during their stay at Dvaitavana, Rukmini. I owed this to her,' Durvasa explained.

'If you meet her again, pray, tell her that Rukmini would now stay with the boys and oversee their well-being every minute, Maharishi. Dwaraka can put up with my absence for a while.'

Something in her eyes, a mix of panic and determination, moved the rishi, otherwise known for his short temper.

'Child,' he paused with a slight shake of his head, 'your resolve is something that makes everyone around you feel proud. But deep down, it will always seem punishing...unless you let go, Rukmini.'

'Let go… Maharishi, you advise me to let go after…' She paused, pointing at the hut where Shrutakarma was resting. 'A stray incident like this could have endangered their lives, right under my watch! Had it not been for you, I could not have faced Krishna and Draupadi.'

'Krishna!' Durvasa sighed. 'He does not share this restlessness of yours, does he?'

Rukmini gave a sad smile and shook her head. 'Incident after incident takes place in my life, Maharishi, giving me a new insight about my husband. I am now resigned to the fact that I cannot know him the way I would have liked to.'

'You are harsh on yourself, Rukmini. And that has caused the illusion of a distance that doesn't exist between you both. And it always feels like you are racing to catch up with him... a never-ending race.'

Rukmini pursed her lips but was unable to control a lone tear.

Durvasa patted her head. 'Rukmini, there are great men, those considered as divinity personified, that walk on this earth. They have the power to envision a change that is not visible to the eyes of common folk. They found new schools of thought that would one day change the outlook of mankind. The second, like Bhagavan Veda Vyasa, not only propound schools of thought, but also word them and disseminate them. Their sheer grace enables men and women to share their vision. Their very appearance gives hope when there is none.' Durvasa paused and looked into Rukmini's eyes. 'Then there are the third and the foremost kind, those who not only envision and articulate but also weld the will and capabilities of those around them to work towards the change they see. The complete ones! Like your husband. Things seem to magically fall into place before their resolve, because they see themselves in this world and the world within themselves.'

'My Krishna...' Rukmini exclaimed, 'stubbornly loves the whole world like his own, is never swayed by adulation or ridicule...'

'Because in his eyes, the adulation is from his own self as is the ridicule,' Rukmini. The sense of exalted abandon that he commands is because of that unwavering sense of oneness, my child, that oneness that makes one, a brahmachari despite being in the company of multiple women, a steadfast ascetic though his potbelly is filled with worldly preparations!' He laughed pointing at his stomach. Rukmini smiled.

Durvasa continued, 'You, Rukmini, should honour him by not thinking of yourself as inferior to him. And you can enjoy sound sleep like he does even if the world seems against you, and still rein in every intrigue before it gets to you!'

Rukmini nodded and touched Durvasa's feet. It would take her a while to digest this, but it was a great consolation to realize that all she had to do was to believe in Krishna's sense of oneness.

Samba's Blunder

It was a tumultuous couple of weeks for the Shoora household. A disturbing news had reached them that Samba, the son of Krishna and Jambavati, had participated in the swayamvara of Lakshana, the Kuru Princess of Hastinapura and daughter of Duryodhana. He had attempted to carry her away, but was overwhelmed by the Kuru warriors who had taken him a prisoner.

Livid at the developments, Balarama wanted to confront the Kurus while Krishna maintained a stoic silence. Upon Balarama's s insistence, Krishna advised everyone to wait. 'They will not harm Samba, Brother Balarama. We must not rush into a retaliatory mode.'

'What if they keep him a prisoner and give Lakshana away to another groom?' Rukmini asked. She sensed a palpable reaction at her question. That would mean a loss of face to the Yadu household.

'If Lakshana is forced into another alliance, we shall rescue her. If she willingly marries another man, it would mean that her heart is not with Samba and we must accept that.' Krishna's tone was grave. When he leaned back against the seat, Rukmini detected traces of disappointment in his eyes.

'Rukmini, talk some sense into him!' Balarama was aghast. 'That is a family which is capable of poisoning and burning their own. How can he think Samba would be safe as their prisoner? Krishna, you are capable of a level of detachment that is even elusive to the yogis. But Samba is your son! Can you imagine the boy's disappointment in knowing that his own family will not lift a finger in his defence?'

Krishna pursed his lips. 'Samba knows us well. I am sure he would see the reason, too.'

'Can't we even negotiate Samba's release, Krishna?' Rukmini's concern for Samba, too, was telling.

'Yudhishtira was no fool, Rukmini. Could he negotiate his way out of the fateful game?' Krishna replied, directing the question at every member present in the small council room. 'That is the thing with the Kurus. They believe what they do is right. They braid together tenets and directives from the Shastras to their benefit and present this uncanny situation and weaken their opponent's position. Balarama, today, the larger Yadava confederacy is divided in terms of siding with the Kurus and siding with the sons of aunt Kunti. If any harm befalls Samba, all the Yadavas would throw their lot against the Kurus, and Duryodhana knows that. Imprisoning Samba instead of killing him is their acknowledgement of the fear of us uniting against them. We should wait it out.'

Balarama walked out wordlessly and Revathi followed him, trying to stop her husband. Krishna rose as if to call his brother back, but checked himself. Rukmini held his arm.

'It is a tricky predicament, Krishna.' She looked at him.

'He is not going to fare better than Yudhishtira, Rukmini.'

'Then stop him, Krishna.' Rukmini attempted to exit.

'No, perhaps this would only…' Krishna left the sentence midway and proceeded towards the military school where their sons as well as the children of the Pandavas were trained.

That very day, Rukmini tried to stop Balarama's departure to Hastinapura.

'Would you tell me the same if it were Pradyumna instead of Samba?' Balarama's words struck her like lightning. She chose to not let the hurt show and let Revathi lead her back inside. Rukmini wished she had Krishna's sense of discretion in deciding between pursuing or letting things be. After all, what was the worst that would happen upon Balarama's visit? Surely, the Kurus would not challenge him to another game of dice. If Balarama pulled off the negotiation, the Yadavas would only have a reason to celebrate.

But it was Krishna's elusive silence that made her feel uneasy.

Balarama did return with Samba and Lakshana, unharmed and safe. The Shooras had a mellow celebration of the wedding through which, Balarama was uncharacteristically quiet, something which Rukmini and Krishna noticed. After the guests left and the newlyweds had retired, Krishna held Balarama's arm. The elder son of Vasudeva avoided meeting his gaze.

'It is alright, my brother. Whatever this cost is, unburden yourself. I know Duryodhana would not have let this pass without a price. What is it?'

'Our military support to Duryodhana in case there is war.'

'What!' Rukmini and Revathi gasped.

'Balarama!' Revathi shook her husband. 'Tell me you aren't going to fight our Subhadra's husband and child. How shall we face aunt Kunti?'

Balarama stared into a vacuum.

'Balarama!'

'Sister Revathi,' Krishna intervened and held Balarama's hand. 'It's alright.'

'No, it is not!' Balarama rose from his seat. 'Bhima, Arjuna, Abhimanyu, sons of Draupadi who grew under our care. We would be forced to raise arms against these. The only way we can avoid that is to somehow influence a peaceful settlement among the Kuru cousins. Stop the war, Krishna. Stop the war. I wouldn't be able to face Subhadra if this comes to be. Stop the war!'

Balarama held Krishna's hands frantically till he reached the point of breaking down. 'Forgive me, little brother.'

Grimness had lately become a characteristic of the Sudharma gatherings. The one following Samba's marriage to the Kuru Princess Lakshana was no different. The most unhappy with the turn of events was Satyaki.

'Brother Balarama, did it not occur to you *once* to consult us before you left for Hastinapura? Samba is like my son too! Krishna, even you did not breathe out a word to me.'

'Samba erred, Satyaki,' Krishna's reply was stern. 'He erred grossly when he forcibly tried to abduct Lakshana, *against her will.*' Krishna's stance was clear; he had not forgiven Samba. Just that none expected him to criticize his own son in the sabha. Rukmini heard a murmur break out, which was full of critical statements against the Shoora family, against Krishna's parenting, comparisons between Pradyumna and Samba, and a lot more that she chose to ignore. She saw that Kritavarma and Hridika, who had been open supporters of Hastinapura, looked content.

Balarama tried to emphasize on the Yadava confederacy taking a proactive role in ensuring peace between the Kuru cousins, an argument that was welcomed by all the Yadava elders, though after a while, they all had to admit that Duryodhana's obstinacy would come in the way. None had the heart to press upon the Pandavas to give up their claim. Finally, the discussion had to come to the sore point—of the Yadava confederacy's stance if the war was inevitable.

Satyaki rose to his feet.

'Revered Grandsire Ugrasena, elders, brothers-in-arms. I, the son of Satyaka, from the household of Shaineyas, reiterate that the Yadava reputation as invincible warriors is paramount to me. But the reputation in the eyes of our future, our progeny, would mean a lot more than the present, full of biases. Arjuna, the Pandava, is my guru. He enabled me to refine my skill on the bow to a level I had never imagined to achieve. During every visit, he patiently imparted his skills to every interested youth in Dwaraka. A lot of times, I told him to ask for a gurudakshina and the valiant warrior smiled my offer away, out of his sheer love for Krishna, Balarama and the rest of us. The least I can do now, to escape the ignominy of gurudroha, would be to not join the side of his enemy.'

'Arjuna himself stands against his own guru, Satyaki,' Kritavarma remarked. 'Is Guru Dronacharya not responsible for Arjuna's dexterity? If he stands to commit gurudroha himself, why does the moral stance concern you so much now?'

Rukmini could not hold herself back any longer. 'If we have to go down to the basics, Kritavarma, Arjuna has more than paid back Dronacharya his due gurudakshina by defeating King Drupada of Panchala. And there have been multiple instances where the descendant of Bharadvaja, Drona himself has failed Arjuna and his brothers when he could have done otherwise and prevented the strife from deepening.' She turned to look at the other Yadava leaders. 'Having to extend military support to the sons of King Dhritarashtra is an undesirable consequence. But let us not delude ourselves with false moral equivalences.'

'Krishna Vaasudeva,' Satyaki implored. 'You are a statesman who can find a way out of the most impossible situations. Is there no way to escape fighting against the Pandavas? Tell us what to do, Krishna.'

Krishna looked up, the heat of his gaze intensifying. 'The current predicament cannot be underplayed or worked around with some diplomatic tactic, Satyaki. Princess Lakshana has gone back to Hastinapura, promising to return only after the armies of the Yadava contingent reach Hastinapura. Our daughter-in-law, she has been forced into this wedlock by our Samba as well as her own father Duryodhana, who used her as a pawn to stop our assistance to the Pandavas. If we fail to stand by our word, we would bear the sin of dishonouring our daughter-in-law. I would advise to let that "reputation" singularly belong to the Kuru family. We must send our armies to Hastinapura as Brother Balarama promised them.'

Rukmini found her lips quivering with a sense of foreboding. She did not even dare to imagine what would have crumbled inside Krishna if he spoke about pledging military assistance to the side that tried to murder his dear cousins, and humiliated his best friend Draupadi. The breath within the confines of her chest whirled around, and she held on to the bolster of her chair to steady herself.

Parameshwari! Show me a way!

'To save the Shoora household from the sin of dishonouring their daughter-in-law, should I take upon my shoulders the sin of committing ingratitude to my guru? This cannot be you, Krishna. This simply cannot be you. Don't decree it this way, I beg of you.'

'Decrees are given out by monarchs, Satyaki. This is a confederacy of Yadu leaders who have stayed true to the ancient republican system,' Rukmini heard herself say and then realized the weight of her own words. She had effectively suggested that Krishna's words were not an order to be followed by all the Yadu leaders if they wished otherwise. As much as guilt stabbed her, she saw it as the only way out. Krishna did not attempt to meet her eye, his stoic silence open to interpretation.

Satyaki looked up straight at Rukmini, partly in disbelief and then in veiled gratitude. Folding his hands as if in a final expression of gratitude, he turned to Ugrasena. 'If my brothers Krishna and Balarama are bent upon saving the Yadava clan from the ill reputation of dishonouring their daughter-in-law, I shall also stand between the sin of ingratitude and this beloved clan of mine. Forgive me, esteemed Yadavas. The household of Shaineyas shall cease to be a part of this confederacy from now on. We shall proceed to Upaplavya as soon as we can. I shall pray to the God of gods, Mahadeva, to ensure the wellness of the Yadu clan even as we shall see each other on the battlefield.'

Kneeling for a moment as a parting salutation, Satyaki rose and left Sudharma with his followers.

Rukmini saw Krishna lock his gaze with Satyaki for a moment and prayed hard that she had not broken him further. He then turned to Ugrasena, almost as if Satyaki's breaking away was a casual event, even as the other leaders tried to come to terms. 'We should also elect a commander who would lead our unit of armies under Duryodhana. He then looked up at Rukmini, as if prompting her to speak up. For a moment, Rukmini was not sure if he was sarcastic, prodding to wreak the damage to the maximum extent. But then she saw Krishna nod, the same way he did when he admired her stances. *Was Krishna happy about Satyaki breaking away? What did he want her to say now?*

'We have you, Krishna…Balarama who has himself taught Duryodhana the skill of wielding the mace…Kritavarma, a maharathi of no mean order…'

'I cannot face Subhadra's husband or son in the battle,' Balarama declared. 'May the world call me a coward. Any reputation of my valour will only be a stab into my heart if it harms Arjuna, Bhima or my Abhimanyu. I shall renounce my claim to be a warrior and leave for a pilgrimage if there is a war.' Unaffected by the mixed reaction his decision caused around the sabha, Balarama turned to Krishna. 'You love them all more than I do, Krishna. Nor do you attach importance to these worldly constructs of valour and cowardice. You are far beyond these attachments, my little brother. Come with me. Let Kritavarma happily lead the armies under his beloved friend, Duryodhana.'

'Let Kritavarma lead the armies,' Krishna repeated. 'I shall renounce the weapon like you do, Brother Balarama.' Looking around him and meeting every pair of eyes that looked at him, Krishna came forward. 'But I shall stay on the battlefield, till the end of this war.'

There were gasps around. 'You shall go to the battlefield unarmed Krishna? What kind of foolhardiness is that?' Kritavarma was surprised.

Balarama stared in disbelief. 'And you don't have to punish yourself for what—'

'I said, I am staying, Balarama,' Krishna declared with a finality that none could contend. 'Let us adjourn the next discussion to after Abhimanyu's wedding at Upaplavya.' He then left the Sabha. Like the one whose body was no longer in her possession, Rukmini followed him, cutting herself away from the million possibilities arising in her mind, about Krishna's decision.

❦

The chariot with the banner of Lord Hanuman drew nearer. Rukmini watched Subhadra and Arjuna alight. They had come from Upaplavya, a principality of Matsya Kingdom where the sons of Pandu camped after the period of their exile and strategized the future course of action. The wedding of Abhimanyu and Princess Uttara of Matsya too had taken place there. After extending the ceremonial welcome, Rukmini saw Subhadra reach out to her, out of Arjuna's earshot.

'What was wrong with brother Balarama during the wedding, sister-in-law Rukmini? Why did he advocate such an undue pacifist stance to Eldest Yudhishtira?'

Rukmini looked at her and shook her head. It seemed like Subhadra was totally unaware of what transpired around the wedding of Samba and Lakshana.

'If not for Satyaki's passionate rebuttal, I would have felt that my natal home totally abandoned my family.'

'It is not that way, Subhadra.' Rukmini shook her head, uncertain about whether it was the right time to brief Subhadra about the undesirable developments following Samba's misadventure at Hastinapura. 'There has been a rather disturbing development,' she added cautiously and then paused, seeing Arjuna join them. 'Rest for today, Subhadra and brother Arjuna. Tomorrow is going to be a long day.'

Early, next morning, Rukmini saw Krishna seated in deep

meditation. There was something mesmerizing about his erect frame, a picture of concentration that created a sense of hope even in the most hopeless situation. Something that instilled faith within people that he would take the reins of steering them out of their predicaments. She had spent a sleepless night wondering what could be the outcome if a war broke out. *How was Krishna going to keep his oath of staying through the war while not taking up a weapon?* At the moment, Rukmini saw him open his eyes. It was the usual timeless moment when his gaze met hers, a moment that took them both away from any impending disaster, detaching them from all the outcomes.

'Are you thinking what I am thinking?' she asked Krishna when he rose. Turning to the eastern window, where dawn was about to break, he smiled. 'There is a belief of our ancestors, Rukmini. The first rays of dawn are not of the sun, but of the reddish hued Aruna, his charioteer.'

And Duryodhana would not complain about a mere charioteer shifting sides. Nor can he complain about Krishna breaking his word if he just drove the chariot of a Pandava!

Rukmini followed his gaze. She almost wished that they were residing at the eastern end of Bharata at that moment. Indeed, the red ball was not visible during the morning while the sunset was always a treat to the eyes. The first rays of a new morning were Aruna's. Even as a prayer slipped through her lips, she heard Krishna blow into his Panchajanya, a low but reverberant note, announcing the start of the new day in the Shoora household.

And a new phase to the whole of Bharata, of his adopting the role of a sarathi, a charioteer.

Dwaraka after the Kurukshetra War

The waves and the sunset were the only consolation against what raged at home. Rukmini steeled herself to turn away from the pristine sight, back to face a world that was ravaged by death and destruction. Despite their victory, the deaths of Abhimanyu and Upapandavas had left a painful vacuum in the lives of the Pandavas and Draupadi, and she, Rukmini, felt as bereaved as the Empress of Bharata. The worst part of the war was that the remnants of rivalries that could not find a closure at Kurukshetra still haunted Dwaraka.

Rukmini had no heart to return to the city even as the last streak of light disappeared into the sea. She sensed a presence behind her. 'Could I sleep at your ashram tonight?' she asked.

'You need not ask, sister,' Acharya Punardatta sounded like he almost knew what ran in her mind. 'Lilavati would of course be overjoyed.' The lost and found son of Guru Sandipani was the groom that Krishna had chosen for Lilavati, the daughter of Acharya Agnidyotana, who had once risked everything in his power to help Rukmini wed Krishna. Punardatta chose to not speak till she turned around to follow him.

But even the atmosphere at Punardatta's ashram seemed tense as a visibly distressed Lilavati rushed to them. 'Father... he looks like...' She stopped with tears in her eyes. The trio rushed to the hermitage that was now the home of the former purohita of Vidarbha.

'Acharya!' Rukmini rushed to Agnidyotana's side.

'Father, it's Princess Rukmini talking to you. Stay with us,' Lilavati pleaded, as Punardatta lit the two earthern lamps in the corner.

Agnidyotana tried to smile as he raised his hand in a blessing and then pointed at Lilavati. 'Thousands of youth, young enough to be my grandchildren, perished in the war and she is sad about this old man, well over a hundred autumns, dying.' He tried to laugh but a fit of cough shook his frame violently. Agnidyotana clutched Rukmini's hand. 'Vaasudeva, is he around?'

Rukmini hesitated. Despite their togetherness in spirit, Krishna's life had become so detached from the household that she had almost stopped wondering about his whereabouts. His silence at the recent killing of Rukma by Balarama during the wedding of Aniruddha and Rukmalochana was something Rukmini still struggled to come to terms with, despite what she had once heard from the Goddess and Rishi Durvasa. Perhaps, the soul-numbing incident was needed to stir a sense of detachment within herself too. That was Rukmini's thought when she managed to mutter an excuse, with some effort. 'He has been on a pilgrimage…'

'Pilgrimage? Which are the Gods this fortunate?' Agnidyotana remarked, making her smile. 'It would have been nice to see him. But even that needs a punya that...' Agnidyotana coughed again. It was a long moment of silence before Punardatta exclaimed

'And here he is!'

Rukmini turned around and saw Krishna rush to Agnidyotana's side. They shared a glance seeking each other's well-being, before turning to the old brahmin. Agnidyotana sought Krishna's hand and then smiled at the couple. 'She had been quite a spitfire before she married you!' The sentence made even Lilavati chuckle and Punardatta joined in.

'Adharma had taken stronger roots than we all had imagined, Vaasudeva. It has fast drained this earth off her strength. Only a fire that can burn this rotting stubble can give hope for a new dawn of dharma to rise.'

'Burning, fire…that's what has been doing its dance of

destruction, Acharya. Since decades,' Rukmini commented, betraying bitterness.

'Did I not tell you decades before, that living the ideal was far tougher than stating them, my child?' Agnidyotana reached to brush Rukmini's hair like the older days when she used to come to him to learn her lessons as a child. 'But I am so proud today, that you did not let the intrigues come in your way, even when they drained you off all the vitality you could command. When the rule of dharma dawns and trust me, by Mahadeva, it shall, the people of Bharata shall worship you! Hold your story dear to their hearts, cling to your memory for hope and faith when times get tough.' He panted for breath and Punardatta anxiously poured water into his mouth, after which Agnidyotana smiled in gratitude.

'I had to have accumulated the punya of multiple lives to have had the opportunity to play even a small role in bringing you both together.' In an unconventional gesture, he brought his hands together in a salutation. 'I am grateful, Rukmini. I am grateful to you, Vaasudeva.'

An unearthly light glowed in Agnidyotana's eyes when he smiled next. 'You both have seen a lot more than any householder would have, you lost more than anyone in life. But still, I pray to all Gods the your names bring joy to anyone who remembers you. That would be the true fruit honouring the sacrifices you made. Stay… till the end of time...as a...symbol of hope, love and delight.'

The brahmin had spoken his last.

Dwaraka in Danger"

'Seems like the longest we spent together.' Rukmini smiled as they ascended the chariot together after the thirteenth-day shraddha rites were performed in the honour of Agnidyotana. 'In many years,' she added. 'And I almost did not have the strength to return to Dwaraka without you.'

Krishna smiled back, drawing her close as the horses picked speed. 'Hatred still continues to burn inside the heart of every Yadava at Dwaraka. And now, each of them has some self-righteous reason to back it up.'

'Like Satyaki calls out to children on the street to avoid the lane where Kritavarma lives lest they meet a similar fate as the children of the Pandavas and the latter warns wandering rishis to not meditate anywhere near Satyaki's house lest he decides to behead them when they are in deep meditation. Kritavarma does not let Satyaki's killing of warrior Bhoorishrava be forgotten either.' Rukmini remembered the bitterness that had spread even to the common households. 'Where one of them is invited, the other is spurned and feared. Both their names have turned into fear-mongering tools, short of abuses. Children younger than ten springs are getting drawn into this mess, Krishna. Can't we do something?'

'You really want to?' Krishna asked with a smile that suggested a million possibilities. 'Haven't given up hope even after what happened across Bharata after our meddling?'

'At the risk of sounding bitter, I sometimes feel, the two old men should meet in a single bout, kill each other and leave the rest of Dwaraka in peace.'

'Like the deaths of Kamsa, Jarasandha and whoever followed solved anything, Rukmini?'

'You are right, that was just my vehemence talking,' Rukmini nodded. 'I just feel for the young children born after the war. They deserve a life free of that hatred sown by their ancestors. Otherwise, every sacrifice made is rendered to a naught. Can't we really do anything, Krishna?' She saw Krishna's well-shaped brows come together. 'Take the case of Kurukshetra. Almost every son who died, did because his father let things go south instead of doing something within his power. Even Bhishma and Duryodhana. Do these innocent young minds have to germinate the weeds of hatred they aren't responsible for, Krishna? The war was fought for dharma. The victory is not of any side. Blood was shed to establish dharma. That purpose gets defeated when mutual hatred between clansmen gets perpetuated this way!'

Krishna nodded and suddenly spoke, 'Rukmini, sometimes, the place and time also play a great role in teaching us a lot of things. Would it do the children any good if say, we all shifted elsewhere?' Rukmini stared at the suggestion which she thought almost made no sense. 'Dwaraka seems vulnerable, Rukmini… Have you noticed the sea turning hostile even while the boats manoeuvre around the islands?'

Rukmini had noticed that the fishing activity had almost stalled around the coastline and the fishing hamlets clustered around smaller islets and coves around Dwaraka. But Krishna mentioning it as a concern was something disturbing. 'What do you mean, Krishna?'

'It has happened before and it can happen again, Rukmini. Dwaraka, when we found it decades ago, was a land that could keep the Yadavas safe from a looming enemy. The sea was its protector. But now, the very sea may turn its destroyer. I sense a deluge coming, Rukmini.'

They were on the road close to the shore and the rumbling of a large tide almost startled Rukmini. Turning back to Krishna, she asked, 'How much time does Dwaraka have?'

Krishna almost grinned at her fearful stare and shrugged. 'I was just suggesting that could be a possibility. That said, I mentioned this possibility to Arjuna and Draupadi and they felt the whole of Dwaraka should now settle at Indraprastha as it is quite vacant after Yudhishtira started to rule from Hastinapura as his new capital.'

'Draupadi too had told me the same.' Rukmini wondered aloud. 'But Dwaraka is our home!'

'A good five decades earlier, it was a dreaded coastal land under the control of fearsome robbers and pirates,' Krishna spoke as he looked into vacuum. 'We the Yadavas, were even ridiculed as deserters of our motherland. When we started strengthening and contributing to the Pandava power centre, Shishupala and others called us cowards who have lost their say as we supposedly "ran away" from our home.'

'Shishupala!' Rukmini chuckled. 'Come to think of it, the man who was the villain of my life is almost a forgotten memory now.' She shrugged. 'Though one can say his death started another bout of...whatever that is refusing to end even after that eighteen-day war. But coming to your point, Krishna, doesn't it bother you? Having to leave the very place you nurtured into a centre of prosperity crumble into—'

'A heap of rocks that would soon sink into the depths of the sea...one has to accept the strength of time and nature, Rukmini. And one has to detach—'

'From the fruits of one's karmas. I know. It is just that...' Rukmini shook her head, unable to suppress her tears.

'You were the one who wanted to protect the children from the actions of the elders,' Krishna pointed out. 'Samba's thoughtless act of kidnapping Lakshana has assumed a form of immense proportions, Rukmini. It has birthed this fault line that keeps tearing the Yadava world apart.'

Rukmini nodded, brushing her tears away. 'You said, Arjuna and Draupadi wanted us to move to Indraprastha.'

'Or rebuild Mathura.'

'I shall look into evacuation. Let us hope that the news of this impending fury of the sea would at least unite the warring factions among the Yadavas.'

Krishna's response—rather the lack of it—was disturbing, like the calm before a devastating storm. She had seen it in his eyes before the war. Now, it seemed even more terrifying.

'I have asked the older Yadavas to gather at Prabhasa. Hopefully for a final attempt to even things out. Perhaps some environment of frolic can…'

They passed through the archway that was once the proud entrance of Dwaraka. Rukmini nodded at the passers-by, most of the commoners whose adulation for Krishna and his family was endearingly unshaken, unlike the swinging emotions of the various house lords at Sudharma.

'Alight, Rukmini. I need to go back to Prabhasa,' Krishna declared, making her look up in surprise. 'When Arjuna arrives, go with him. Don't wait for me.'

Rukmini found herself nodding till a knot in her chest assumed a magnitude that was beyond her. She had almost alighted from the chariot but she turned around and looked at Krishna.

'No.'

'Rukmini…'

'I shall do everything to evacuate Dwaraka, Krishna. But I cannot go to Indraprastha with them, or anywhere…not without you!' It was a sudden vehemence that broke out within her. Like the restlessness she used to feel before her wedding. She saw Krishna's eyes close for a moment and open again. Everything felt surreal and it furthered the inexplicable fear within. 'Krishna, please!' By this time, her heaving chest had become so visible that Krishna had to hold her close and tight. 'Come for me.'

Krishna pursed his lips, in an effort to withhold something beyond all her speculations and nodded. He kept nodding when he wiped the tears that flowed out of her eyes. Then there was something in his glance that compelled her to alight. She stood at the foot of the stairs that led to her mansion, till the chariot bearing the eagle banner was out of her sight. Her tears dried and the resolve got stronger, like it always did when she held the fort for him. Just that this time, a sense of loss engulfed Rukmini—a feeling that clung to her even as she was greeted upon her return by a bustling household. Her sons, daughters-in-law and grandchildren came to welcome her home and she felt no apparent cheer within to match their affection.

'Where is Father?' Pradyumna asked her when Rukmavati led her to the dining room.

'He left for Prabhasa,' Rukmini answered absent-mindedly, explaining about Krishna's final attempt to secure peace among the warring groups among the Yadavas. Her reverie broke only when she felt the couple stare at her in horror.

'Why don't we know anything about it?' Pradyumna sprang to his feet.

'What if something untoward happens out there, Mother? Father and Uncle Satyaki are going to be outnumbered!' Rukmavati, too, pointed out. 'Take Aniruddha and the others with you too,' she added, turning to Pradyumna.

'Wait, you both!' Rukmini protested. 'A job awaits us here. Dwaraka faces peril from the sea. We need to evacuate the old and the vulnerable and make plans to relocate back to the northern plains. Arjuna is expected to arrive from Hastinapura. Krishna said that we should make all arrangements to leave Saurashtra for good.'

Pradyumna halted and considered the task ahead. Rukmini saw him contemplate and plan, his expressions almost matching that of his father's. Except that she could easily guess his unwillingness to let Krishna go alone. 'Rukmavati...help mother evacuate Dwaraka, love.'

She saw Rukmavati nod with the same emphasis that she, Rukmini, used to do when Krishna entrusted her with something.

'I shall also send a message to Prabhavati and Mayavati to bring back Vajra to Dwaraka,' Rukmavati planned aloud. 'As soon as you all return from Prabhasa, we can leave for Hastinapura.'

Rukmini saw the discussion continue between the couple, spanning from the availability of chariots, carts, palanquins to the guard needed for the whole journey ahead. For the first time, she saw them assuming control and she could not bring herself to override them. Secretly, she wished that she and Krishna left for an idyllic destination to spend their last phase of vanaprastha. They had overstayed the phase of grihastha and it was truly time to let Rukmavati assume the power and responsibility.

'I shall inform mother Satyabhama right now,' Rukmini heard Rukmavati continue as Pradyumna left. 'She will want to carry every single thing. Have you told Uncle Arjuna that we shall need another township only to accommodate her belongings?'

Rukmini chuckled at the obvious attempt to bring cheer. She knew that deep within, Rukmavati felt a similar pang of separation at Pradyumna's sudden departure and was attempting to laugh it away. 'Rukmavati, child.' She smiled at the younger woman. 'Call Pradyumna back. Krishna promised me that he will return. I am not worried. Call your husband back and...'

Rukmavati shook her head, brushing a tear away. 'I cannot stop him when he is determined, Mother. I can only pray that everything goes well at Prabhasa, and that I shall be laughing at these fears, soon. And I am sure I shall be. You have told me how Pradyumna withstood an attack by Shalva when he was barely thirteen. I have seen him fight every other suitor at Vidarbha when he brought me here. I should not be entertaining fears, lest I slight the warrior that he is!' Rukmavati sighed. 'Mother, you have led an evacuation before the Rajasuya too. Tell me everything. I shall start upon the task right now.'

Work was only a ruse to keep Rukmavati's fear in check. Rukmini wanted to tell her it was alright to fear, to express the unexpressed love, to vent the pent-up fury, to let out the insecurities. As a woman, the least she could do was to support another woman, this time her own niece and daughter-in-law, face her battles. But she knew that words would not do the task.

Nodding with the same resolve, Rukmini took a deep breath. 'Alright, let us start.'

He Shall Come Back

It was the end of the second day after the men of the Shoora household had left for Prabhasa. A messenger sent by Pradyumna had returned in the morning saying that the proceedings had been peaceful and this day was meant to go in some frolic. They were all expected back in Dwaraka the following day. Rukmini saw Rukmavati visibly relieved and took on the task of evacuation with greater cheer. Seeing everything catch momentum, Rukmini allowed herself to retire early in the evening. Past twilight, she sat in the garden, in front of the platform where her Tulasi plant was planted. It had dried up and Rukmavati had told her about her efforts to revive it going in vain. Perhaps, it was a signal from the Goddess too, that the time had finally come for Rukmini to leave this home of hers.

She felt a hand upon her shoulder and smiled. 'Came back early?'

'Leaving everything you have made and nurtured, to succumb to the fury of the sea is not easy, Rukmini. It is like the grief of the parents seeing their children die before their eyes. Like a harsh reminder from the forces beyond our control that nothing, Rukmini, nothing is here to stay.'

'Who can say that better than you, Krishna?' Rukmini clasped his hand, kissing it. 'I was in fact wondering what would it take for you to actually accept the impermanence.'

'Rukmini.'

'Many of our near and dear called the other Yadava house lords ungrateful when they used to oppose your intentions and initiatives to strengthen dharma and then quickly lay blame upon you when things went south. But we have been lucky to have them as a part of our lives too, Krishna. A totally grateful Yadava confederacy, I am afraid, may have made me a lot more attached than I am now.'

'You speak like you have decided to—'

'Renounce, Krishna. It is high time we did.'

'Renounce?' Krishna's voice had a tinge of amusement. 'Are you sure that you are ready?'

'Of course, I am.'

'Wonderful. Come with me.' Krishna tugged at her arm, almost dragging her to her feet.

'Wait!' Rukmini laughed. 'There are things that still need to be done. Krishna, I meant, we should renounce as soon as everyone is safely on their way to Hastinapura.'

Krishna laughed. 'I thought you said you are ready. Apparently, there is still some attachment.'

'It is called responsibility, love. We can't leave tasks incomplete and, you know, "elope" this way to vanaprastha.' Rukmini grinned at her own joke and rested her head on his lap. 'Or should we start a trend there, too? Makes it exciting.'

Rukmini's eyes closed, but she could feel his gaze upon her. The same warmth and love that he wrapped her in during her early days at Dwaraka before the political intrigues of the rest of Bharata called for them.

'Attachment assumes various forms, my love,' Krishna said after a long while. 'And the most treacherous form it can assume is that of responsibility. It binds you with a clouded sense of righteousness and before you know, there is no escape.'

'Continue this way, and I shall fall asleep,' Rukmini said without opening her eyes. 'And you would actually have to abduct me.' She smiled.

'Rukmini, you seem satisfied and happy with the way Rukmavati is handling it. Stop being that controlling mother-in-law. Exit when people still want you to stay.'

'Alright!' Rukmini sighed, stretching herself. 'Just let me be till the moment I actually see them all safely on the road to Hastinapura. Just till that moment. You can even drag me away by force if I resist then. Happy?'

'You promise?'

'Yes, love. I mean it.'

❦

'Princess Rukmini! Wake up! By all Gods above, Rukmini, open your eyes!'

It was rather a rude awakening and when Rukmini opened her eyes, she saw a distraught Malathi, close to breaking down. She sat up and realized that she had fallen asleep in the garden itself. *And where was Krishna?*

'What happened Malathi? And where is Krishna?'

'Rukmini!' Malathi collapsed and broke down trying to hold Rukmini's arms. 'Brace yourself. Gods have been truly unkind! The men of the Shoora household. All of them...It happened yesterday evening…' Malathi could not speak any further.

'All of them, what?' Rukmini held her back, looking around for Krishna. 'Krishna came here yesterday night.'

'Rukmini!' Malathi exclaimed. 'My Princess, he too...Daruka found his…pierced by a poisonous arrow at the toe.'

'What? No, you have heard it all wrong. Who all? Malathi, stop weeping and tell me everything.' It seemed like her friend had lost her mind. Rukmini then saw Daruka stand at the back entrance of the garden. The gloom on his face echoed what Malathi had wailed about. 'Daruka, what happened?'

Brushing his tears aside, Daruka tried to narrate. 'It was going very well between the two hostile factions, my Princess. Or so it seemed till yesterday afternoon. And then, Lord Satyaki started it. He said something like "someone give more wine to this son of

Hridika, lest some innocent children get murdered in their sleep tonight". Or something of that effect. Things went...awry and they all attacked Lord Satyaki... Lord Pradyumna went to save Lord Satyaki... Young Lord Aniruddha too.'

Daruka had to pause as he unsuccessfully tried to stop his tears and had to lean against the pillar. 'It turned into a war bloodier than the one at Kurukshetra! It looked like the earth thirsted for the blood of every Yadava man! Lord Balarama gave up his life, unable to see the bloodshed!'

Rukmini stood rooted to the spot. *Pradyumna and Aniruddha! If only she had stopped them from going. How would she console Rukmavati and the young Rukmalochana?* Her quivering palms clenched into fists. She had to console the younger women before bereavement engulfed her. 'Daruka, where is Krishna? Have you informed him of this?'

'Princess Rukmini...' Daruka started and looked helplessly at Malathi who was equally nonplussed. 'Pray, come with me.' He staggered outside the garden along the long corridor that led to the main entrance where Krishna's chariot stood, without the eagle banner fluttering in the wind like it always did. Rukmini's feet froze. Placed on the terrace of the chariot, Rukmini saw the lifeless body of the man who everyone thought of as a god. The eyes that mirrored the unravelled mysteries of the universe, were closed. The face that had spread only joy around whoever saw it had lost its lustre. The arms that granted assurance and protection to anyone who sought them, the arms that had fought the monstrosities of many wayward kings and lords, lay limp.

'Krishna!'

Malathi held Rukmini, bracing herself for a reaction. But to her shock, none came from Rukmini. To her further dismay, Rukmini stoically turned back to go into the mansion.

'Princess!'

Rukmini shook her head without turning. Inaudible to Malathi and Daruka, she whispered, 'He shall come back for me.'

❦

'He shall come for us, Satya. Believe me. He promised so!' Rukmini almost pleaded. But her co-wife was a picture of determination.

'I don't command the faith that you do, elder sister,' Satyabhama replied with a conviction that nothing could deter. 'Beg you, Rukmini, don't try and stop me. I want to follow him.'

'He has not gone anywhere, little one. It is a promise he would not fail to keep! What more can I say to convince you all?' Rukmini's voice broke.

'Meet you in a better world, elder sister.' Satyabhama embraced her.

'The Shastras don't encourage this even for women who truly lost their husbands and you all are—'

'Rukmini, the Shastras also don't come in our way when we want to follow our love, our Lord. Some of us want to join the pyre with him. I am retiring to a life of tapasya. I have reaped the benefits of my past punya in this life, sister. I have to work to reunite with him again.' Satyabhama managed to extricate herself from Rukmini's grip and proceeded towards the exit.

'That body is not him!' Rukmini could only whisper. She cleared her throat for a final attempt to dissuade her other three co-wives who had become more than her own sisters in Dwaraka, from ascending the pyre. 'Foolish women, you would only be displeasing him.'

'Not the first time,' were their last words. Satyabhama walked away and Rukmini never felt more helpless in all her life. She tried hard to convey the realization that had dawned upon her gradually with every encounter she had with Krishna, the vision that Yogamaya had granted her, and the last meeting she had with her Krishna, to Satya and the others, but in vain. She averted her gaze when Vajra, the lone survivor of the massacre, approached the pyres with a flaming torch.

The world went dark.

Dark... that was the hue of her beloved, her Krishna! He is everywhere.

Even as her body succumbed to a faint, Rukmini smiled.

Epilogue

The deafening sounds of birds going back to their nests was just the cover that he needed. The setting sun across the horizon gave him the perfect view from his hiding spot. Vajra stared in the direction of the stream that disappeared into the wild patch. Raising his hand, he gave the signal to his faithful band followers, the young Yadava boys, who had escaped the fateful massacre at Prabhasa. They lay in wait. Vajra trusted his instincts, which told him of a certain hidden hamlet nearby. This had to be the one. His relentless search of over a month was to bear fruit. This was meant to be a surprise attack and not much hostility was expected. He nimbly moved from thicket to thicket, signalling those behind him to follow his suit and not blow their cover. The wilderness gradually thinned and he turned back to tell his men to wait before he emerged out of his cover. His guess was right. Vajra held his breath seeing the settlement, quite close to where he could hear the waves of the sea. It has claimed quite a part of what used to be called Dwaraka. Noiselessly, he leapt to block the entrance of the largest hut. Holding his weapon close, he kicked at the door, which gave way. But there was nobody inside.

Again? Vajra despaired. This was his fifth raid on an Abhira hunting hamlet and this, like the earlier ones too, was deserted. *Where could they have gone?*

Steeling himself to keep his search on, the grandson of Krishna turned to leave. Then he heard it, the familiar jingle of bangles. Vajra's eyes misted over at the flood of memories.

As a child, he could sense and differentiate between the characteristic jingle of the bangles of his mother Padmavati and that of his grandmother Rukmini, of the mother who nursed him,

Mayavati, and of his jovial stepmother Rukmavati. His heart missed a beat at what he heard. As noiselessly as he could, Vajra followed the sound. It came from behind the hut, along the path towards the sea. And he saw her. Alone.

Something within him froze for a long moment before he gathered himself to approach her, close enough to hold her arm. She turned around and words failed him. Saying nothing, he turned around, in a bid to take her with him. 'I cannot, Vajra.'

Pursing his lips, he suppressed a sob. 'It will be nothing like before, I promise you.'

But the woman stood like a rock. 'Trust me, grandmother Rukmini. It is a new home, a happier one.'

Rukmini smiled, her eyes betraying pride and joy. 'As immense a delight as it sounds, that is no place for me, Vajra.'

'Why? A home free of intrigues, conspiracies and adventure sounds like a bore to both of you right?' Vajra gave way to his annoyance. 'His behaviour is understandable, but not yours, Grandmother!'

Rukmini chuckled like she used to do at his theatrics as a child. 'How did you find out? Everyone other than me believed that he is gone.'

Vajra sighed. 'A warrior like Arjuna gets shot while on a moving chariot, right beside his artery, like the arrow missed it by a hair's breadth. It was clearly not a missed aim, grandmother Rukmini. The one who did it wanted to spare Arjuna. Who else can do it?' Vajra demanded. 'Though I am short of hating him for the grief he let the Pandavas go through. They did not deserve that from him!'

Rukmini laughed at his uncontrolled indignation. And he was the only man in this world who had the liberty to berate her husband before her. Grandsons enjoyed the unique privilege.

Vajra shook his head. 'Coming back to the topic, Grandmother,

Emperor Yudhishtira is about to renounce the world along with his brothers and Empress Draupadi. Before they leave for their final journey, they want to crown me as the King of Indraprastha.' Vajra held Rukmini's arms, his eyes pleading. 'I want you to be there and bless me. If you come with me, he will be compelled to come too! Please, Grandmother.'

Rukmini smiled as if she was moved, but to Vajra's dismay, she shook her head.

'Grandfather...he spent his life trying to secure dharma so that not only the Yadavas but everyone on this land would walk on the path of cosmic order, without lust, greed or hatred overpowering them. If this is the start of a new era, he deserves to see it, Grandmother. And so do you. And what would I know of dharma? I am the youngest in the family to survive. And now I am expected to lead the rest of my clan and kingdom without guidance?'

'Alright that is enough, Vajra.' Rukmini frowned. 'You have completed your education in the Shastras. And you have near history of your immediate ancestors as a practical reference. Trust me, you will do far better than you think you would.'

Vajra let out an inaudible sigh, reconciling to the fact that his grandparents had decided their course of future and it was not to join the surviving Yadavas. Kneeling on the ground, he pressed Rukmini's toes, at a loss for words, unable to either argue or leave without her. He stayed that way for long enough for Rukmini to shake him by his shoulder.

'Go, Vajra, we shall watch over you, child. Let Krishna live forever through your rule of dharma so that every citizen hears his words when they need to, sees him in action when the time comes, has him in their hearts every moment...Let him live forever, so he is not forced to take birth in this human form again.'

The crown placed on his head, the cheer, the chants of auspiciousness, the blessings, the hope in the eyes of the common folk and the whole hustle-bustle around him did not succeed in distracting Vajra. He acknowledged the presence of the scions of Satyaki and Kritavarma's households, each of them crowned as kings of their own principalities after the disbanding of Sudharma. They had met the previous night though, and resolved to keep the spirit of Sudharma alive while adhering to the monarchical structure. He had already sought the blessings of Yudhishtira, the Emperor, his brothers and Draupadi, the Empress. He had secured the friendship of the soon-to-be emperor, Pareekshit. Smaller than its original size, the extended Pandu-Yadu-Kuru family was finally rid of its past baggage and the land was ready to enter the new era of dharma. As Vajra turned to salute the crowds, his subjects, and the people of Indrapastha, he saw them.

Rukmini and Krishna. *They had heeded his request!* Vajra held himself back, fighting the urge to rush to them for he knew that would only disappoint them. Hands still joined in salutation, he let his tears speak out his commitment to the task ahead.

They would live through him, as the Timeless.

Acknowledgments

The idea to write a novel on Goddess Rukmini came to me on an auspicious Friday, supposed to be dear to Goddess Lakshmi. I thank Team Rupa for being a constant support.

No mention of Rukmini Kalyanam to a Telugu heart goes without the immortal poetry of Bammera Pothana-Amatya in his Andhra Mahabhagavatamu. I am fortunate to have parents like Smt. Usha Krishna Swamy and Krishna Swamy Kumar who taught me these poems since my childhood. The beauty of that poetry has constantly influenced and inspired my writing, not just in this book but in all my other literary endeavours as well. My parents have also been my first beta readers and have ensured that they find a resonance in the draft before I could finalize the same.

My husband, Arvind Iyer, the 'Krishna' of my life for his all-encompassing support, right from helping me with my routine to taking care of our toddler daughter and holding the fort of my household when I am away travelling for lit fests and so on. (Wait, he is to me, what Rukmini was to Krishna!).

Abhirami, my hyperactive little bundle of joy, for her part, was a regular 3 p.m. napper throughout my writing phase, which ensured that I could complete the draft.

I am grateful to my in-laws for putting up with my dreamy self, lost in a world that existed at least four millennia ago.

No writer makes it through multiple books and still lands up with the enthusiasm to write her next without the support of selfless individuals. In my case, Lord Krishna has blessed me abundantly with a mentor like Harikiran Vadlamani, founder of Indic Academy, an organization committed to nurturing civilizational writing and Indic thought processes. I sincerely thank

Dr Bibek Debroy, Amish Tripathi, Sanjeev Sanyal, Prof Makarand Paranjpe, Gautam Chikermane, Hindol Sengupta, Sumedha Verma Ojha and Aravindan Neelakanthan for their kind endorsements after going through the book despite their very busy schedules. Yogini, managing editor of Indic Today, Pramod Buravalli, and team at MyIndMakers and Nithin Sridhar of IndiaFacts have been wonderful friends in exchanging ideas right from research and referencing to publicity and marketing.

Debdatta Sahay, Vishnu Chevli, Shashank Davanagere, Santhi Pasumarthi, G.V. Shivakumar, Dimple Kaul and K.V. Subramaniam are my bookworm friends who have regularly promoted my books, reviewed them on various portals and their blogs. My Twitter family as I call them, my followers, have been another source of support, for it is there where I gush or rant about my writing highs and lows.

My memory has surely left out some names but they are all in my prayers and best wishes. Last but not the least, a huge thank you to my readers who have stayed with me through this journey.